About the Author

Thomas R. Boniello is a native of the State of New Jersey, USA. He holds a BA from Amherst College, a JD from the Seton Hall University School of Law, and a master's degree in education from the College of St. Elizabeth. He currently serves as the Director of Admissions at Oratory Preparatory School, Summit, NJ.

BookMarck

Thomas R. Boniello

BookMarck

Olympia Publishers
London

www.olympiapublishers.com
OLYMPIA PAPERBACK EDITION

A CIP catalogue record for this title is
available from the British Library.

ISBN: 978-1-80439-410-6

This is a work of fiction.
Names, characters, places and incidents originate from the writer's
imagination. Any resemblance to actual persons, living or dead, is
purely coincidental.

First Published in 2023

Olympia Publishers
Tallis House
2 Tallis Street
London
EC4Y 0AB

Printed in Great Britain

Dedication

Dedicated to S. Cocchiaro

Acknowledgments

I thank the late authors Alexandre Dumas of *The Three Musketeers*, Sir Arthur Conan Doyle of *The Adventure of the Reigate Squire*, Mary Shelley of *Frankenstein; or The Modern Prometheus* and H.G. Wells of *The Time Machine* for creating some of the characters that populate *BookMarck*. It was my intention in writing *BookMarck* to pay homage to these authors and to honor their characterizations. I hope that I have in some small measure met that task. My learning curve as a first-time author has been considerable. I was supported by my cousin, Adrienne DiGiovine of DiGiovine Design who put me in touch with the reliable Janet Byrne from whom came referrals to source materials from which I could vet agents and publishers. I am grateful to Mr. James Houghton, Kristina Smith and staff at Olympia Publishers for seeing enough merit in my writing and in the narrative arc of *BookMarck* to publish me. Tess Forte, editor and copy director, was among the first professionals to whom I disclosed that I'd a story to tell. She provided me with the initial enthusiasm to launch my project and her occasional "look-ins" were valuable reminders that I'd not been forgotten. I thank two of my friends and colleagues at Oratory Preparatory School, Francis Kearns and Matthew Klarmann, for their considerable efforts in editing the second draft of BookMarck. Among the classmates whom I have been privileged to call friends, it is Christian G. Appy, author and professor at the University of Massachusetts, to whom I have always looked when aspiring to publish. I have been influenced by many fine teachers and instructors including George Kateb, Hadley Arkes, Richard Fink and the late George Armour Craig. My partner in life, Susan Cocchiaro, has had to listen to the generation of this novel from its infancy through the processes of publication, and she has remained supportive, mirthful, wise, loving and amused throughout. It is to her that I dedicate this book.

BOOK ONE

Chapter One

The Library

Cameron Taylor untied the front flap of the red rope folder, raised it from its resting place on her lap, and emptied its contents across the length of the library table. Her gaze shifted from her son, Abisai, who was sitting across from her, to her former husband, Gus, who was sitting next to her.

Abbie waited as the various college brochures and pamphlets spread and settled across the table, then flipped them about with a single index finger as if higher education was a communicable disease.

Gus finally interrupted their shared silence.

"This is a little dramatic, isn't it, Cameron?" Gus asked.

Abbie loved his father's voice. Gus had been raised in Martinique. He had spoken French and French Creole in their home to encourage their trilingualism.Abbie wondered if he'd lost any of his facility with French since his father's departure from their home after the divorce.

"No, Gus. I am **not** being overly dramatic," Cameron responded testily.

"College deadlines are slipping away."

Cameron turned her attention back to Abbie.

"I have not seen a single application from you, Abisai Taylor. Not a single college essay."

Abbie could not bring himself to meet his mother's eyes.

Abbie had often heard his mother described as *focused* and *relentless*, usually in the context of qualities he did not have.

"Have you considered UMass? I hear that they have an impressive literary department," asked Gus, attempting to conciliate.

Gus briefly shuffled through the disarray of papers in hopes of finding the UMass brochure.

"Well then," said Gus, responding to his own question. "How about Stanford? Maybe continue your fencing career?"

Abbie, provoked by the absurdity of his father's question, finally spoke.

"Dad. You know that's silly. I don't have the skill set to be a Division I fencer and that is where the scholarship money is."

"I didn't think that this conversation was about money," responded Gus as he turned toward his ex-wife.

"Is it?"

"Not if you help pay for his tuition," responded Cameron, unable to hide her skepticism.

"What about financial aid?" asked Gus, attempting to sidestep their continuing dispute.

Cameron sighed with resignation.

"We'll never qualify for financial aid."

Abisai's younger sister Charlotte had been diagnosed with Multiple Sclerosis after her eighth birthday. Since that day, Cameron and Gus had mobilized into *Team Charlotte*. They researched MS. They translated what they'd learned into family strategies. They economized the family's spending to save for treatments yet to be discovered. And if an accumulation of money was a measure of success, then Cameron Taylor was indeed a success, having amassed a small fortune over a number of careers.

In Abbie's opinion, it was the financial imbalance between his monetized mother and his modest father that led to their divorce.

Abbie tuned out his parents as their conversation followed a familiar spiral into an argument. He knew that the real reason for their having invited him to this 'family meeting' was so that he could serve as their buffer. He knew that their decision to meet at the North Orange Public Library was an embarrassingly transparent attempt to encourage one another to negotiate using their 'inside voices.'

Abbie shifted his chair ninety degrees and pretended to stretch out his legs, furtively scanning the room to see if his parents were attracting attention.

Mom has to be annoyed with how empty this place is, thought Abbie. Cameron Taylor had developed a national reputation as a fighter for freedom of expression and as an obstruction to the closure of public libraries. Abbie found it ironic that the North Orange School Board was that evening to entertain two motions: one motion to exclude from his high school curriculum several books deemed to be 'controversial,' followed by a motion to permanently close the North Orange Public Library.

School Board Member Ron Luck had self-identified on the town website as a prophet, foreseeing a time when all local libraries would be rendered obsolete by e-resources and pandemics.

On this particular afternoon, Luck's opinion was hard to refute. Here they sat as living evidence to the obsolescence of public libraries, accompanied by a lone librarian who was shamelessly leaning upon the reference desk with both elbows, giving the Taylors' argument his full attention.

15

Abbie side-eyed the librarian. He looked familiar. Had they met? The librarian's facial features were fascinatingly asymmetrical. His thinning black hair had been combed over his scalp to camouflage his thinning pate. The man's skin was pale and cratered; his mouth expressionless.

The librarian's attention finally drifted to Abbie. Realizing that he'd been caught eavesdropping, the librarian hastily pushed off his elbows and walked away.

Abbie turned his attention back to his parents' conversation, and to the annoyance in the voice of his normally unflappable father.

"What are you accusing me of? Being financially unsuccessful is not a crime!" Gus punctuated his remarks by jabbing his index finger into the surface of the table.

"Enough," sighed Abbie.

Abbie pushed his chair back from the table, enjoying the ease with which his chair slid across the floor.

"Mom, you don't have to advocate for me.

"Dad, you don't have to defend yourself.

"I'm sorry that I've put you two in this position."

Cameron exhaled and instinctively reached across the table to her son.

"This is not your fault," she said.

Gus waited a beat, then teased him.

"It's all your fault."

Normally, Abbie would have rewarded his father with a smile or laugh, but not today.

As Abbie rose to leave, Gus called after him.

"Here. Don't forget this."

Gus slid a copy of *The Three Musketeers* across the table to him.

Abbie had pulled this copy of *The Three Musketeers* from the library stacks when he had first arrived at the library with his mother. Doctor Haley, the instructor of his honors literature class, had assigned the class the first ten chapters for reading. Abbie had already read *The Three Musketeers* several times over previous years, including a Gus-driven read-through entirely in French. Yet, he looked forward to again acquainting himself with characters he considered to be friends.

Abbie had been drawn to this particular edition by the cover illustration of an elaborate sword. As a member of the North Orange High School Fencing Team, Abbie appreciated the acknowledgement of swordsmanship by the publisher. Even so, the artist's depiction had become almost entirely obscured by the accumulated grime on the book's aged cellophane jacket.

As Abbie reached for the book, Gus gently placed his large palm over Abbie's outstretched hand. Abbie's annoyance ebbed away as the warm, well-worn creases of his father's skin enveloped his own.

Abbie was reminded of his father's encouragement to read from printed pages and not from screens. To his surprise, he had begun to appreciate his father's admiration of books as sensual objects. But Abbie was also a realist and knew that his classmates perceived him as an eccentric for his appreciation of the printed word.

Maybe Mr. Luck was right. Maybe it was time to move on.

"We're proud of you, son," said Gus as he squeezed his son's hand.

"This… this… *positioning…* that your mother and I do. It's because we see a great literary future for you and your sister."

Abbie stood patiently as his father struggled to complete his thought.

"You know, son," continued Gus. "Every time you open a book, you give literacy one more chance to survive."

Whatever that means, thought Abbie.

Gus released his son's hand.

"Is that it?" Abbie asked flippantly.

Inexplicably, he felt himself starting to cry.

"Abbie. Are you still available to drive me to the school board meeting tonight?' asked his mother. "My car is still being repaired."

"Yes, Mom. I didn't forget. Do you need a ride home now?"

"No thank you, Abbie," she responded sheepishly, as if conceding that Abbie was at that moment the most mature of the Taylors.

"Your father can drive me home."

Abbie approached the reference desk. The librarian had turned away, pretending to be oblivious to his family's contretemps. Abbie thumped *The Three Musketeers* onto the desk, hoping that the sound would draw the librarian's attention.

The librarian turned toward the sound of the book.

Abbie blinked rapidly as if to clear his vision. This was not the same librarian who had glanced in Abbie's direction just moments before. Instead of the jaundiced, asymmetric face of his predecessor, this librarian glowed with wind-swept exuberance. His carefully trimmed, snow-white beard lined his strong jawline and provided a dramatic contrast to the dark canvas of his sun-tanned skin.

As opposed to the reticence of the previous librarian, this man appeared to relish the chance to socialize. His eyes twinkled as if prepared to take on all comers.

The librarian paused as he picked up the weathered copy of *The Three Musketeers.*

"Is anything wrong?" asked Abbie, suddenly concerned that he'd been discovered as a scofflaw of late fees.

"You know?" began the librarian as he tapped the cover of *The Three Musketeers*. Literature is sacred in Paris. *La Belle Époque* and all. I've had some fine times in Paris. Yes. Fine times."

The librarian opened several drawers until he found an antiquated book stamp and inkpad. He carefully spun the dials on the book stamp to a due date seven days forward, then pressed the stamp onto the pad to load it with ink.

The librarian opened the book to its back cover. He seemed perplexed by the bar code that appeared on the last page. Abbie grinned as the librarian searched for an appropriate landing spot for his book stamp.

"Why don't you use the scanner?" asked Abbie, gesturing to the scan gun sitting on the desktop to his right.

As if in an act of defiance, the librarian stamped the due date over the bar code and shut the back cover of the novel.

"Enjoy it!" cried the exuberant librarian as he slid *The Three Musketeers* across the reference desk to Abbie.

Abbie opened his knapsack. At the bottom sat a paperback copy of *Frankenstein; or The Modern Prometheus* by Mary Shelley which he'd borrowed from the library two years prior. It had sat embedded in the bottom of his knapsack for so long that he now considered it to be untouchable.

As Abbie turned to go, the librarian held the book stamp aloft, searching for a suitable resting place for it. He circled and surveyed the surrounding desk surfaces several times before finally abandoning his search, casually tossing the book stamp over his right shoulder with a harrumph, ignoring its clatter as it bounced on the laminate floor, spitting ink drops as it caromed about.

Chapter Two

Charlotte 1.1

Abbie arrived at his mother's condominium before her. He called for his sister, but she didn't respond. If he moved quickly, he could devote the next thirty minutes to his homework before having to chaperon his mother to the school board meeting.

Abbie closed his bedroom door behind him, admiring the proper fit of door into frame and the clinical click of a proper lock. His mother's townhouse was still a curiosity to him. Things worked with precision.

Things had not worked so well in the classically weathered Elizabethan manse where his family had lived before the divorce. Abisai had overheard a realtor say that the house was a charmer to look at but a disaster to live in. Abbie had begun every morning in that house with a battle to pry open his bedroom door from its misshapen frame. During his invariable next stop in the bathroom, he would risk a toilet flood or no flush at all on a daily basis. Since neither his mother nor his father were enthusiastic about home repair, their deteriorating house was an easy metaphor for their disintegrating marriage.

Abbie emptied the contents of his prized knapsack onto his bed. Gus had bought the knapsack for him years before when they'd visited an Army-Navy store for Scout equipment. Its authentic Second World War vintage would often attract the attention of Vietnam war veterans who would introduce themselves and then share stories of how their respective knapsacks had saved their lives by taking a bullet or shielding them from an explosion.

Now, this knapsack held the secrets of Abisai Taylor, including an overdue library edition of *Frankenstein*.

Abbie propped his two pillows against the wall where a headboard should rightfully have been, and sat. He opened his laptop to the screen that listed his weekly calendar:

NEXT DAY

Prepare for assessment: Product and Power Rules of Derivatives.
Read the first ten chapters of *The Three Musketeers*.

And, he reminded himself, *I have to drive Mom to the school board hearing tonight.*

Abbie grabbed his library copy of *The Three Musketeers*, intent on skimming through the first ten chapters to refresh his familiarity. As he paged toward the first chapter, a cache of pages tumbled forward.

There, stuck securely in the binding of the spine between page 121 and page 122 was a bookmark.

A bookmark was a rare find in Abbie's electronic world, so he paused to savor its existence, pulling it from its berth as much to satisfy his curiosity as to procrastinate. Holding it between his thumb and index finger, Abbie was surprised by its delicacy. Although it appeared to be made of paper or cardboard, the bookmark felt as if it had no density at all, as if he might be holding a thought or a dream.

Abbie found its appearance to be even more intriguing than its lack of weight. The bookmark seemed to be composed of interlocking sequins, reminiscent of medieval chainmail worn by European knights. Holding the bookmark toward the dimming daylight from his bedroom window, Abbie turned it in his hand and watched it reflect patterns of primary and pastel colors onto his bedroom walls.

I wonder if this is what confused the librarian? he asked himself.

Suddenly, at a particular angle in its rotation, the bookmark disappeared from his hand. Startled, Abbie repeated the motion several times in order to convince himself that he wasn't mistaken. Each time he hit that precise angle, the bookmark's coloratura would blend with the colors of its background and "disappear." Abbie could feel it in his hand, yet it had become invisible to his eye.

Abbie turned the bookmark over, searching for a product name or trademark. There was no imprint. *Is it valuable?*

"Dope," he said aloud.

Then he lay down, one arm behind his head, the other rotating the bookmark in the air, mesmerizing himself.

In what seemed like a matter of moments, Abbie heard the sound of his father's car door. He bolted into an upright sit. His mother was home. He must have fallen asleep. He checked the digital clock on his nightstand. Thirty valuable minutes had passed.

He used the back of his free hand to wipe saliva from a corner of his mouth. Then, he remembered the bookmark.

Where is it?

As he frantically searched his bed, he heard his sister's familiar knock on his bedroom door.

"Just a minute!" he called out to her.

Shit. If it's angled toward invisibility, I might never find it.

But Abbie did find it on the bedspread. Having been chastened by this near loss, he hurriedly re-set it between page 121 and page 122.

"Dinner time. Your trough is ready!" Charlotte yelled impatiently from the hallway.

Charlotte's voice invariably melted him. When she was a toddler, Abbie had placed the intonation of her voice somewhere between "troll" and "chipmunk." Although she'd grown to be far more athletic, independent and derisive than he, her voice had retained that innocence.

Abbie coughed out the vestiges of sleep in his throat and responded to his sister.

"Charlotte. Come in for a minute?"

He heard the door knob turn.

"It's locked, idiot," Charlotte said, using the French pronunciation for *idiot*.

As Abbie bounded off the bed to unlock his bedroom door, he was met with a kaleidoscope of memories.

Charlotte had been eight years old when she'd had her first MS attack. Early on a school day morning, she had cried out to him from her bedroom.Abbie had never before heard that level of distress in his sister's voice, so he had bounded out of his bed in a similar fashion.

Back in that moment, any delay in unsticking his bedroom door had deadly consequences, so he'd forced it open with both his hands on the doorknob and his foot pressed to the wall for leverage.

By the time he'd gotten to Charlotte, she had collapsed. He remembered calling for his parents. He remembered the effortlessness with which Gus scooped Charlotte into his arms and ran her to the car.

When his parents returned from the hospital that evening, they shared with him that Charlotte's doctors were *substantially certain* that she had Multiple Sclerosis. Abbie realized that their lives had irrevocably changed.

Charlotte entered his bedroom and sat at his desk chair. Abbie watched his sister with appreciation as she used assiduous care not to touch anything nonessential, and wrinkled her nose at what he assumed was the boy-smell of his bedroom.

"What?" she asked, her patience with him already exhausted.

Abbie recounted to her the context of his meeting with their parents, but focused on his encounter with the two near-simultaneous versions of a reference librarian, one ashen and asymmetric, the other glowing and exuberant.

"Maybe you were delirious," Charlotte suggested by way of a self-serving solution.

"I'm starving. Let's go eat."

"Wait. There's more," begged Abbie. He opened his copy of *The Three Musketeers* to page 121 and handed to her the bookmark.

"Have you ever seen anything like this?"

"It looks like the golden ticket from *Charlie and the Chocolate Factory*," she quipped, citing one of her childhood favorites.

Her self-satisfied smile quickly faded as she was absorbed by the beguiling effervescence of its mesh of cells.

Then, the bookmark disappeared from her hand.

"Holy shit!" Charlotte gasped. "What is this?"

"I don't know, but it was in the library book that I borrowed this afternoon," Abbie replied.

"Look here," she said. Abbie moved to a spot behind his

sister and bent to her eye level, peering over her right shoulder. As she tilted the bookmark away from herself, he could see an imprint lightly embossed on the impossibly thin surface.

"BookMarck 501.23," they said in unison.

Their examination was interrupted by the voice of their mother from the base of the staircase.

"Abbie! Get your homework! We have to go! Charlotte! Your dinner is on the table. Buh-bye!"

"Charlotte," Abbie said as he rose from his bed. "Put that back in the book and throw it into my knapsack when you're done with it? Pages 121 and 122. I've gotta go."

Abbie grabbed his calculus book and left the room.

Charlotte was still examining the BookMarck when she heard the front door smoothly shut into its proper frame.

Chapter Three

The School Board

The North Orange School Board held its meetings in the Town Hall, which was only minutes away from his mother's townhouse. Cameron had briefly considered asking Abbie to walk with her to the meeting, but walking would have required a rapid hike up the steep ascent of Ivy Hill. Rejecting the idea of arriving at the meeting in a sweat, she slid into the passenger seat of Abbie's Subaru and tried not to envision him as a six-year old driver.

Although Abbie did not identify with his Subaru station wagon, he did not dispute how conveniently it had fallen into his hands. Abbie had a small side hustle tutoring French to high school freshmen and sophomores, and a desperate couple had offered to him their used Subaru in exchange for a semester's worth of French II support for their failing sophomore. At the end of the semester, she earned a B- and asked him out to her sophomore prom, to which he drove her in his slightly used Subaru station wagon.

Abbie's motivation to chaperon his mother to the school board meeting wavered somewhere between beneficence and procrastination. He enjoyed driving and felt no desire to study for his calculus assessment.

As he slid into the driver's seat and buckled his seatbelt, he did his best to allay his mother's unease by deflecting her with conversation.

"Mom? What is it about these books that threatens the School Board?" he asked. Abbie anticipated that his mother's answer would extend through the duration of their short car trip. He was so familiar with his mother's cadence that he could tune her out yet remain sensitive to a break in her rhythm that might signal that she'd asked a question or had offered an instruction.

As his mother's voice buzzed in the back of his head, Abbie visited vague memories of his mother's previous career in New York City. He remembered her frenzied, late departures for work on school mornings, the scent of her exotic perfumes, and suits that his father had described as "sharp." He remembered howCameron and Gus would welcome wide varieties of eccentric guests into their home, how their guests would become more animated as the evenings wore on, and how they would become most raucous once he and Charlotte were dismissed to bed.

"Watch out for the stop sign at the top of the hill," he heard her say.

"Yes, Mom," he responded.

Shortly after Charlotte's MS diagnosis, Cameron stopped commuting to work. She redirected her energies toward the preparation of breakfasts and lunches. She no longer smelled of Chanel but of fresh strawberries. Visits from exotic friends became less frequent and then not at all.

Although Cameron would tell Abbie that she had left her work to be home for Charlotte, Abbie had always suspected that her departure had been for another, less voluntary reason.

Intent on enriching their lives, Cameron would pick up Abisai and Charlotte after school and accompany them to the library for play dates and book readings. Abbie knew that it was only a matter of time before his mother's charisma would catch the attention of the library director. Cameron was soon running the library's after-school daycare, book drives and fundraising events.

Abbie had looked on with appreciation as his mother took on the mantle of local advocate for library science. On those evenings when the family watched the evening news, she would identify how some reportage sought to devalue science and sensationalize speculation.

"Turn left here, Abbie," she instructed.

"Yes, Mom," he answered.

Before long, it was Cameron who appeared on local news telecasts as she led demonstrations protesting library closures in underserved communities. She had morphed into a local celebrity before their eyes. On the day she opened her Twitter account, she was joined by three thousand followers.

When two high school seniors tweeted their plan to burn the charter of the Center for Disease Control and Prevention as a political statement, the event sparked interest across social media networks around the world. On the night of the proposed bonfire, several nationally affiliated news outlets had cameras in place to broadcast the event.

Cameron, exuding undeniable on-air charisma, suggested to the protestors that the destruction of the printed word had social consequences far beyond their youthful considerations, and that setting their protests into a written manifesto would memorialize their objections with far more clarity.

In the days that followed, news outlets, both storied and irreverent, sought comment on how she had defused the conflict. Cameron Taylor catapulted from local news into the national spotlight. She became the super-cool and super-chic talking head when networks and news affiliates needed a sound bite about freedom of expression.

As Abbie pulled the Subaru into the least conspicuous

parking space he could find, it seemed supremely ironic that the town's leadership would seek to censure the high school reading curriculum, knowing that they would draw his mother into the fight.

An impartial observer might characterize it as purposeful.

A conspiracist might consider it a trap.

The front of the North Orange Town Hall was ringed by seven wooden desks in a semi-circle facing the audience. The desks sat on a dais elevated at least four feet above floor level. This was the location from which the School Board would conduct its hearings.

A microphone and stand was centered in front of the seven imperious desks to record public comment. Ten rows of ten folding chairs had been set up with military precision behind the microphone for the public, each row bisected by a middle aisle. Every folding chair was painted the flat putty color of institutional regimentation.

The Board members were in various stages of arrival when Abisai and Cameron walked into the room. Several of them placed name plates on their desks as they sat.

"The lettering on the name plates is so small that it's hard to read," Abbie whispered to his mother.

Cameron nodded in agreement, her lips pressed in a thin smile.

"We're being gamed, Abbie. If you look closely, this entire room is set up to preserve anonymity, even though these demagogues will tell you how transparent this process is."

Cameron's comment activated Abbie's curiosity.

How many other ways might these guys be hiding their identities in plain sight? he asked himself.

Although the meeting room had been renovated several times since having been built in the 1700s, the diffused lighting from the chandeliers suggested that the space was still lit by candle.

Recessed lights had been installed above and slightly behind the desk of each Board member in grudging acknowledgement to twenty-first century illumination. But by backlighting their heads, the shadows under their browlines claimed their eyes as if absorbing them into black holes. The dark shadows under their nostrils and lower lips contributed to Abbie's apprehension of their faces as death masks.

The occupant of the last empty seat climbed onto the dais and sat at the center desk. His long, gaunt face was made indistinguishable by shadows. Abbie assumed him to be the Board Chairperson.

The man attached a microphone to the lapel of his jacket and performed a sound check by clearing his throat. Cameron turned to Abbie and wrinkled her nose. They smiled at one another in mutual disgust.

"May I have a motion to open this April 21 meeting of the North Orange, New Jersey School Board?" asked the man.

"So moved," said a voice to Abbie's right.

"Do I have a second?"

A voice came through the speakers positioned on the walls on either side of the room.

"I second."

"Let the record reflect that the motion was seconded by Mr. Chambers, who is attending this meeting remotely. All those in favor say 'aye?'" requested the Chairperson.

All of the seven responded.

"Aye."

"All opposed?"

Silence followed.

"The motion is carried unanimously and we are in session."

Abbie noted to himself how only Mr. Chambers had been identified by name.

"Mister Secretary. Has the roll been called?"

"Indeed, it has."

"And do we have a quorum?"

"Indeed, we do."

"Let the minutes reflect that the roll has been called and a quorum has been approved," noted the Chairperson.

Abbie had not heard the roll called. He looked about to see if anyone else shared his confusion. He had been looking forward to the chance to apply names to the semi-faceless.

Before Cameron could stop him, Abbie had risen to his feet.

"I didn't hear the roll taken," he called out.

"You're out of order," growled the Chairperson.

Several adults in front of Abbie turned toward him to locate the source of the impertinent comment.

"But while you're on your feet, young man, let's all stand for the Pledge of Allegiance."

Embarrassed by the decisiveness and dismissiveness with which his objection was dispatched, Abbie was relieved to be swallowed into the obscurity of the standing audience.

As the crowd began to recite the Pledge, Abbie pivoted to his right and side-eyed the crowd to see if he'd embarrassed himself in front of anyone he knew.

The room had filled quickly and almost every seat was occupied. Abbie's scan caught the image of a large figure sitting five rows back. The hulking silhouette was surrounded by a ring of empty seats, as if audience members thought it better to keep their distance.

Something about the individual's appearance held Abbie's

attention longer than he'd intended. The head appeared to be disproportionately large for the body and was covered by a gray hoodie, pulled tightly and tied under a massive chin.

Before Abbie could turn back to the dais, the figure returned his gaze with an impassive stare. Unnerved but not wishing to appear rude, Abbie casually reversed his pivot back toward the front of the room, pretending to admire the outdated paintings on the aged walls.

I didn't know they made hoodies that size, Abbie thought.

After the Chairperson invited the audience to be seated, the projection screen above the dais filled with the image of a document titled *Agenda – Township of North Orange School Board Meeting – Thursday, April 21.*

"Do I hear a motion to accept the agenda for tonight's meeting?" asked the Chairperson.

"So moved," came a voice from the dais to Abbie's left.

"Seconded!" said the disembodied voice of Mr. Chambers from his remote location, already sounding vexed and impatient.

The Chairperson called for a voice vote, and the motion quickly passed.

"We will hear comments on non-agenda items for the next hour. Please feel free to use the microphone in the center of the dais. We are recording this meeting and need you to be on mic in order for us to record your comments.

"Also, we ask that you limit your comments to three minutes.

"Finally, please note that the Board will not respond to any comments at this time but will consider them in closed session for inclusion in a future meeting. Please do not identify any individuals by name during your remarks. If you need to identify any individual, please notify the Board Clerk."

The Chairperson concluded reading from his notes and looked up into the audience for the first time that evening, scanning the room over the rims of his eyeglasses. No one approached the microphone.

"Not hearing any comments, let us move on with our agenda," said the Chairperson, his eyes returning to his notes.

"We will now hear from Mrs. Mauriello, sixth grade teacher at Washington Elementary School and chairperson of our Pandemic Defense Team, with a status report."

Abbie opened his calculus book to study for his next day's assessment.

Mrs. Mauriello was followed by Mr. O'Brien and his report on preparations for a possible virtual graduation ceremony. After Mr. O'Brien completed his remarks, an unidentified Board member acknowledged Superintendent of Schools Martha Wittington for her leadership through the pandemic.

After a brief round of applause from the audience, the School Board swung through a series of discussions, the evening descending into a repetition of motions and votes.

"Are you asleep yet?" Cameron asked.

"Terminal boredom," he responded, but grinned back in response.

"It won't be too much longer," she whispered.

"Do I have a motion to discuss the high school curriculum and reading list?" asked the Chairperson as if on cue.

Abbie could sense his mother preparing to stand.

"So moved," offered a Board member.

"Seconded," added another.

"No one has signed up for public comment. Is there any comment from any Board members before I move to have the high school curriculum and reading list accepted?"

Cameron rose and attempted to slide through their row of seated adults into the center aisle. As he watched his mother negotiate her way past each set of knees, Abbie noted at least five heads in the front row turn toward her, then rise from their seats. By the time Cameron had managed herself into the center aisle, all five adults from the front row had stationed themselves in a column in front of the microphone.

"The Chair recognizes Mr. Luck," said the Chairperson in response to a raised hand to his right.

Finally, a name I recognize.

Abbie recalled Mr. Luck as having forecasted the library's closing to the newspapers.

"Thank you, Chairman Skantz," responded Mr. Luck. Abbie wondered if anyone else had caught Luck's breach of gender politics by referring to Skantz as a Chairman rather than a Chairperson, and whether Luck had done so intentionally.

"I want to bring to the Board's attention that this curriculum includes at least five books that are categorized as 'controversial.' I object to their being included in our curriculum."

Abbie's focus shifted from his mother to Mr. Luck. Mr. Luck was hunched over his microphone, throwing his entire face into shadow.

"It seems to me that we dealt with this question last year," continued Mr. Luck. "I continue to be confused as to why we must present this material to our students."

Mr. Luck's words started to accelerate. He spoke without hesitation, as if he were reading from a prepared statement.

"Parents trust us to put before their children material that is age-appropriate. We have an obligation not to violate that trust. Were I to read excerpts of these books into the record, you would likely admonish me and censor the public record of this meeting.

"So, I move to have these books removed from our high school curriculum. I identified the objectionable books in copies of the amendment that I submitted to this Board before this meeting."

"Chairperson Skantz. I would like to respond," came a voice from the darkness.

Abbie recognized the voice of Superintendent Wittington who sat on the far end of the dais.

"Wait a moment, Doctor Wittington. I need to ask for a second on the motion before we begin discussion," responded Chairperson Skantz.

But Doctor Wittington did not wait.

"I suggest that, once we begin to label books as controversial or non-controversial, we slide down a slippery slope. Mr. Luck is correct in that we had this discussion last year. But I thought we'd resolved this by including these books only in our elective classes. The reading lists for those classes are posted on our website, so parents have the chance to read the books that you've generalized as 'objectionable,' and decide whether they want their child to participate in that class."

"Mr. Chairman? May I speak?" the voice of Mr. Chambers resounded from the speakers.

"We still need a second on this motion," pleaded Chairperson Skantz.

"If you wait for a family to raise an objection after being exposed to this material," thundered the disembodied voice of Mr. Chambers, "the horse will have already left the barn and you have already breached a trust. And parents? Parents don't have the time to do their due diligence and pre-read these books. They are too busy paying mortgages, shopping for food or trying to keep their families healthy. It's our obligation to be their partner in education, not their adversary."

"Mr. Chairman," interrupted Mr. Luck, feeding off of Mr.

Chambers' momentum. "I ask that my amendment to remove these books as "controversial" be seconded."

"Seconded," boomed Mr. Chambers from the loudspeakers.

Chairperson Skantz affected his best monotone.

"All those in favor of amending the motion so as to remove all books categorized as 'controversial,' please indicate by saying 'Aye.'"

Ayes resounded from the dais.

"All opposed?"

Doctor Wittington realized that she'd been outvoted and that public discussion on the amendment to remove the controversial books would now follow. Seeing Abbie's mother waiting patiently at the sixth position behind the microphone encouraged her.

"Nay."

"The proposed amendment has passed six to one. We now open the amendment to the floor for public comment."

Abbie suspected that the five adults in front of his mother had conspired to get to the mic before her in an effort to discourage her.

But he knew that his mother had done the math. If she remained in line and waited patiently, there would be time enough for her to speak.

As Abbie expected, all five adults who had beaten Cameron to the microphone spoke in support of the amendment, echoing Mr. Luck's desire to protect their children from "offensive" material.

Finally, Cameron Taylor gained the microphone. Abbie saw several cell phones raised to record her remarks.

"This curriculum was vetted by professionals," began Cameron Taylor. "To discard the advice of educational specialists on what books should, and should not, be included in a high school curriculum would be analogous to ignoring a doctor's advice on what medications to take."

As she said this, Abbie made a mental note that no member of the school board was wearing a mask other than Dr. Wittington.

"Dr. Wittington has already said that our use of controversial books is limited to elective classes. This gives students and their families the freedom to choose whether they want their children reading these books. It is, if you will, an exercise in democracy. To deny access to these materials is to be repressive and to deny freedom of choice.

"How is a student to develop critical thinking skills without being challenged by critical texts? How is an adolescent to understand abuse or trauma unless our teachers and our books define what that is? These books dramatize and inform so that our children come out of their literary experience better educated, better informed and more able to protect themselves."

Abbie knew that his mother had lost.

But his attention was drawn toward the left side of the dais. He saw his mother look left. As she did, Mr. Luck and the rest of the Board rose to their feet. The crowd was standing and craning their necks.

Someone had fallen to the floor in the second aisle in front of Mr. Luck. Abbie started to overhear the words "heat," "fainted," and "water" bubble up through the crowd.

"This meeting will be adjourned for the next fifteen minutes," announced Chairperson Skantz.

"What now?" boomed the voice of the remote Mr. Chambers.

Abbie's mother disappeared into the scrum of bodies in the

front of the room. He assumed that she was aiding whomever was in distress. His aisle had quickly cleared, its former occupants moving either toward or away from the commotion. Several uniformed EMS workers pushed through the crowd down the center aisle toward the dais.

Faced with a fifteen-minute adjournment and with his aisle having cleared, Abbie rose to shop for "dinner" from a vending machine in the lobby.

As he stood, Abbie's senses were jarred by the odor of something ancient.

"You should consider the consequences before you participate in these events."

Abbie felt a massive presence loom over his right shoulder, essentially pinning him in the narrow aisle and preventing him from turning. The large stranger with the hoodie must have slid into the row behind him during the confusion.

"Abisai Taylor. You and your sister are destined to become the stuff of legends. So be it."

Abbie could feel the deep sonority of the voice vibrate the bottoms of his feet as if reverberating through the colonial timbers supporting the floor.

"But if you continue to assist your mother in her fool's errand," continued the voice, "our pathways will cross. And it will end poorly for you.

"Think of your family. Think of Charlotte."

The interloper's familiarity with his family startled Abbie. The direct threat to his sister froze him in place. The mustiness of medievalism sucked the oxygen from the room.

"I just want to go to the lobby," Abbie said aloud, unintentionally, as if delirious.

Abbie waited for the presence to recede. *Wasn't that the protocol of threatening behavior?* he asked himself. Instead,

Abbie felt the intimidating torso lean further into his space as a massive hand descended toward his calculus book.

A gray, desiccated finger opened his textbook and flipped through several pages. Abbie was reminded of his previous one-fingered treatment of college catalogs earlier in the day.

"Are you confused by college, too?" mumbled Abbie.

The mountainous figure spoke, ignoring Abbie.

"You know, Nikola Tesla performed integral calculus with his imagination. No textbooks. No instructors. We have, at the Institute of Abandoned Knowledge, several of his 'missing notebooks' in which he describes *picturization*. Were we to work out our differences, I could make this notebook available to you.

A pause.

Then.

"And go to college."

Abbie was pinned, so running was not an option. Instead, he remained absolutely still and quieted his breathing to minimize any additional contact with the hulking presence at his back.

Still, the absurdity of the moment did not escape him. Here he was, pinned by a giant whose interest had been piqued by his high school calculus book.

I am being offered a settlement, thought Abbie.

Just as suddenly as it had arrived, the presence behind him withdrew with unnatural grace and speed. Abbie did not turn to watch it go, but remained absolutely immobile, afraid that his acknowledgement might prompt a return.

"So how'd I do?" suddenly said a cheery voice to his left.

"Wha…?"

As Abbie slowly turned toward the sound of his mother's voice, his left knee buckled. He felt himself falling into her.

"Abbie. ABBIE! Sit. Sit down."

Cameron used her entire body to leverage her much larger son back into his chair.

"What's the matter? Are you not feeling well? You haven't

had any dinner, have you?" she scolded.

"A man in the second row just passed out as well."

Abbie paused and swallowed whatever saliva he could accumulate. The top of his head hurt and his eye sockets pulsed as if he were about to succumb to a migraine. But he managed to speak to her.

"Did you see it?" he asked.

"See what?" she responded.

Abbie paused for a moment, then thought better of disclosing the events of the last few minutes to his overprotective mother.

"Just let me sit for a minute. I'll be okay in a minute."

His next sensation was that of Cameron pressing an opened water bottle into his hand. He must have blacked out for a moment.

"Here. You're dehydrated. I think the air conditioning system is broken. It's so warm for April! They are going to postpone the vote on eliminating the books until the next meeting. Mr. Luck and Chairperson Skantz and a bunch of others are really annoyed. They think I had something to do with it. A little moral victory for us?"

Abbie lifted the water bottle to his lips and swallowed deeply. Somewhere in the distance, he heard the voice of Chairperson Skantz calling for a motion to suspend the meeting until May.

A postponement of the Board's vote was indeed a small victory for his mother. The hearing had provided her with a chance to measure her adversaries and the delay would give her time to mobilize the community.

"Abbie. Do you mind if I speak to a few people before we go? Will you be okay?" she asked.

She's already working the room, he thought.

"Sure, Mom. You go ahead. I'll be fine," Abbie replied.

Abbie dropped his head to diminish the strobe-like effect of passing bodies on his throbbing eyes.

Just as he thought he was beginning to recover, his field of vision, previously limited to the floor in front of his feet, filled with the appearance of another pair of shoes.

"Abbie. Might I have a moment? I'm Ron Luck."

Using the back of the chair in front of him for support, Abbie slowly pulled himself to his feet. He did not raise his head to acknowledge Mr. Luck's greeting and could only really "see" Mr. Luck from the periphery of his lowered eyelids. But he was able to focus enough to recognize that Luck had masked the lower half of his face after leaving the dais in grudging acquiescence to the North Orange Health Code.

"Sorry. I'm not feeling well," Abbie mumbled.

Mr. Luck took a half-step back but continued to speak as if pressing an agenda.

"Abbie, I appreciate your mother's sense of civic responsibility. In fact, I've been a fan of hers for quite some time. But you and I both know that she is going to lose and these books are going to be eliminated from our reading lists. And eventually we are going to be successful in closing the library."

Luck waited for Abbie to respond, but Abbie remained still and silent.

"I've been having this conversation with myself: 'How might the library acknowledge your mother's commitment to education?' And I have an idea.

"The library owns some valuable first editions of the 'controversial' books on tonight's list, and I'd like your mom to have them in recognition of her commitment to our town. I think we've got two or three boxes of them. I wondered if you might stop by the library after hours tomorrow night to pick them up:

41

Say nine-ish? If she doesn't want them, you could always sell them. I'd think that they'd go a long way to paying your first year's tuition."

Abbie's head began to throb again. How could Luck know that his family had a disagreement about tuition payments? He was confused as to whether to be grateful for Luck's offer or offended by his blatant attempt to bribe his mother.

"Why come to me?" asked Abbie. "She's right here. Why don't you ask her?"

"Your mother is a political liability to me. I don't want it to look like I'm patronizing her, or trying to buy her off," responded Luck.

"Besides, there are too many mobile phones in the room and I don't want to be photographed with her. That's why it is ultimately a better idea if I extend this gift through you.

"Agreed?" asked Luck hopefully, and he extended his hand.

Abbie was too tired to object and took Mr. Luck's hand in response, postponing his analysis of the evening's events until his head had cleared.

"Good. It's settled. I'll see you in the library tomorrow night at about nine. I'll have the back door unlocked for you."

With that, Luck moved toward an exit. Abbie took another pull from the water bottle, closed his eyes and inhaled deeply.

Moments later, he heard his mother's voice next to him once again.

"How are you feeling?"

She didn't wait for him to answer.

"C'mon. Let's get you home. Give me your key. I'll drive."

Cameron collected Abbie's calculus book while he slowly turned to scan the room for large, outsized heads and torsos.

Once out in the parking lot, Abbie slumped into the front passenger seat of the Subaru and turned the air conditioning vents

42

toward his body.

It's so warm for April!

I'll ask Mr. Luck more questions when I see him tomorrow night, thought Abbie.

Chapter Four

Honors Lit

Adam Goldberg and Adrienne Saleh were already in their seats when Abbie arrived at classroom 201. Adam and Adrienne had had their previous class in Room 201, so the only traveling they'd had to do was from one assigned seat to another.

As Abbie slid into his seat, he savored the relief accompanying his having completed his first period calc test, and the possibility that he might have done well.

Feeling in the moment for the first time since he'd awakened, Abbie felt a hunger pang and opened his knapsack to search for something to eat.

Then, the thought occurred to him.

Where is the BookMarck?

Before that moment, Abbie had not given the BookMarck a thought. He'd had no reason to open his knapsack that morning. His mother had prepared his lunch and packed it in appreciation for his having accompanied her to the school board meeting. After he'd slung his knapsack over his shoulder, he'd carried his calc textbook to school by hand to allow himself a quick review before class.

But now that the anxieties associated with his calc assessment were behind him, the bizarre nature of the previous day came rushing back at him.

Abbie grabbed the straps of his knapsack, trying not to

appear as frantic as he felt. After hauling the bag up and onto his lap, Abbie reached in and pushed aside his laptop and his lunch bag.To his relief, there was his library edition of *The Three Musketeers* lying upon the overdue copy of *Frankenstein*. And poking between page 121 and page 122 was the exposed edge of the BookMarck.

Thank you, Charlotte, thought Abbie.

Curiously, the BookMarck seemed to acknowledge Abbie at the same time that Abbie focused upon it. Although only a fraction of its surface area was exposed, that splinter of the BookMarck pulsed with color as if to greet him.

Abbie raised his head furtively to see if either Adam or Adrienne had noticed.

"What was that?" asked Adam, who had turned toward him to start a conversation.

Abbie pressed the BookMarck deeper into the pages so that it was no longer exposed. Then, he did his best *nonchalant* and lowered his knapsack between his knees to the floor.

"What was what?" asked Abbie innocently.

"I just saw some colored lights inside your backpack," responded Adam.

"It's a knapsack," corrected Abbie.

"Whatever," responded Goldberg.

Abbie's correction had annoyed Adam sufficiently to cause him to lose interest in pursuing his inquiry.

Mission accomplished, thought Abbie.

Abbie began to feel that he'd finally persevered through the headwinds of the previous day. His mother had moved past her annoyance to reach an appreciation for his having sacrificed his evening for her. The BookMarck was secure and his sister had miraculously followed his instructions. Even the impression of the massive interloper in the North Orange Meeting Room was receding.

Yet, as his day settled into a familiar rhythm, he felt an unexpected appreciation for the previous day's excitement.

So Abbie allowed part of himself to relax and part of himself to remain vigilant as he waited for the arrival of classmate Priscilla Stern.

Priscilla arrived in the final scrum of students pushing through the classroom doorway, to be immediately followed by their instructor, Dr. Haley.

"Good morning to all," said Dr. Haley cheerfully as he dropped an armful of books onto his desk.

Dr. Haley did not wait for a reply. He turned and wrote on the whiteboard behind him the instructional agenda for class:

The Three Musketeers:

Historical Context
Real Locations
Who was Alexandre Dumas?
Instant Expert Reports

"If you haven't done so already, please shut off your cellphones. Put the food and drinks away," said Dr. Haley with his back to the class.

Abbie watched as several of his classmates thumbed-out last minute conclusions to their text messages. He knew that Dr. Haley would need to issue at least one more admonition before class could start.

Dr. Haley turned to face the class.

"Cellphones away. Now!" repeated Dr. Haley, raising the

volume of his voice. Abbie's classmates dropped their phones into bags or squeezed them into pockets.

"I understand that several of you had a calc test during first period today. I hope that you all did well.

"In acknowledgement of your exhaustion, I will do the heavy lifting for the first half of class and will address three of the four topics behind me: the historical context in which *The Three Musketeers* was written, a virtual tour of Parisian locations mentioned in the book, and a brief biography of the author.

"After that, I will randomly select students to give their instant expert reports."

Abbie had forgotten to prepare an instant expert presentation. Dr. Haley had posted the assignment to the class website during the previous week, and Abbie had forgotten to carry it forward in his planner. As Abbie casually lifted his laptop out of his knapsack and onto his desk, he said a silent prayer that it was sufficiently charged to allow him to research his assignment.

Abbie opened Google Search and furtively eyed his classmates in hopes that he was invisible. As he scanned the room, he realized that everyone in the room was on their laptops as well, scrambling to complete the assignment.

Abbie looked up at Dr. Haley with renewed appreciation. In electing to "do the heavy lifting," Dr. Haley was giving them the time necessary to pull together the reports that they'd failed to previously prepare.

Abbie's reverie lasted only a moment. He knew that he had to move quickly. He anticipated being among the first to be called upon to speak. He was the logical choice. His topic, the source material used by Dumas in writing *The Three Musketeers*, fell naturally into an introductory class.

Besides, Dr. Haley knew his students well enough that he could predict the tone that he or she would project into the classroom. If he was seeking wit, he might call upon Micaela Griffin or Seamus Sullivan. If he were seeking stoner humor, he might ask Dan Geer.

But if he sought reliability bordering on predictability (*read: monotony,* thought Abbie), Dr. Haley would call upon him.

After twenty minutes of research and writing, Abbie felt prepared.

In the interim, Dr. Haley had muscled through the politics of early seventeenth century Europe, and had dimmed the classroom lights to share a Google Slide presentation of Parisian landmarks referred to in the narrative of *The Three Musketeers.*

When Dr. Haley finally turned the lights back up, Abbie's sightline to Dr. Haley was disrupted by a choreography of student limbs in varieties of stretches and poses.

"Let's take a five minute break. When we come back, we begin our expert reports."

"Mr. Taylor?"

Abbie raised his head.

"Would you be kind enough to start us off with the source material that Dumas relied upon in developing the story of the Musketeers?"

"Yes sir," replied Abbie.

"Thank you. We are adjourned for **five minutes**," said Dr. Haley, emphasizing the duration of the break.

As Abbie heard the buzz of liberated voices around him, he saw several heads turn toward him with grins of commiseration.

"The curse of being conscientious," Adam said as he passed his desk.

It took ten minutes for all of Abbie's classmates to return to their seats. As Priscilla turned to drop her phone into her bag, their eyes met. She smiled and gestured a thumbs up.

Dr. Haley invited Abbie to the front of the room.

Abbie began his remarks in his customarily dry monotone. But today he had a plan. Today, he would be different. The previous day had inspired him to appreciate the uncontrollable nature of his life. Today, he would try spontaneity.

As Abbie identified individuals or locations by name, he began to use the authentic French inflections that he'd learned under his father's tutelage. By the time Abbie brought his unassailable accent to the *Pont Neuf*, *Cardinal Richelieu*, and the *Bibliotheque Nationale*, he'd begun spinning out entire sentences in French. His classmates, catching onto his routine, began to encourage him, hooting with laughter and clapping their approval. Abbie concluded by speaking exclusively in French for the final minute of his presentation.

Abbie's classmates applauded.

Dr. Haley folded his arms, dropped his chin to his chest in mock capitulation, and smiled.

As Abbie returned to his seat amid raucous comments, Priscilla interrupted her enthusiastic clapping to wag her finger at him in mock disapproval.

Dr. Haley asked for the next speaker.

Abbie tilted his chair back (no easy thing with an attached desk), linked his fingers behind his head, and exhaled in satisfaction.

Chapter Five

The Aginbyte of Inwit

By the conclusion of his school day, Abbie had begun to fantasize about the largesse he was to receive from Mr. Luck.

Will my car be big enough to carry all of the books? Should I have rented a truck? Could the books pay for Dad's share of my tuition?

Abbie's mind crossfired between realistic expectations and overinflated hopes. In an effort to find a happy medium, Abbie settled on bringing his mother's hand truck to his meeting with Mr. Luck.

But where was her hand truck? He didn't see it in the clutter of her garage. It was only after he had searched the rest of her townhouse that he found it during his second pass-through of the garage, buried among the unpacked boxes. He was already fifteen minutes late by the time he extricated the hand truck, wrestled it into his Subaru and drove to the North Orange Public Library.

Abbie attempted to recreate the adrenaline rush he'd experienced earlier in the day during his successful presentation by repeating the words of Dr. Haley:

I'll do the heavy lifting.

But the energy that had accompanied his successful presentation was gone. Instead, Abbie felt his stomach flutter as he pulled his Subaru into the empty parking lot of the North Orange Public Library.

Maybe Mr. Luck has been delayed, he reasoned.

Maybe Mr. Luck is already inside waiting for me with a set of invaluable first edition classics. Maybe he got a ride to the library and I'll offer him a ride home to show my appreciation.

Or maybe Mr. Luck had to leave, but left three boxes of books inside the library, one box stacked atop another along with an appraisal and a note of thanks to my mother.

Abbie tried the door handle of the rear door entrance, expecting it to be locked. It turned easily in his hand. No alarms sounded. Abbie interpreted this as a good sign and stepped into the hallway, pulling the hand truck behind him.

The only illumination in the corridor was from the red luminescence of the Exit sign and the reflection of parking lot lights through the three small windows in the door. But Abbie knew this hallway. He wheeled the hand truck down the corridor to the elevator and elbowed the "UP" button. The elevator responded brilliantly. As its door slid open, the corridor was brightened by harsh LED lighting. Abbie stepped inside and punched the green diode for the first floor.

As the elevator door opened to the first floor, Abbie paused. If Mr. Luck were here, Abbie would have expected to find him in a well-lighted room standing among boxes of antiquated and valuable books. But there were no boxes of books. And the room was illuminated only by the light of the opened elevator, soon to be extinguished when the door closed behind him.

Maybe I should go, he thought.

Abbie stepped into the room.

"Mr. Luck?" he called as he stationed the hand truck outside the elevator.

The automated door closed behind him.

Abbie could hear the whir of the fans of the ventilation system.

Abbie reached into his pocket for his phone.

I'll text Mom and see if she has Mr. Luck's cellphone number.

As Abbie pulled the phone from his pocket, he unintentionally exposed the BookMarck to the darkness as well.

Abbie had brought the BookMarck with him with the intention of asking Mr. Luck about it. Surely a member of the school board would have an explanation for it. So Abbie had retrieved the BookMarck from between page 121 and page 122 before he'd left the house and folded it into his pocket.

The BookMarck responded to its exposure with a modest combination of diffused colors. It bathed the cinder block walls of the gallery with a soft palette of pastels. Although Abbie appreciated the light, he noticed that the colors radiating from the BookMarck were far more muted than its previous light-shows. Was it trying to give him a warning?

Still, Abbie felt emboldened by the BookMarck as if he had a partner in his enterprise, lighting the way and providing an early warning system.

Abbie walked to the library table where he'd previously sat with his mother and father. He trailed the tips of the fingers of his left hand along the table surface to seek out their vibration and felt a pang of regret for having disappointed them.

Abbie's gaze settled upon the two-storeyed windows along the elevator wall. Suddenly, he became aware of the possibility that the lights from the BookMarck might attract the attention of a neighbor or the local police. Abbie folded the BookMarck in half and returned it to the front pocket of his jeans, but not before it twice pulsed out a white light with strobe-like intensity.

The room darkened.

Abbie was familiar with the main gallery of the North Orange Public Library. Ten parallel aisles of books ran along the first floor wall across from where he stood, organized alphabetically by author's last name.

A massive catwalk was suspended over the first floor of

aisles. The second floor consisted of another exposed set of parallel aisles consecutively numbered eleven through twenty and concluding with the last names of authors starting with "XYZ."

As his sight adjusted to the darkness, Abbie focused on the circular staircase connecting the first and second floors below aisle Twenty.

Behind him was the door to the elevator.

Why am I identifying escape routes? he asked himself.

Abbie caught his breath. A massive figure was standing halfway down "Aisle Three – Floor One – Author's Last Name E-F," the torso backlit by the window at the end of the aisle. Abbie easily identified the figure as the stranger who had threatened him during the school board meeting. Broad shoulders filled the aisle from book stack to book stack. The oversized cranium was partly hidden by the hoodie.

Abbie did not move, fixated by a combination of fear and fascination. The darkness around the figure was occasionally interrupted by random combinations of yellows, greens, blues and reds, all originating from under the fabric of the hood.

The figure moved down the aisle toward him. But it did not appear to walk. It seemed to glide, its fluidity at odds with its size.

Once it had halved the distance between them, the figure stopped moving.

"Good evening, Abisai Taylor. We meet again."

It paused as if in no particular hurry. Or was Abbie being measured?

"Allow me to introduce myself. I am the Aginbyte of Inwit."

The Aginbyte of Inwit raised its massive hands to its cowl, hooked thumbs inside the hem and deftly pushed back the hood to reveal its face and skull.

Even in the dim light of the library, Abbie could see that the craggy face was more gray than flesh-toned. Its thick, dark lips were settled in an emotionless slash across its face. Deep crevices framed its mouth, curving upward toward nostrils until the folds dissipated into the pallor of its skin. The crow's feet that extended from the corners of its eyes suggested the tributaries of great rivers. Round its granite-like forehead and skull was a metallic headband punctuated by bolts. The headband secured a transparent dome to its skull. The dome was made up of two interlocking, watertight panels, seamed from front to back.

Inside the fluid-filled dome was the exposed brain of the Aginbyte of Inwit. Electric-like flashes previously muted by the hood now lit the darkness as the dynamism of the Aginbyte's thoughts fired from synapse to synapse.

Abbie could not pull his eyes away from the dome.

"I represent the Repositors. The Repositors are an organized group of conspiracists who have undermined cultures for centuries by seeding doubt into their sciences and scholarship. Once the Repositors have successfully debunked or discarded an intellectual property, they cull the information and reposit it into their unique data banks. They then repurpose that valuable knowledge and profit from it. Ironically they dominate cultures using the very knowledge that these cultures have themselves eschewed."

Abbie wasn't sure that he understood everything that the Aginbyte was saying.

Sensing Abbie's confusion, the Aginbyte offered an analogy.

"You might associate the Repositors with the Carpetbaggers of the American Civil War," offered the Aginbyte.

Abbie nodded his head, recalling stories of scurrilous opportunists who migrated from the North to the South after the American Civil War.

"The problem that you present to the Repositors and, by

54

extension, to me," continued the Aginbyte of Inwit, "is that, in supporting your mother's efforts to oppose censorship and fight library closures, you encourage the democratization of knowledge.

"That makes you, your mother and your sister, our adversaries."

"My sister?" Abbie repeated.

Charlotte had never participated in any of his mother's protests or events. Why would the Aginbyte include her in the list of offending parties?

"Where is Mr. Luck?" asked Abbie. Abbie silently evaluated whether he could make it to the staircase before the Aginbyte.

"Luck is gone," responded the Aginbyte impassively, either unaware of or unwilling to acknowledge the double entendre.

"Can I have my books?" asked Abbie innocently, reverting to absurdity as a defense.

Another pause. Then.

"Where did you get that BookMarck?" asked the Aginbyte of Inwit.

"Wha—?" Abbie was initially dumbfounded. "Oh. You must have seen me using this as a flashlight. Do *you* know what this is?" asked Abbie as he pulled the BookMarck out of his pocket.

Once liberated, the BookMarck bathed the room in a golden aura as if to defuse a dispute.

"It is called a BookMarck. A BookMarck is a tool of the Repositors and their agents, such as myself. We use BookMarcks to enter the BookStream, analyze the contents of a writing, and then use this interior knowledge to develop propagandas to discredit it. Then, once abandoned by your populus, we usurp the information into our coffers and profit from it."

"The BookStream?" whispered Abbie, not so much asking a question as allowing the word to roll off his tongue.

"The banks into which you reposit this discredited

knowledge? Is that the Institute of Abandoned Knowledge that you mentioned to me last night?"

"Why, yes. Yes it is," replied the Aginbyte, impressed by Abbie's having made a connection.

But the Aginbyte quickly returned to its agenda.

"You have no idea of the danger that you have invited into your family while you possess that BookMarck. Give it to me."

The Aginbyte extended its meaty hand to receive the BookMarck.

"Does it belong to you?" asked Abbie.

"In a manner of speaking, it does," replied the Aginbyte.

"Then what is its serial number?" asked Abbie.

The Aginbyte blinked once. Several synapses in its amygdala fired red. Its ancient mouth moved again.

"I extend this offer to you once more before I take the BookMarck from you. Give the BookMarck to me."

The Aginbyte began to glide forward toward Abbie. The exposed brain fired off synaptic discharges from ear to ear, accompanied by a salvo of white flashes closer to the Aginbyte's forehead. Shadows fluttered against the walls of the library.

The emanations from Abbie's BookMarck abruptly changed from golden hues to harsh primaries as if it were creating a luminescent smoke screen to camouflage Abbie.

Abbie took his cue from his BookMarck and, in the momentary kaleidoscope, ran toward the spiral staircase. He had an escape plan, but it required him gaining the second floor.

The Aginbyte closed the distance between them quickly, and Abbie did not think that he would reach the staircase in time.

Then, the visual confusion galvanized by the BookMarck was compounded by a figure running out of aisle four. The man purposefully slid to a stop between Abbie and the Aginbyte, separating them. Abbie recognized him as the bearded librarian from his previous visit to the library. Abbie's BookMarck celebrated the space around the librarian with a spray of incandescent confetti.

"Shame on you, seeking to intimidate a boy," snarled the librarian, squaring off and lowering his shoulders in the direction of the Aginbyte. "This boy. His sister. We both know that they are to be the stuff of legend. Their story has been set, even though their book may not have yet been written.

"As has your finale been written, Aginbyte," concluded the librarian, as if giving voice to a known, shared postscript.

Abbie thought he saw a moment of indecisiveness in the Aginbyte. The librarian had spoken with such assurance that Abbie took heart that he might yet escape.

"He and his sister will **not** be legendary if I stop them," threatened the Aginbyte.

The Aginbyte slid forward with an agility so incongruous with its size that it surprised both Abbie and the librarian. Their appreciation was short-lived, as the Aginbyte backhanded the librarian with a blow so brutal that it lifted him off the floor and across the room.

The librarian landed upon his back just before the reference desk, his hand immediately going to his chin.

"My jaw, you bastard," groaned the sprawled librarian.

Abbie watched as the Aginbyte menacingly glided across the floor toward the fallen librarian, speed no longer a tactical necessity.

The librarian saw the Aginbyte as well, but could not avoid the descent of the Aginbyte's massive boot upon his extended right ankle. The librarian's cry of pain echoed throughout the library.

For the second time that day, Abbie tried to make himself invisible as he backed his way up the spiral staircase toward the second floor fire exit.

As the librarian reflexively reached toward his ankle, the

Aginbyte grabbed the librarian's shirt front, hoisted his torso off the floor, and tossed the librarian across the laminate floorboards as if rolling a bowling ball. Abbie watched the librarian slide toward him, his head narrowly missing the steel bar fixing the spiral staircase to the floor. The librarian's left shoulder absorbed the blow but halted his slide.

With the librarian below him, Abbie realized what was happening. He was witnessing a demonstration. The Aginbyte was illustrating what would befall Abbie once the librarian was finished.

Abbie's scenario-building was interrupted by the outstretched right hand of the librarian.

"Mate. Your BookMarck?"

Abbie suddenly became aware that he still held his BookMarck in his right hand, and quickly handed it to his defender.

The librarian sought out Abbie's eyes as if to say: *Watch and Learn.*

Then, after sharing what was becoming a familiar grin and wink, the librarian raised Abbie's BookMarck.

"*The Odyssey.* Homer," said the librarian with a purposefulness that would leave no mistaking his destination.

The gallery blazed with arcs of lightning from Abbie's BookMarck.

Then, the librarian's right arm morphed from substance to colored light, a sequence that progressed through his shoulder and neck, and down his torso until his entire silhouette had become a melange of the incorporeal colors of the universe. The light, as if possessed of its own intelligence, collapsed into a stream, whipped across the room and down aisle four into what Abbie assumed to be the nearest location of Homer's *Odyssey.*

The Aginbyte watched the librarian's departure with a studied nonchalance, as if it were a phenomenon it had seen many times before.

The Aginbyte of Inwit gave Abbie a stare of intimidation, then pulled what looked to be an identical BookMarck from the left sleeve of its massive hoodie.

"*The Odyssey*, Homer," repeated the Aginbyte.

Abbie watched with a greater sense of expectation, admiring the phenomena of traveling into a BookStream via a BookMarck. He watched as the Aginbyte's cellular structure degraded into a lightform and then compressed into a light stream, finally departing in a swift wave of color down aisle four in pursuit of the librarian and his BookMarck.

As the room finally darkened, Abbie sat down on a staircase step for the first time in what felt like hours and attempted to process what he'd seen and heard.

"Holy shit," he said aloud, his voice bouncing about the now empty gallery.

Chapter Six

Charlotte 1.2

Abbie rarely, if ever, woke Charlotte from her sleep. But there he was, sitting at the foot of her bed, shaking her foot without having asked to enter her bedroom.

"Is it morning already?" she asked, wiping the drowse from her eyes.

"What are you doing in my bedroom, you infidel?"

"No, it's not morning. Wake up. I have to talk to you," he responded with deference, hoping that she'd not be so angry with him as to dismiss him.

"Well, could you at least get me a bottle of water?"

Charlotte stretched, then drank, and then listened as Abbie unspooled his story about the Aginbyte of Inwit, at first a threatening curiosity at the school board meeting, and then a fearsome deliverer of harm in the North Orange Public Library. He told her about how a librarian who had referred to them as the "stuff of legends" came to his defense by luring the Aginbyte into *The Odyssey*.

Finally, he described what it looked like to be disassembled atom by atom and transported by BookMarck into the BookStream.

The only thing he held back from his sister was his impression that a BookMarck might be self-aware. Was it his imagination, or were the colors accompanying the departure of the Aginbyte less fervent than those accompanying the librarian? Could a BookMarck tell good from evil? Did it take sides? Abbie could not yet bring himself to believe that a BookMarck had a sentient intelligence, and so he decided to not yet share his theory with Charlotte.

Charlotte watched her brother. She weighed whether to cut him with cynicism or to dismiss him as absurd. But somewhere in her core she knew that something serious had happened.

"You must have dreamed this," concluded Charlotte. "This is the psychological fall-out from your meeting in the library with Mom and Dad," she continued.

Abbie had been leaning forward in earnestness as he spoke to his sister. Her response caused him to tilt back and distance himself from her.

"How can you be so, so—" Abbie paused as he searched for his words.

"...So emotionally detached from everything?" Charlotte offered, completing her brother's question. "I am emotionally detached because I am so profoundly self-absorbed," Charlotte pronounced.

Charlotte laughed her gerbil laugh. For the first time since he'd arrived home, Abbie felt normal.

"Okay. Okay. You are never going to believe me, are you?" He grinned.

Charlotte smiled but did not respond.

"Do me a favor?" he asked.

She waited.

"Humor me. If we are being pursued, can we develop some sort of accelerated notification system to contact each other?" he requested.

"Why are you so preoccupied with speed?" she asked.

"Because the Aginbyte is so deceptively fast for its size. And because it doesn't walk. It surfs the earth's surface."

Charlotte considered this information before she responded.

"Okay. I promise not to add any new apparitions to the crazies already populating my life," she smart-assed back at him. "But seriously, Abbie, if I do run into trouble, I will call you. I will not text you. I will call you. And I never call anybody. So that way, you'll know I'm in serious shit. Okay?"

Abbie nodded in agreement.

Then, as she rose from her bed, she stomped upon his foot.

"You can call me the Aginbytemyass from now on," she snarked as she moved toward the bathroom.

"Now get out of my room."

Chapter Seven

A Reunion

During the week following his confrontation with the Aginbyte of Inwit, Abbie's sneakers were stolen immediately before gym class and he received a zero for unpreparedness. Cameron had asked if he'd seen her hand truck, and he denied knowing its location, knowing full well he'd left it behind in the gallery the night he'd fled the library. Priscilla Stern ignored him. He aced his calculus test.

He'd not had to warn Charlotte that he was being pursued by the Aginbyte of Inwit.

In other words, life had moved on with some normalcy.

At the conclusion of that week, Abbie's copy of *The Three Musketeers* came due for renewal. Had it been scanned through the library's lending software, he could have easily renewed it online. But since it had been manually checked out, he would need to renew it personally.Any residual anxiety that Abbie carried about his confrontation with the Aginbyte had been diluted by the events of his week. He was even a little curious to see if there remained any evidence of that night of mayhem.

It was a convenient coincidence that Abbie's independent study class fell on the morning of the library book's renewal date, because Abbie would not have to report for school until mid-morning. He might even get to return to his mother's townhouse for breakfast before reporting to school.

So, on a day when the morning sunlight seemed to bathe the earth in gold, Abisai Taylor returned to the North Orange Public Library, superstitiously entering through the front door so as not to duplicate the rhythms of his previous visit. He was reassured by the appearance of at least five other library patrons. But their presence did not come as a surprise to him. He had reconnoitered the parking lot and counted at least five cars other than his own.

The gaunt librarian with the combover was working the reservation desk. Abbie could have quickly renewed his book and exited. But he hung back. He was curious to see if the room evidenced any indications of the fight from the week before.

Abbie did his best impression of casual. First, he loitered about the perimeter of the gallery to browse the magazines in the wall racks. Then, he moved over to the kiosks of graphic novels. Finally, he made his way over to the spiral staircase, looking for gouges in the laminate flooring or damage to the base of the staircase.

Emboldened that his inspection yielded no evidence of a fight, Abbie approached the reservation desk to renew his copy of *The Three Musketeers.*

The librarian did not look up as Abbie stood before him. He accepted Abbie's book and opened the back cover as if to stamp the renewal date. But instead of recording an extended return date, the librarian leaned toward Abbie and spoke down into the pages as if to share a confidence.

"Aisle Twelve," whispered the librarian.

Abbie repeated the words back to the librarian.

"Aisle Twelve?"

"Aisle Twelve," repeated the librarian, and he raised his head in a slight nod toward the second floor stacks.

Abbie turned to look over his left shoulder and read the signage on the aisle.

Aisle Twelve - Floor Two

By Author's Last Name

"W"

Abbie placed his hand on the reservation desk for support and stepped up onto his toes to try to peer down aisle twelve, but his sight line was blocked by the height of the second floor landing.

"What's in aisle twelve?" Abbie asked as he turned back to the librarian.

But the librarian was gone, and he had taken *The Three Musketeers* with him.

The room is bright. There are other people in the building. There's no way that the Aginbyte is attempting to hide back there.

Abbie climbed the spiral staircase and walked across the second floor platform, staying on the balls of his feet to minimize the sound of his footfalls.

He stopped his forward progress at the stack for aisle thirteen. He gripped the vertical columns supporting the book shelves, leaned his body forward and peeked down the corridor of aisle twelve.

He immediately recognized his white-bearded defender from the previous week.

The librarian stood casually, one elbow resting at shoulder height on a partially empty shelf, his legs crossed at his ankles.

"Oh my God! It's you! You're alive! Are you all right?" Abbie exclaimed, striding excitedly down the narrow aisle toward the librarian.

The tanned figure grinned. He wore a short-sleeved safari shirt as if ready for adventure. He raised a single finger to his lips.

"Shhhhhh. Quiet, mate." He grinned.

"It is, after all, a library."

The librarian stepped toward Abbie and offered his hand in greeting. The librarian had obviously concluded his Aginbyte business with his vitality intact, impressing Abbie with the muscularity of his wide forearm and the strength of his grip. Yet, it was not lost on Abbie that the librarian supported his weight on his left foot as he stood.

"How can you even be on your feet?" asked Abbie.

"Aye. How can I be walking indeed?"

The librarian rested both of his elbows on an empty portion of a bookshelf to relieve the weight on his right ankle.

"Who are you?" Abbie finally asked.

"A friend," he replied with not a small amount of mischief in his voice.

"What was that thing that attacked us?"

"That is the Aginbyte of Inwit. It is an agent of an organization that seeks to discredit the value of scholarship, and then appropriate that discredited knowledge for profit."

"An agent?" asked Abbie. "You mean that there are more of them? What do they want with me?"

The librarian sighed, as if weighing how much information to divulge.

"The future suggests that you and your sister will join us and become powerful defenders of scholarship. There will be books written about you, and some of your history will be exaggerated into folklore. All of that threatens them."

"Us? Them?" asked Abbie, confused yet a little impressed that he might someday be considered a colleague of this impressive man.

The librarian raised his hand and stroked his beard, pausing to consider his words before he spoke.

"Them? Let's call *them* the Repositors," the man finally responded.

"Us?" he continued. "We are WordSmythes."

"This is like science fiction," responded Abbie.

"A meritorious genre," the man responded with a telling grin, "but not my *metier*."

"How did you escape from the Aginbyte?" asked Abbie.

"Your ankle was broken."

"No. Not quite broken. But damaged. Your BookMarck is of the 500 series. 501.23 to be exact. The five hundred series of BookMarcks are very reliable. Perhaps not the speediest, but dependable."

"What does this have to do with your escaping the Aginbyte?" pressed Abbie.

"Patience, Abisai Taylor. There is value in a well-spun story, don't you think?" the librarian suggested.

"So, your BookMarck's registration number of 501.23 indicates that it falls into the five hundred series of BookMarcks, and that this particular BookMarck has twenty-three properties. One of these properties, fortunately for me, is a healing factor.

"Are you familiar with red light therapy?" continued the librarian.

He did not wait for Abbie to reply.

"Wavelengths of light can reduce inflammation, produce new blood vessels, new fibroblasts, new tissue. Your BookMarck is the equivalent of red light therapy on steroids. As soon as you handed your BookMarck to me, it recognized that my ankle had been compromised and bathed my ankle in extraordinary frequencies of light. Those light frequencies initiated an accelerated healing process, allowing me to quickly recover and to elude our flummoxed adversary. And so, here I am."

"Healing properties," Abbie repeated to no one in particular, and shook his head in fascination.

With that, the bearded man unbuttoned the flap of his shirt pocket and extracted the BookMarck. Once liberated, the BookMarck emitted a steady pulse of light.

"Repositors covet BookMarcks. It allows them access to the interior of all written materials. From the inside of books, articles and researches, the Repositors identify or create vulnerabilities in logic, then publicize and exploit those flaws to the public until that scholarship is perceived to be worthless. The Repositors then collect the debunked material, use it, profit by it, apply for copyrights and create monopolies.

"The Aginbyte of Inwit, and the Repositors, will not rest until they have recovered your BookMarck.

"You and your sister are in real danger. I speak to you today so that you might learn to use the BookStream to elude your pursuers."

"My sister? How does she—?" began Abbie.

The librarian intentionally ignored Abbie's interruption and continued.

"When you are in the BookStream of a novel or a piece of writing, you may live in between its paragraphs, and participate in the lives of its characters, but you may not disturb the storyline or interfere with its narrative. So, it makes sense for you to enter only those novels with which you have familiarity. This will allow you to anticipate events and avoid disturbing them."

"What happens if I interfere with a narrative?" Abbie asked.

"The book will disintegrate and cease to exist. It does not happen often, but it has occurred. To their credit, Repositors value the integrity of the books they invade, and they are careful not to disturb a narrative. If you are skillful enough, you can use the Repositors' respect for books against them as a tactical advantage."

"What happens to you if you are in the novel when it disintegrates?" Abbie asked.

"Let's not worry about that right now, shall we?" responded the librarian. "Finally, when you travel in the BookStream, elapsed time in your 'present' will toll. Your 'present' will move exceedingly slowly until you return from the BookStream, so you need not worry about 'missing' your life."

The librarian paused to look at Abbie and assess whether he could absorb anything else.

"You'll need this as well."

The librarian reached into the book stack behind Abbie and withdrew a copy of *The Time Machine*.

He opened the copy of *The Time Machine*, slid the BookMarck deeply between page 121 and page 122 to secure it, and handed the book to Abbie. The pulse of the BookMarck began to accelerate as one's heart might beat faster when reunited with a valued friend.

The librarian winked as he tapped his index finger upon the cover of the book.

"H.G. Wells," he said, referring to the author. "He fancied my third wife, you know."

As he handed Abbie the book, the librarian's smile grew distant, as if surveying the absurdities of life.

Then, he snapped back to the necessities of their meeting.

"In order for you and your sister to ultimately exit from the BookStream, you must return to your present using Wells' Time Machine. It is the best exit plan that I can offer you right now.

"Now, it is time for us to part ways," said the librarian, his gaze scanning the spaces between the rows of books to ensure they'd not been overheard or spied upon.

"Did you return here using the Time Machine?" pursued Abbie.

"GO!" barked the librarian. "Now. You see? You've forced me to violate the 'Librarian's Oath of Silence.'"

The librarian smiled warmly, winked and extended his hand to say goodbye.

"Do librarians really take an 'Oath of Silence?'" Abbie asked.

"No."

Abbie exited the aisle and hurried down the spiral staircase toward the exit, his book in hand. He needed to speak to Charlotte to update her on all that he'd learned.

Before he could reach the front door, the woman standing behind the front desk cleared her throat.

"Aren't you forgetting something?" she asked, and she nodded toward *The Time Machine*.

"Oh yea. Sorry. I forgot," apologized Abbie.

"You seem distracted. I pray you, don't dwell on your dreams."

Abbie stopped and looked at her, aware that every word spoken to him could be part of the larger narrative that swirled around him. She, too, appeared to be familiar, her red hair falling gently upon the shoulders of her powder blue blouse.

"I think that I left the *Three Musketeers* back here somewhere with the other librarian," he said to her, quietly and carefully.

She stamped the return date on the back page of *The Time Machine*, and pushed it toward him along with his copy of *The Three Musketeers*.

"Enjoy," she said innocently.

As Abbie turned to leave, he heard the remote scanner fall to the floor, a victim of the sweep of the back of the librarian's hand.

Chapter Eight

BookMarcks

The interior headband of Charlotte's racing helmet was irritating her forehead, so she unstrapped her chin guard and removed her helmet. She hoped that the telltale red mark it always left across her forehead would fade by first period homeroom.

I wonder how the Aginbyte of Inwit deals with a steel band bolted to its forehead? Charlotte shook her head to dismiss the thought, as if the details of her brother's incredible narrative from the previous evening were dust she could shake out through her ears.

She looked at the racing app on her smartwatch to distract herself. According to the app, she had raced to the small cupola at the top of Ivy Hill in 34:32.8. Charlotte dropped her helmet to the ground and slowly leaned back until her spine touched the backrest of her speedchair.

That's a fast time, she thought. *I guess anxiety is a great motivator.*

With her training regimen completed for the morning, Charlotte paused to focus on the vista below her. To her right, she could make out the roof of her high school, her ultimate destination that morning.

Far below her, she could see her mother's townhouse at the base of Ivy Hill.

Her mother's townhouse reminded her of her parents' divorce.

Did they divorce because of me?

Charlotte caught herself before she spiraled downward. Over her years of counseling, her sports psychologist had provided her with strategies to reroute dispiriting thoughts into positivity, but this morning Charlotte was having a hard time finding her way out.

So she turned her chair away from the downhill, let her arms dangle to her sides, and bent her head back to savor the first rays of the rising sun.

She inhaled deeply. The cool, moist air of the dawning day had not yet lost its newness to carbon emissions and heat. She repeated deep breathing for several cycles, imagining the tissues of her challenged body being vitalized by pure air.

As her body began to cool, Charlotte began to inventory her muscle groups for pain. Her mind wandered back to the consequences of imbalance that she'd endured growing up: skinned knees, abused elbows, falls and concussions.

I can't fight off my past today, she said to herself. *It's claiming me. Stop fighting it. Just go with it and see where it leads.*

Having given herself permission, Charlotte began to replay the highlight reel of her life with Multiple Sclerosis. She remembered Saturday mornings with her family, entering the local diner and tripping over obstacles that didn't exist. Then came the turned heads and the forward rush of strangers seeking to assist. Finally came the tears of her embarrassment, easily misinterpreted as pain.

She saw the varied faces and demeanors of her examining physicians: young and old, female and male, serious, some inauthentic, some sincerely friendly. She compared suburban treatment centers with the more historic, traditional, urban hospitals squeezed in among the intimidating buildings of New York City.

Charlotte knew where her mind was taking her. So she accelerated her thought process to *the moment*.

She remembered the voice of Grandma Anna, calling her name from the entryway of their home. Charlotte exited her first floor bedroom off the kitchen to greet her grandmother, passing her seated parents and brother at the breakfast table.

"Were you expecting Grandma?" asked her mother.

"No. Were you?" asked Charlotte as she passed through the kitchen to the foyer.

After exchanging a hug with her grandmother, Charlotte stepped back and watched Anna open the front door as if drawing open the curtain at a Broadway opening.

There sat a wheelchair, the primal scream of its de rigueur fluorescent rental tag fluttering in the light morning breeze.

My life in a wheelchair.

Abbie, Gus and Cameron froze in momentary indecision about who to help first: Charlotte, who was hurling a string of unimaginable expletives in all directions, or Grandma Anna, whose blood had drained from her face as she realized the enormity of her massive miscalculation.

But when Gus sprinted forward to lift the chair off the porch and spirit it away, Charlotte screamed at him.

"Leave it, Dad! Leave it RIGHT THERE!"

For months, guests would navigate around the wheelchair to enter the house. Among neighbors, the shorthand description of the Taylor residence became "the house with the wheelchair."

Charlotte used that moment define herself as an independent and uncompromising woman. She abandoned using her brother as her benchmark for success, surpassing his record of honor roll mentions to lock down the highest GPA in her grade. She eclipsed

Abbie's modest fencing career to be named to the all-state gymnastics team on the uneven bars. She insisted that her parents relocate her bedroom from the anteroom off the kitchen to the second floor, engaging the challenge of their staircase every day. As she walked to school every morning, she would good-naturedly wave to her classmates as their school bus passed by.

But in her private conversations with herself, Charlotte was unable to deny that her lower body was breaking down with increasing frequency.

It was Adam Goldberg's younger sister Amy who summoned the courage to share an advertisement she'd seen on Tumblr:

> WANTED: Children who require support to walk,
> yet seek the excitement of speed.

At Charlotte's request, and after a series of emails, Cameron and Gus were able to arrange an introduction with the owners of Uber Ergodynamics, LP.

The offices of Uber Ergodynamics were located in a corporate office park of low slung buildings with sandy brick exteriors, one as nondescript as the next. The lobby of their offices was painted stone blue with a low pile carpet to match. There was no receptionist to greet them. So, while Cameron attempted to announce their arrival by depressing a white button on the lone desk in the lobby, Gus signed the guest book and Charlotte began to pace off the length of each lobby wall.

They were greeted by a woman who immediately focused on Charlotte's activity.

"I'll save you the effort, Charlotte. This room has the dimensions of a double cube—" started the first woman through the interior doorway.

"...And bravo to you, Charlotte, for seeing that

74

straightaway," said the second woman through the doorway, close on the heels of the first woman.

"We think that the previous tenants had hoped to build out an art gallery in this space. Anyway, allow me to introduce my spouse and business partner, Ms. Maggie Wright—" said the second woman as she gestured toward the first.

"...And allow me to introduce **my** spouse and business partner, Dr. Ursula Wojszek," said Maggie Wright as she gave Wojszek's elbow an affectionate squeeze.

"You must be Charlotte Taylor."

Maggie Wright oscillated Charlotte's arm in an overenthusiastic handshake, followed by Dr. Wojszek who seemed to have mistaken Charlotte's outstretched arm for a water pump.

Charlotte's face creased with an involuntary grin.

In the two weeks of interviews that followed, Charlotte was enchanted by the synchronicity of Maggie Wright and Ursula Wojszek. Both of them unfailingly attended all of her interviews with unassailable punctuality, dressed and styled identically (white lab coats with their hair pulled up in buns), as if to present to the world one intelligence separated by two bodies.

Charlotte felt that they were at their best in conversation. Maggie might introduce an ingenious concept or thought, but would only allow herself one phrase to do so, then defer to Ursula to finish the thought. Ursula would then extend the same deference to Maggie, the result of which was a comic duet of alternating insights. Charlotte felt as if she were audience to a Greek chorus. To Charlotte, this pushed Wright/Wojszek into the realm of loveable eccentrics.

Most importantly to Charlotte, Wright/Wojszek celebrated their gay marriage with transparency and comfort, providing her

75

with an affirmation of love that was missing from the emotional fall-out plaguing her parents.

Wright and Wojszek treated Charlotte's final interview with the pomp of a graduation ceremony, inviting Gus and Cameron to attend.

"Charlotte Taylor—" began Maggie Wright. She tried to continue, but had to pause to collect herself. Dr. Ursula Wojszek gave Maggie's elbow a squeeze of encouragement.

"Charlotte Taylor," began Wright once again. "You have surpassed all of our expectations as a candidate…"

"…And we would like to invite you to join our team as our test pilot," said Dr. Wojszek, completing the thought. "But then, we knew you were the right candidate from the moment we met you…"

"…As you attempted to confirm that our reception area was a double cube. That kind of intellectual curiosity…"

"…Combined with the courage to pace out a strange room among strange people speaks volumes about who you are. So…"

"…Will you join us?"

"Join you to do what, exactly?" asked the perplexed Charlotte for what seemed to be the hundredth time.

Wright/Wojszek bowed and excused themselves, but not before asking their intern, Amy Goldberg, to escort the Taylors to the building's test track.

Gus, Cameron and Charlotte followed Amy down a long hallway. As they walked toward the rear of the building, they passed several laboratories and offices, some of which Charlotte recognized as rooms in which she'd been interviewed.

Pushing through two double doors, the party was again greeted by Wright and Wojszek, each now carrying identical clipboards.

"Charlotte, this is the prototype VLCT 1200," said Wright. The VLCT 1200 sat under a pool of stage lamps, its highly polished surfaces reflecting stars of light. An indoor test track sat behind the dais, its synthetic cedar plank flooring and banked curves a shallower version of velodromes that Charlotte had seen during telecasts of Olympic bike racing.

"This is not a wheelchair. This is a speedchair. We built it not as an accommodation but as an extension of a person's desire for speed," said Dr. Wojszek.

"In building it, we combined specialized strength-to-weight materials with state of the art gearshift engineering," said Ms. Wright.

As Gus, Cameron and Amy listened politely to the Wright/Wojszek presentation, Charlotte walked around the VLCT 1200 to the oval test track behind it. She peered down the first straightaway.

Once Charlotte was satisfied with the track, she walked back toward the VLCT 1200. She hesitated at first, thinking the three-wheel frame would be unstable.

Then, she poured her body into the seat, surprised by how naturally her body folded into the tapered "V" of the three-wheeled cockpit, two twenty-four inch cambered wheels beside her and a single spoked wheel in front. The low backrest forced her center of gravity forward, encouraging her to push on the grip rims of the exterior, cambered wheels.

Charlotte's anxiety disintegrated, and she felt the excitement associated with speed. It was a feeling that she'd thought was lost forever.

She looked up at the pair as if to say, "Let's go."

"Oh no—," started Dr. Wojszek, reading Charlotte's eyes.

"…Not without racing gloves—" advised Maggie Wright.

"…And a helmet," concluded Dr. Wojszek.

Charlotte dutifully strapped on her gloves and helmet, impressed but not surprised that both had already been custom-fitted to the specific contours of her hands and head.

With Charlotte strapped into the cockpit, Maggie and Ursula gently guided the speedchair onto the track.

"The VLCT 1200 has an anti-rollback brake system—" started Dr. Wojszek.

"…That will allow you to race-climb hills that might otherwise have seemed insurmountable," said Ms. Wright, concluding the thought.

Now on the track, Ursula and Maggie gave Charlotte their final instructions.

"Just take it down this straightaway," advised Dr. Wojszek.

"No surprises," advised Maggie Wright.

"When you reach the first curve, there is a decline," counseled Wojszek.

"You'll feel yourself accelerate going into the banked turn," alternated Wright.

"What then?" asked Charlotte.

Dr. Wojszek looked at Maggie Wright, then back to Charlotte.

"Then, punch it."

Over the years that followed, Maggie Wright and Dr. Wojszek would repeatedly strip down the VLCT to its lug nuts and recreate it, attempting to build a vehicle that would complement Charlotte's capacity for speed.

Charlotte's life accelerated into a new direction as she immersed herself in the world of speedchair racing. Her parents retained trainers who devised devilish regimens to develop

Charlotte's deltoids, pecs, triceps, forearms and lats. She punched the push rims of her speedchair in an infinite dance of repetitions, pulling her elbows behind her ribcage, then extending her triceps to drive forward. She worked with flexibility coaches to increase her lumbar and thoracic flexion, and to extend her shoulders. She was treated by a corps of health care professionals to address her inevitable shoulder joint irritations and rotator cuff injuries.

She swapped out her mental health professional for a sports psychologist.

As Charlotte developed as an athlete, she shed the trappings of girlhood. Although she'd forever be grateful for her brother's protectiveness, she'd now pushed through her need for it.

But I did agree to call him, she said to herself, *if I bump into the Aginbyte of Inwit.*

The dewiness of morning had suddenly begun to melt into the heat and humidity of an accelerated summer. At the top of Ivy Hill, Charlotte closed her eyes and allowed the perspiration under her eyes to steam. She briefly considered removing her racing gloves but thought better of it. In a moment, she would need to return to her mother's townhouse, shower, inhale breakfast, apply some makeup and walk to school.

Let's take one more moment, she breathed to herself.

Suddenly, the reflection of orange light through her closed eyelids darkened. Too sudden to be from the effects of a passing cloud, her heart skipped as she realized that something had moved in front of her and blocked the light of the rising sun.

She opened her eyes. A large figure had positioned itself to use the backlight from the sun to obscure itself.

The Aginbyte, she said to herself.

Charlotte pivoted her speedchair ever so slightly, hoping to draw the gaze of the Aginbyte to her left hand while she moved her right hand to seek out the small can of mace belted to her waist.

"Good morning, Charlotte Taylor."

"Allow me to introduce myself. I am the Aginbyte of Inwit. Perhaps your brother has spoken of me? We are colleagues."

The Aginbyte of Inwit, Charlotte repeated to herself. *Quite the introduction. You've managed to patronize me and lie to me in the same breath.*

"Who are you? And what do you want?" she asked, stalling.

"I watched your ascent up this grade. It was an impressive display of strength and athleticism."

"I'm an athlete. My upper body strength took years of exercise and training to develop." Charlotte threw as many words at the Aginbyte as she could, hoping to buy time and develop an escape plan. She analyzed the distance between them and concluded that the trajectory of her mace spray would fall short of the Aginbyte's height.

"Yes. I am familiar with upper body strength," said the Aginbyte, agreeably.

"Do you require this vehicle all the time, or can you walk?"

Charlotte noted her first advantage: the Aginbyte did not know that she could still walk passably well. She might be able to use that uncertainty to her advantage.

"There are more efficient ways to travel," advised the Aginbyte.

"Like so."

The Aginbyte slid to its right as if surfing on a wave of air. Then, the Aginbyte repeated the maneuver, but this time to its left, appearing to simulate the swing of a pendulum.

"That looked like a half pipe without a skateboard,"

observed Charlotte, impressed with the maneuver despite her apprehension.

"Indeed," the Aginbyte replied. "Imagine. Freedom from your chair. I could give you this technology, were you to cooperate with me."

The absurdity of the moment did not escape her.

I am in a negotiation, thought Charlotte.

"What do you want?" she asked again.

Charlotte tensed her body in the event of an attack, recalling the Aginbyte's assault on the librarian as recounted by her brother.

"Do you recognize this?"

The Aginbyte bent at its waist so that its large hands were at Charlotte's eye level. Then, it pulled a BookMarck out of the left sleeve of its hoodie. In the sunlight atop Ivy Hill, the BookMarck pulsed with violets and blues.

"Wha…?"

Charlotte squinted and moved her face forward, as if unable to focus on the BookMarck in the sunlight.

The Aginbyte attempted to accommodate her by moving the BookMarck closer to her face.

"That's my brother's," Charlotte said matter-of-factly.

Charlotte snatched the BookMarck out of the outstretched hand of the Aginbyte and stuffed it down the front of her T-shirt. While bent forward in the direction of the Aginbyte, Charlotte gripped the bottommost section of her push rims and pulled as mightily as she could.

At first, the tires of her VLCT 1200 skidded on the dry, loose stones beneath her wheels. Charlotte could find no traction and thought her escape was lost. But then, the tire treads shed the last of the detritus of the sidewalk, gripped the pitted concrete, and moved her backward down the hill away from the Aginbyte.

The Aginbyte's hood could not suppress the colors of surprise that rocked its cranium. Charlotte stole a glimpse forward to see the Aginbyte bend its knees to initiate a surf in pursuit.

Charlotte sped backwards down the street and toward her mother's townhouse. Although she knew the idiosyncrasies of this downhill run, she had never attempted to ride it backwards. Appropriately frightened by the Aginbyte, Charlotte continued to pull at her wheels while glancing over her shoulder to steer.

Within moments, Charlotte was inside the shade of a large saucer magnolia tree. Normally, she'd curse the uprooted tree as having raised a section of the macadam. The crust of the street had been buckled and split like a giant boil, coerced by an ascendant tree root.

Today, it would serve Charlotte.

Charlotte maneuvered the left tire of her speedchair to roll up the uneven gravel of the erupted street surface. As she crested the slope, the left tire of the chair lifted off of the ground. Once the tire was airborne, Charlotte threw the weight of her body into the backrest, jerking her single front tire off the ground as well. With only her right tire grounded, Charlotte pulled her brake and pushed her body into her right shoulder blade. The chair pinwheeled on its immobile rear right tire, spinning Charlotte into a hundred and eighty degree pirouette and turning the chair to face downhill.

Charlotte folded her torso forward to ground all three wheels, releasing her brake as she did so The unlocked wheels briefly skidded on the loose macadam, then gained traction. Charlotte punched her grip wheels with both hands to reaccelerate forward and down the street. She directed a silent

82

prayer of thanks to Maggie and Ursula. The VLCT 1200 had held true.

Charlotte did not look back to check whether the Aginbyte had closed the distance between them, fearing that twisting her torso might slow her. Instead, she tucked her head between her knees and punched her grip wheels to minimize her wind resistance and maximize her acceleration.

"Since you don't have your helmet—" she heard Miss Wright observe in her head.

"...Don't brake with your head," advised Dr. Wojszek, completing the thought.

Charlotte unbuckled her seatbelt and detached her mobile phone. Head down, eyes forward, she thumbed in her passcode and punched the automatic dial-up for her brother, never once looking at the dialpad.

Abbie, having returned from the library, answered her call immediately, as they had agreed.

"What's wrong?" he asked over the speaker function.

"MayDay!" she screamed. "The AginBiteMyAss is after me. Meet me in the front yard. I'm crash landing!"

Cameron Taylor's townhouse was about a hundred yards up and beyond the hill bottom, and Charlotte hoped that the short climb up the incline on the opposite side of the trough would provide her with a small amount of deceleration. A slight decrease in speed was all she sought.

Charlotte reached the trough of the hill at full speed. She angled her chair up the apron of the neighbor's driveway to allow gravity to slightly decrease her speed, veered up the slope of her mother's front lawn to slow herself further still, and then directed herself toward the cement retaining wall separating her mother's townhouse from her neighbors. She saw her brother run out of the front door with his knapsack in one hand and Charlotte's school backpack in the other.

He has a plan, she thought.

Abbie jumped down the front steps and focused on his sister. Then, he looked back up Ivy Hill.

Charlotte had about a twenty foot lead on the Aginbyte.

Once at the top of the lawn, Charlotte threw her weight to her left side and intentionally dumped the VLCT into a sidelong skid. The chair flipped onto its side, then skimmed across the front lawn until it collided wheels first with the retaining wall, jettisoning Charlotte onto the lawn. Her brother was at her side in moments.

"He's not the only fucker who can surf," she yelled.

"Only he's not surfing," he yelled back at her.

Charlotte looked up to see that the Aginbyte was not gliding after her, but executing the most awkward attempt to run downhill that she had ever seen. The Aginbyte was struggling not only with the downhill incline but also with its own stability. It paused after each massive step forward as if to avoid blowing out its knees, wavering from left to right as it did so.

Charlotte's emotions caught her by surprise. She felt a pang of remorse for the struggling Aginbyte.

As she pushed herself into a sit, Charlotte reached into the front of her T-shirt and pulled out the BookMarck.

"I got this back for you!" she yelled proudly to her brother, triumphantly waving the BookMarck in the air.

"What do you mean?" he yelled back at her, and held his own BookMarck in front of her face.

"Oh shit!" Charlotte said, realizing that she'd stolen the BookMarck of the Aginbyte of Inwit. Abbie watched as Charlotte's righteousness drained from her face, her confidence in having avenged the theft of her brother's BookMarck evaporating.

"Charlotte, you've got to get out of here," Abbie continued, his protectiveness kicking in. "Your BookMarck will send you into the BookStream of any book you choose!"

"What's the BookStream?" she yelled back at him.

Fighting against his adrenaline, Abbie pushed his face into Charlotte's ear so that only she could hear him.

"Just say aloud the book title and its author and you'll be absorbed into the narrative of a novel. You can live within its narrative and among its characters, but you cannot disturb the plot.

"Where do you want to go? Jane Austen? F. Scott Fitzgerald? Just be quiet when you say it so the Aginbyte doesn't follow you!

"And take this!" he added as he pushed her backpack into her arms. "The librarian said that our way home is through Wells' *Time Machine*! It's in your bag."

Charlotte dug into her school backpack and pulled out her copy of *The Memoirs of Sherlock Holmes*, exchanging it into Abbie's knapsack.

"This is where I'll be," she whispered back.

Charlotte reached around her brother's neck and embraced him, pressing her cheek to his. But before he could reciprocate, she held the BookMarck of the Aginbyte before her face.

"Sir Arthur Conan Doyle. *The Memoirs of Sherlock Holmes*," she whispered to her BookMarck, out of the earshot of the oncoming Aginbyte.

Charlotte's hand, arm and shoulder transfigured into a rainbow of sparkles, then transformed her entire body into a stream of light, arcing her into the air and flying back into Abisai's knapsack to seek out her copy of *The Memoirs of Sherlock Holmes*.

As the Aginbyte lumbered forward, it took note that Charlotte's pathway of escape had taken her into a book in Abbie's knapsack.

Abbie pivoted on his knees and faced the oncoming Aginbyte of Inwit.

"Why are you chasing me?" yelled Abbie, waving the BookMarck in his hand as if he held a talisman.

The Aginbyte stopped moving and put both of its massive hands to its knees as if to collect itself.

"I seek your BookMarck so that you do not follow the path of your parents," replied the Aginbyte between gulps of air.

"My parents? Do they know about all this?"

The words tumbled out of Abbie as he tried to process this information and form an intelligible question at the same time.

"'Do they know about all this?'" repeated the Aginbyte, rhetorically.

"Who do you think gave you that BookMarck?"

Abbie had always assumed that the BookMarck had been mistakenly left in his copy of *The Three Musketeers*, or slipped to him by one of the librarians. He'd never considered that his parents had secreted it into his library book. As he replayed the events of their meeting in the library, he focused on his father having slid the copy of *The Three Musketeers* to him.

Then, he remembered his father's words.

"Every time you open a book, you give literacy one more chance to survive."

Were he and Charlotte literacy's last chance to survive?

Abbie's reverie was interrupted by the Aginbyte who had renewed his bull rush toward him. Abbie threw himself back against the white retaining wall and sat next to the twisted frame of the VLCT 1200, hefting to his chest his knapsack with its three books.

He held his BookMarck before him.

"Let's see how good your French is! *The Three Musketeers*! Alexandre Dumas!"

Abbie recalled how the bearded librarian had lured the

Aginbyte into *The Odyssey* and hoped that his declaration would do the same to draw the Aginbyte away from Charlotte.

The Aginbyte of Inwit watched impassively as Abbie's corporeality transformed into a light signature and made good his escape.

The Aginbyte of Inwit paused to consider the events of the morning. A wisp of a child had managed to steal its BookMarck and escape. Her destination had been effectively concealed, the only clue to her whereabouts being inside the knapsack of Abisai Taylor.

The Aginbyte nodded its massive cranium in self-agreement.

The legend was true.

Charlotte Taylor would be a formidable foe.

BOOK TWO

Chapter Nine

Abisai in Paris

As Abbie's vision cleared, he found himself sitting astride the haunches of a metal horse suspended high above the ground. His muscles stiffened in momentary panic. Hoping to avoid a long and disastrous fall, Abbie tightened his embrace around the metallic waist of the immobile rider in front of him.

Where am I? he asked himself.

Abbie allowed himself a moment of disorientation, appreciating that he'd just been disassembled atom by atom, then reassembled atop the statue of a horse and rider.

He tried to piece together the recent events that had led him to this moment. He remembered developing an escape plan for Charlotte should she be threatened by the Aginbyte of Inwit. He remembered receiving his sister's frantic cellphone call that activated his escape plan for her. What Abbie had not been prepared for was Charlotte having stolen the Aginbyte's BookMarck. Still, he'd had just enough mindfulness to stuff a copy of *The Time Machine* into Charlotte's backpack and to coach her into a BookStream, hoping to hide her from the Aginbyte and the Repositors.

As he loosened his grip from around the midsection of the rigid rider before him, he felt the dampness of the cold, wet metal beginning to seep through his clothing. He could smell the scent of lavender in the high air about him. Early morning sunlight reflected off of the two channels of water on either side of the monument upon which he sat.

"Bonjour, Monsieur," he heard someone call from below.

A fellow with a round face had called up to greet Abbie.

Abbie estimated that a small crowd of ten or twelve observers had collected around the pedestal far below him.

"Bonjour," Abbie responded, attempting to remain as casual as one might while astride a metallic horse suspended twenty feet aboveground.

"Could you tell me where I am?" Abbie continued in French.

Abbie's question provoked several chortles and guffaws from below. The quizzical looks exchanged among several of the observers suggested to him that his French pronunciation was amiss.

The kindly-faced gentleman ignored the ribaldry around him.

"You are in Paris, Monsieur," he gently responded in authentic French. "You are sharing a horse with King Henry IV."

Abbie was momentarily stunned by the possibility that he might be existing within the pages of *The Three Musketeers*. But before he could entertain that thought, a young lady accompanying the gentleman called up to him.

"Please come down before you are seen by the police and arrested," she urged in her native French.

Abbie wasn't sure that he'd understood everything she'd said. But her outstretched hand, combined with his having understood the words *descendre* and *gendarmes*, suggested to him that it was time to dismount.

He evaluated his predicament and identified three obstacles that he'd need to overcome. He needed to descend safely. He needed to descend contritely to minimize the perception that he had been disrespectful to King Henry IV and the culture of Paris.

And he needed to descend quickly, if only to avoid being easy prey for the Aginbyte of Inwit.

The gentleman moved toward the base of the pedestal and held his hands aloft as if to caution him to descend slowly.

"Lentement. Lentement," the man repeated.

To avoid tumbling to the pavement below and sustaining a serious injury, Abbie would have to control his slide off the slick haunches of the bronze horse. So, while hanging onto the waist of good King Henry IV, he swung his right leg around the back of the horse as if to dismount, pressing his knees and thighs into the torso of the metallic steed to create separation between himself and the statue. Aware that the crowd below had a premium view of his butt, Abbie's plan was to release his hold of the King's torso while pushing away from the statue with his knees. Abbie bid a grateful *adieu* to the historic royal, released his grip and dropped to the first platform, banging his head on the horse's undercarriage. Abbie could only guess the number of rude jokes circulating below. But he had managed to land safely upon the first platform.

After he steadied himself, Abbie carefully rotated his body and folded his legs under him. Now facing the assembly below the pedestal, Abbie could see that his audience was dressed in the garb of manual laborers. Abbie guessed that they had been on their respective paths to open shops, cook food and clean homes before he'd distracted them with his horsemanship. Although attired modestly, it was apparent to Abbie that many of his observers had dressed with an attention to detail. The crown of a large man's head was complemented by a jauntily-tipped hat. The lapel of a woman's overcoat was accentuated by a gold broach reflecting the rays of sunrise. Abbie was embarrassed that his unintentional mischief had disrupted their morning routines.

Anxious to descend and claim anonymity, Abbie noticed that

each of the four corners of the pedestal was decorated by a statue. Each corner statue had been sculpted to appear seated, but bent forward at the waist to suggest supplication or captivity. To Abbie, their broad backs offered a perch upon which he might execute a bounce to the ground. So Abbie sidled toward the front corner of the pedestal and prepared to drop himself onto the broad, muscular back of an unyielding Captive. As Abbie leaned forward from his seated position, several members of the crowd perceived his intention and raised their arms and hands to catch him.

Abbie pushed himself off the platform. His feet landed on the back of the Captive as he had intended, but the soles of his sneakers slipped off of the slick metal surface, pitching Abbie forward. Before his chin smashed into the metal figure before him, Abbie felt sets of hands gripping his arms and shoulders, guiding him safely if inartfully to the ground.

Abbie allowed himself a grin while ducking his head in embarrassment, saying *"Merci"* repeatedly as he planted his feet.

Satisfied that the show was over, the crowd began to disperse. But the kind man and the young lady loitered about until only the three of them remained.

"Je m'appelle René et voici ma fille Simone," said the man slowly, introducing himself and his daughter.

As opposed to her curious gaze while he was up on the statue, Simone would now not raise her eyes to him.

"Je m'appelle Abisai. Merci," Abbie replied to René and his daughter Simone, grateful for their intervention.

Abbie scanned the Square for the Aginbyte of Inwit as they spoke, hoping to do so without alarming his new acquaintances. He did not yet want to share the news of his being pursued if he could avoid it.

"Allez, Monsieur," advised René, seeing through Abbie's poorly concealed uneasiness.

The trio set off. Gently, René steered Abbie away from the Square and into the street.

"Monsieur. We are now crossing the Pont Neuf," said René as they were absorbed into the crowd of pedestrians.

Paris, said Abbie to himself in disbelief. Abbie knew something of the geography of Paris. He had hoped to accompany a group of his classmates to Paris the previous summer, and had studied the neighborhood around the Louvre in preparation for that school-sponsored trip. Ultimately, his parents decided against the trip, electing to save the money for college.

As they walked, Abbie tried to make himself nondescript. He kept his head down and avoided eye contact with passersby, navigating himself using his peripheral vision. He could tell by the positioning of passing feet that his appearance in a golf shirt, jeans, and precision haircut was attracting some notice, but no one stopped them.

Abbie was grateful for the obscurity provided by the Parisians around him. *If I can disappear into Paris,* thought Abbie, *I can make it difficult for the Aginbyte to find me.*

Abbie welcomed the slow and unobtrusive gait of his hosts.

Once René felt that Abbie was beginning to relax, he began to ask questions.

"Monsieur, would you pardon my curiosity? But where are you from? I ask because, as a tailor, I have never seen vestments such as yours. I don't recognize the material. I don't recognize the stitching. Pray, young master, where did you come from?"

Although René spoke exclusively in French, he had observed Abbie's struggles with acclimating to his dialect and so slowed the tempo of his phrasing to assist Abbie in his comprehension.

"I am from America," responded Abbie truthfully.

Although Abbie had only been in Paris for a few moments, he was forcing himself to process as quickly as he could manage. Embracing the fantastic possibility that he might be inhabiting the Paris of *The Three Musketeers*, he began to anticipate questions he might be asked, and rehearsed in his head responses in French that would not alarm his hosts.

"My clothing is made by machine," Abbie added.

"By machine!" exclaimed Simone, speaking for the first time since they'd left the Square. "We know of machines!"

In her enthusiasm, Simone impulsively placed her hand upon Abbie's arm, then quickly withdrew it, realizing the error of her informality. Her eyes returned to focus upon the ground at her feet.

"Pardon my daughter," laughed René, recognizing Abbie's confusion with the alacrity of Simone's speech pattern. "Simone is very passionate. Her friends tease her that my career as a tailor may soon be concluded by a machine. Can you imagine? Absurdité!"

As Abbie considered a number of replies, an alarm bell went off in his head.

Where is my knapsack? Where is my BookMarck? It is my only way of getting to Charlotte!

Abbie abruptly turned to look back at the base of the statue of King Henry IV, but his view was obscured by the crowds of Parisians walking over the Pont Neuf and passing the gates surrounding the statue.

It was now Abbie who hurried his words.

"Did you see my knapsack?" he asked René in English.

René looked at Abbie with confusion.

"Knapsack?" René attempted to repeat the word phonetically.

Abbie repeated his question in French but struggled to find an equivalent to "knapsack" until he fell upon the word *valise*.

"Ahh, Monsieur." René patted Abbie's shoulder in an attempt to comfort him. "When Simone and I first approached you, you had dropped your valise. It fell to the ground."

René spoke slowly in hopes that Abbie would understand his narration.

"As the crowd developed, a local swordsmith with whom I am familiar picked up your valise. He went through your bag briefly and, after doing so, left the Square."

"Why do I not remember any of this?" asked Abbie, raising his hands to his head as if preparing for the onset of a headache.

"Before you dropped your valise, you appeared to secure an object into the binding of a book. Then, once you dropped your valise to the ground, you briefly passed out. We thought surely you would fall from the statue. You must have dropped your valise in a moment of étourdissement."

"Did the swordsmith take my valise with him?" asked Abbie.

"Oui," responded Simone and René in unison.

Abbie could hear the panic rise in his voice.

"Je dois trouver cet homme," Abbie urged.

"But yes. We can certainly help you find him," René reassured.

"He has his shop right here on the Quai de Feraille."

Chapter Ten

Aubergois

Abbie, René and Simone had only to walk about fifty yards before arriving in front of the swordsmithing shop of Roland Aubergois. As they approached, René repeatedly pronounced Monsieur Aubergois' name to Abbie and encouraged Abbie to repeat the name aloud. After coaching Abbie through several adjustments in inflection, René felt confident that Abbie's pronunciation would not offend.

"Allow me to enter alone and make the introductions," René volunteered. Abbie noted that René, at least a head shorter than himself, still had to stoop to avoid hitting his head on the low doorway.

Now alone with Abbie, Simone was at a loss as to what to say. She was not a natural raconteur as was her father, and so she needed several moments of silence to search for a suitable idea for conversation.

"Monsieur Aubergois is well known in Paris as a maker of great swords," she finally managed. "He makes swords for both the King's Musketeers and the Cardinal's Guards."

"The Cardinal?" repeated Abbie.

"Cardinal Richelieu. Surely the Cardinal is known in America, no? He is a great man, and commands the best swordsmen in France."

"And the Musketeers?" asked Abbie.

"The Musketeers are the best swordsmen *in the world*," she offered, shading her comment and hoping that Abbie would catch her distinction.

"The Musketeers have sworn their allegiance to our King."

"Are the Musketeers and the Cardinal's Guards rivals?" Abbie asked, knowing full well of the contention between the Cardinal's Guards and the King's Musketeers.

"Hush, Monsieur. Please do not speak so boldly in public! What one knows and what one says on the streets of Paris are very different things."

"Do you know any of the Musketeers personally? I am looking for three of them—" Abbie asked Simone.

But Simone's answer was interrupted by the appearance of two men stooping to exit the shop. As René took his place next to his daughter, the other man pulled himself up to his full height and looked down at Abbie.

"Bonjour, Monsieur. Je m'appelle Roland Aubergois."

"Bonjour, Monsieur Aubergois. Je m'appelle Abisai Taylor."

Abbie bowed to Roland Aubergois in appreciation for having received him.

"Abisai Taylor." René and Simone smiled at one another and repeated the name in an attempt to fit it on their tongues. Abisai found himself appreciating the singularity of his first name. It made it difficult for people to associate him with a particular land or culture, and gave him greater flexibility should he ever need to build a story around himself. Like today.

"He is from America!" confided Simone to the swordsmith, unable to contain herself.

Aubergois had permitted himself a slight smile as he heard René and Simone practice their pronunciation of *Abisai Taylor*.

"America, eh? I saw you earlier this morning. You rode into Paris with King Henry IV?"

Aubergois' comment was more witticism than question, but

it did beg for an explanation from Abbie to dispel the impression of disrespectfulness.

"Yes. No. I apologize if I distracted you this morning. I was suffering from—"

"…Étourdissement," volunteered René.

Abbie directed a quick smile of gratitude toward René.

"I am a stranger in Paris and sought a convenient height from which to survey the City." continued Abbie. "But I recognize that I must have appeared to be disrespectful, and I apologize."

In reality, Abbie had had no control over his arrival, having been under the thrall of his BookMarck. Thinking it too early to trust anyone with the true circumstances of his arrival, Abbie fabricated a story around regrettable mischievousness.

"Oui. And how are you feeling now?" asked Aubergois.

"I am much better, Monsieur. Thank you for your concern."

As he attempted to satisfy the etiquette of introductions, Abbie struggled not to ask about the location of his knapsack. But his unease must have been more obvious than he thought, prompting René to speak.

"Monsieur Abisai Taylor." René savored the opportunity to say Abbie's name, so he repeated it. "Monsieur Abisai Taylor has misplaced his valise. He recalls last seeing it at the base of His Majesty's statue. Might you have any information about this article, Monsieur Aubergois?"

Aubergois surveyed his three guests before directing his remarks to Abisai.

"Monsieur Taylor. I appreciate the self-restraint that you, René and Simone have demonstrated. In engaging in polite conversation with me, the three of you kindly forebore from accusing me of theft."

Then, Aubergois waved his long hand as if dismissing a triviality.

"Do not be concerned, Abisai Taylor. I recovered your valise. I have it in safekeeping."

Abbie attempted to respond as casually as he could manage, hoping to mask his anxiety.

"I am in great need of it, s'il vous plait."

"A curiosity it is, Monsieur Aubergois. Although I saw it only briefly, and from a distance, I appreciated the precision of its workmanship," remarked René the tailor.

"It was sewn by a machine," offered Simone helpfully.

"Yes. Quite so," observed Aubergois.

"Monsieur Abisai. Paris can be a dangerous place. And you have undoubtedly heard that my customers include the finest swordsmen in the world. As such, no one dares steal from me, else they incur the wrath of my clients."

"I have a proposition for you, Abisai Taylor," offered Aubergois. "I see that you do not carry a sword. And in my casual inspection of your valise, I found that you have no clothing except that which you wear. I hope that these observations have not offended you?"

Abbie attempted to internally translate Aubergois' French into English as quickly as possible and so did not immediately respond. Aubergois took Abbie's silence as license for him to continue.

"My apprentice recently became ill with lovesickness. His illness was then compounded by the blade of a rival's sword. He had to abruptly discontinue his employment with me. I have made arrangements for a new apprentice, but he will not arrive for several weeks. In return for my protection of you and your valise, I offer you a position as my temporary apprentice. In exchange for a full day's work, I will provide you lodging here, your meals, and protection of your person and your few belongings."

"What say you, Abisai Taylor?"

Abbie hadn't given lodging or food a thought since his arrival.

"May I see my valise?" he asked.

"Mais oui, Monsieur. That is a reasonable request."

As Aubergois disappeared into the shop to retrieve the knapsack, René and Simone moved to Abbie.

"Do you understand what he is offering?" asked René excitedly. "This is a prestigious assignment, Abisai Taylor of America!"

"You'll be safe here. Perhaps you will allow us to visit?" Simone asked hopefully.

Before Abbie could respond, Aubergois returned and placed the opened knapsack at his feet. Abbie knelt and briefly peered into his knapsack. Stacked inside his knapsack was the copy of *The Memoirs of Sherlock Holmes* that Charlotte had shoved at him, his library copy of *The Three Musketeers* and the copy of *Frankenstein* entombed into the bottom of his bag. As if to reassure Abbie that all was well, an exposed margin of Abbie's BookMarck greeted him with a display of primaries.

Abbie resisted the urge to *hush* his BookMarck.

Abbie rose to his feet.

"If you agree to serve my shop," said the swordsmith, "I will keep your valise as collateral to ensure that you fulfill the terms of your apprenticeship. When your apprenticeship satisfactorily concludes, I will return your valise to you."

"Merci, Monsieur Aubergois," said Abbie. "I am flattered by your generosity, and by your concern to keep me and my few possessions safe.

"I accept your offer. I am at your service."

With that, Abbie lifted his knapsack and handed it back to Aubergois in a gesture of trust.

"Bon," responded the swordsmith.

As if to acknowledge Abbie's trust, Aubergois made a show of stowing Abisai's valise in an easily accessible cupboard just inside the front entrance of his shop.

"Abisai. I will show you where you will sleep. You will start the fires at dawn and close the shop in the evening. Please come in so we can get to work."

With that, Aubergois gave René and Simone a short bow, stooped and walked back into the shop.

Abbie turned toward René and Simone, and bowed.

"Thank you, both. I look forward to seeing you again."

Simone kissed him gently on both cheeks. As she stepped away, Abbie could have sworn he saw her blush. The thought of Priscilla Stern briefly came to his mind.

René embraced Abbie and clapped him on the shoulders as he released him.

Then, Abisai turned and followed Roland Aubergois into his shop.

Chapter Eleven

Cardenio

The Aginbyte of Inwit stood in front of the reference desk of the Institute of Abandoned Knowledge. Aisles of books and materials began from behind the desk and seemed to stretch back into the infinite, reminiscent of rows of infantry marching in formation. Similarly, The Great Hall was devoid of clocks, calendars, maps and windows. It could have existed anywhere at any time. The Aginbyte of Inwit was always impressed by the Institute of Abandoned Knowledge.

Behind the desk stood the Chancellor of Abandoned Knowledge, for whom the Aginbyte did not share a similar regard.

Despite the formidable appearance of the Aginbyte of Inwit, the Chancellor managed to appear busy and oblivious to the waiting giant.

The Aginbyte finally cleared its throat.

"Good morning, Aginbyte of Inwit," the Chancellor finally said without raising his head from his reading.

"Good morning to you, Chancellor. I apologize for disturbing you. What of note?" asked the Aginbyte.

The Chancellor exhaled, his breath sodden with impatience. Then, he ran his index finger down a long list to his left.

"The news is good," he finally said cheerlessly. "Both the Impact Factor for scientific journals and the H-Index of citations have reached ten-year lows. One might argue that this declining readership reflects a worldwide lack of confidence in scientific research."

The Aginbyte paused to consider the significance of this news. The decline in the metrics quoted by the Chancellor suggested that the Repositors' centuries-old quest to discredit the value of pure research was gaining momentum.

The Chancellor paused for emphasis before continuing.

"Also, believe it or not, we have finally obtained and cataloged the only known copy of *Cardenio* in existence. Would you care to see it? I believe that you can find it in Aisle 12,102 index 35.042."

That the Repositors had secured a copy of *Cardenio*, a lost play of William Shakespeare, portended decades of profit.

"Thank you. Some other time, perhaps," responded the Aginbyte.

"Ah yes. You are not here to read Shakespeare, are you?" suggested the Chancellor, his voice taking on the tone of a reprimand.

"No. That's not why I'm here," the Aginbyte confirmed.

"You are in need of another BookMarck. Am I correct?" asked the Chancellor.

"Yes, Chancellor. I am in need of another BookMarck," responded the Aginbyte.

The Aginbyte was aware that news traveled quickly in the world of the Repositors. The Aginbyte was prepared to be chastised.

"I understand that a little girl has taken your BookMarck."

There it was.

For the first time that day, the Chancellor raised his head and peered up at the Aginbyte. The Aginbyte looked down at the Chancellor, hoping to appear impassive. Although the Aginbyte had drawn its hood tightly around a knitted skullcap, it was unable to mask the synaptic expressions of annoyance occurring in its brain.

"With the theft of BookMarck 333.7, you've lost your gliding factor," added the Chancellor. "I daresay that Charlotte Taylor will appreciate gliding, what with her MS and all."

The Aginbyte of Inwit did not respond, but continued to peer down at the Chancellor.

"You must apply for a temporary BookMarck while you attempt to recover BookMarck 333.7," advised the Chancellor. "Your sponsor will have to approve your application. But you may as well get it started."

The Chancellor disappeared behind the desk to open the drawer closest to the floor. The Aginbyte could hear the Chancellor fumbling about. BookMarcks were rare and valuable. To the Repositors, an agent's loss of a BookMarck implied a lack of responsibility or professionalism. The Aginbyte had no doubt that the Chancellor's delay was to exact a silent reprisal on behalf of the Repositors.

When the Chancellor finally stood, he held a yellow pad of paper attached to a clipboard. The paper was devoid of any printing except for narrowly-ruled horizontal lines as one might find in a middle school composition book.

The Chancellor slid the clipboard across the desk to the Aginbyte.

"I can't seem to find the applications for BookMarck replacement," said the Chancellor. "It happens so infrequently, don't you know? You can use this pad to request a replacement."

Then, the Chancellor reached back down into his bottommost desk drawer and produced a small cardboard box of golf pencils.

"Thank you," said the Aginbyte.

As the Chancellor returned to his reading, the Aginbyte reached into the box and attempted to extract a single pencil. As the Aginbyte lifted its massive hand out of the box, it held three pencils between its fingers while spilling five others about the counter.

The Aginbyte peered at the clipboard and considered how to explain how Charlotte Taylor had stolen its BookMarck and then escaped.

As the Aginbyte considered explanations, the Chancellor looked over the Aginbyte's mountain-like shoulder.

"If you intend to complete the application here, could you at least step aside and clear the queue?" requested the Chancellor.

The Aginbyte dutifully stepped aside to accommodate the next patron in line. After several moments had passed and no one assumed the spot, the Aginbyte turned and looked back toward the entrance. The cavernous chamber was empty except for himself and the Chancellor. A single synapse fired red somewhere in its cranium.

The Chancellor watched the Aginbyte spend several minutes composing a tortuous essay, then concluded the Aginbyte's lesson in humility.

"There are currently no BookMarcks available for loan."

The Aginbyte involuntarily snapped the little pencil into shrapnel, half of which pinwheeled on the desk before coming to rest.

The Chancellor slid the Aginbyte's clipboard around to read the handwritten narrative.

"You're in luck," suggested the Chancellor. "I see that you have requested access into the BookStream of *The Three Musketeers*. This morning I ran into The Censorium who mentioned that he would be departing into the BookStream of

107

The Three Musketeers as well. Perhaps if you contact him, you could travel with him on his BookMarck."

The Aginbyte politely returned the remains of the broken pencil into the small box. As the Aginbyte turned and labored toward the exit, the Chancellor called out after him.

"Remember, Aginbyte. You may share the Censorium's BookMarck to travel **into** your destination, but at a considerable cost to the energy field of the BookStream. For you to leave on the same shared BookMarck would dissipate the entire energy field of the BookStreams. So, you'll have to find another BookMarck in order to leave the *Musketeer* BookStream, or you'll be marooned in *The Three Musketeers* until we can retrieve you."

The Aginbyte's hand was on the push bar of the Exit door when it heard the Chancellor's voice one last time.

"And please keep your carnage to a minimum and within the context of the novel?" requested the Chancellor.

"As you wish," answered the exiting Aginbyte.

Chapter Twelve

The Apprenticeship of Abisai Taylor

"René referred to me as a swordsmith, and so I am. But I do not repair all parts of all swords. I *hilt* swords. Do you understand what it means to hilt a sword?"

It was obvious to Abbie that Aubergois had slowed his explanation as a courtesy. Abbie nodded that he'd understood.

"We accept all requests for repair," said Aubergois. "But, in this shop, we only attach swords to pommels. If there is anything else to be done, we accept the commission but send the work out to another swordsmith."

Aubergois did not wait for Abbie to respond before he turned his back and walked to a wall upon which hung a variety of swords and weapons.

"Épée," said Aubergois as he pointed to a sword with a bell-like guard.

"Fleuret," continued Aubergois as he gestured toward a sword with a shallower guard.

"Sabre."

Abbie noticed how the guard of the sabre offered greater protection to a swordhand than the épée or the fleuret.

Aubergois pulled a sabre down from the wall. He held it aloft with his right hand, gesturing with his left.

"Point," he said, and he touched his finger to the tip of the sword.

"Foible," he said as his left hand swept across the third of the blade closest to the point.

"Forte," he said and he gestured to the third of the blade closest to his grip.

Aubergois returned the sabre onto the wall, then lifted a sword awaiting repair from a nearby anvil. Aubergois tucked the broken blade under his arm and extended the forte toward Abbie.

"This is the handle," said Aubergois, and he extended the distressed sword closer to Abbie so that he could see the detail.

"The handle and blade are separated by a guard. The blade is locked into the handle with this end piece, the pommel."

Abbie nodded again, understanding.

"This sword blade has shattered. The handle on this sword is exquisite, but with half a blade, it is useless. We fit a new blade into the existing handle and, *voila,* off goes monsieur to impale someone."

Aubergois returned the damaged sword to the anvil, and reached for a nearby whisk broom.

"For now, this broom will be your sword. Your first duty every morning will be to clean out the debris from the forges, saving any scraps of iron from the previous day."

Aubergois picked up several pieces of cold iron from a forge to show Abbie what recyclable fragments might look like, then tossed the fragments in the direction of a bin in a corner of the shop.

"Follow me."

Aubergois led Abisai to a rear room, then through a back door and into a courtyard, the perimeter of which was lined with ten-foot-high wooden planking. Abbie wondered about fire safety among Parisian swordsmiths.

"After you've cleaned the forges, grab an ax from the

110

courtyard and split the charcoal so that it will fit into the ovens. You can use that wheelbarrow to haul it into the shop."

"Then start the fires in the forges and have them going before I arrive. Do you know how to start a fire with a flint?"

Abisai did not understand the French word for *flint* until Aubergois picked up a piece and held it before him. Abisai nodded in assent.

Aubergois continued.

"After you've lit the fires, you'll spend the balance of your day sweeping and picking up debris and tools."

"Oui, Monsieur," responded Abbie. "Je comprends."

"Good," Aubergois continued. "There are several journeymen who will be in the shop on any given day. On some days, I pay them to assist me. On other days, they pay me to use one of the forges for their own profit. I will introduce you to them tomorrow."

Aubergois walked out of the room and quickly returned with an armful of blankets which he dropped upon several bales of hay lined against the far wall. Abbie's mind again returned to flying embers.

"This is your bed, unless you prefer to sleep on the ground. I will bring you breakfast in the morning when I arrive for work. If you eat all of your breakfast at once, you'll have no food until the evening, so conserve your food. I will arrange for your dinner to be delivered to you every evening after you've closed the shop. Let me see your hands."

Abbie held out his hands, palms up, as if carrying a stack of his mother's placards. Aubergois ran his thumbs across Abbie's palms. Noticeably unimpressed, Aubergois started to release Abbie's hands when he abruptly stopped after having run his thumb across Abbie's right palm.

111

"You've the calluses of a swordsman," he observed.

Aubergois' eyes left Abbie's hands and focused upon his face.

"Who exactly are you?"

Abbie did not respond immediately, appreciating Aubergois' thought as more commentary than question. But Abisai requested an audience with Aubergois as he prepared to leave for his dinner.

"Monsieur Aubergois," began Abbie. "Me and my sister are being pursued by a ferocious adversary. I elected to flee to France from America in order to decoy the pursuer away from her."

In offering this explanation, Abbie had elected to hew as close to the truth as possible, but not to disclose to Aubergois the existence of BookMarcks, Repositors, WordSmythes, and Aginbytes.

Aubergois found himself wanting to believe Abisai's backstory. The boy seemed so well-intentioned.

"Merci, Abisai Taylor."

As he made his final arrangements before leaving, Aubergois feigned dissatisfaction with Abbie's preparation of the charcoal, and sent him back into the courtyard to re-organize it. As Abbie attended to his errand, Aubergois removed Abbie's valise from the front cupboard and departed.

When Aubergois returned that evening, he found the boy deeply asleep on the bales of hay and assumed him more exhausted than hungry. He left Abbie's dinner on a nearby anvil before leaving for the evening.

The following morning, Aubergois arrived to find that Abbie had cleaned the shop and lit the forges. But Aubergois did not pause to assess the work. Instead, he sent Abbie off into the courtyard to split more charcoal. Once Abbie had left the room on a fool's errand, Aubergois furtively returned Abbie's knapsack to the shop cupboard.

Aubergois's overnight inspection of Abbie's valise had not

yielded the reassurance that Aubergois had sought. Instead, the swordsmith's suspicions were compounded by his discovery of a book titled *The Three Musketeers* in the valise. Written in what Aubergois assumed to be English, the words were largely indecipherable to him. Its title, however, was unmistakable.

By midday, Abisai was multitasking with aplomb, sweeping debris, salvaging fragments of metal, carrying in new loads of charcoal and stoking the forges. As the journeymen departed for the evening, Abbie set about to clean their stations. Aubergois raised his palm to interrupt him.

"I am going to leave to dine with my wife and children at my home," he said. "Then, I will return with dinner for you. Once you have cleaned the floors and cleared the forges, you may conclude your day and wash for dinner."

With Aubergois' departure, Abisai found himself energized but alone for the first time since he'd arrived in Paris. In the solitude of his second evening in the French capital, he allowed himself to consider the questions he'd avoided: *Is Charlotte safe? Was I successful in luring the Aginbyte of Inwit away from her? Should I retrieve my BookMarck and chase after her, or would she be better served if I stay here in Paris as bait for the Aginbyte? Is enlisting the aid of the King's Musketeers even remotely possible? How much more can I disclose to Aubergois?*

The voice of the Aginbyte insinuated itself back into his head.

"Who do you think gave you that BookMarck?" had said the Aginbyte.

Did Mom or Dad slip me the BookMarck? Did they both? Was it intentional, or a mistake? Do they yet realize that me and Charlotte are in the BookStream? Or is our absence imperceptible, as the librarian had suggested?

113

Abisai was grateful for Aubergois' return, if only to distract him from his bewildering self-interrogation. Aubergois threw a blanket over one of the many anvils in the shop and set out Abisai's meal. He put out a large heel of bread, a pungent cheese whose aroma managed to penetrate even Abisai's charcoal-laden nostrils, and a whitefish wrapped in paper.

Aubergois motioned for Abisai to pull up a bench from a corner. Before he sat, Aubergois placed two forged goblets on the anvil, uncorked a bottle of red wine, and filled both goblets to their brims. Although parched and hungry, Abisai recalled the conventions of the era and waited for his mentor to sit before he sat.

"After you, Monsieur," Abisai said, deferring to the master swordsmith.

"I've eaten, Abisai, but thank you. Let us drink to the day."

Abisai raised his goblet and drank deeply, hearing the voices of his parents' disapproval. Then, Abisai broke off a mouthful of bread from the heel and grabbed at the whitefish. He was ravenously hungry.

Aubergois interrupted Abisai before he could stuff the food into his mouth.

"Forgive me," the swordsmith said. "You'll find that your fingers are still fouled with charcoal, despite your having washed them. The utensils are in the top drawer of that desk."

Aubergois allowed Abisai to eat without further interruption, his eyes glazing over as if deep in thought. Possibly he was enjoying the breezes of evening, finally cooling the interior of the shop. Possibly he had focused on the sounds of horse hooves on the cobblestones exterior to the entrance.

Abisai had eaten half of his meal before Aubergois broke out of his reverie and spoke again.

"This pursuer you have mentioned. This adversary. You described him as large. Would you say he is my height?"

The swordsmith stood up from the bench. Abbie stood as well and measured Aubergois with his eyes to approximate the height of the Aginbyte of Inwit.

"Yes, Monsieur. He is about your height, but he is much broader. His shoulders are the width of the doorway."

Aubergois walked to the wall upon which hung the swords.

"Have you ever fought an opponent who was significantly taller than you?" he asked Abisai.

Abisai paused and thought back to his high school fencing career. It felt as if he'd already been away for a million years.

"Not that I recall."

Aubergois took two sabres down from the wall.

"There are several things that you should know before you duel a taller opponent," said Aubergois.

Then, he offered Abisai the handle of a sabre.

Chapter Thirteen

Charlotte 2.1

The Commissioner of the Saint-Étienne Department of Police slid the revolver across the table to the woman seated across from him. An empty tea cup and saucer sat an arm's length away from her. Behind the seated Commissioner stood Louis Lepine, Prefect of the Loire. Two gendarmes, armed and at the ready, stood to either side of the seated woman.

It was the Commissioner's opinion that the glory of his native France had been diminished by spies for decades. The Commissioner would connect the dots for you, were you to ask. He would suggest that the seeds of distrust were planted as far back as 1806 and Napoleon's defeat of Prussian forces at Jena. Or he would argue that France's having to cede most of the province of Alsace and parts of Lorraine to its Prussian rival fueled a national desire for revenge. But on this April day of 1887, the Commissioner would lay France's displacement as a military and manufacturing influence at the feet of the superior spy game of the German State.

Which brought the Commissioner back to the woman who sat across from him, and the revolver upon which his hand rested.

"We can end this interview one of two ways," suggested the Commissioner.

He raised the revolver and gestured toward the papers on the table in front of the woman.

"You can tell us the truth."

"Or you can use this." He again slid the revolver toward her, his hand resting firmly upon it.

The Commissioner considered himself a skilled interrogator. Still, he was grateful to have Prefect Lepine in the room serving as a witness.

The woman remained silent. The only suggestion that she was weakening after her second hour of interrogation was that a few locks of her thick, auburn hair had escaped from her hair pin and had fallen to her cheek.

The Commissioner continued, again raising the revolver. He separated several pages one from another using the barrel of the gun.

"On the table before you are plans for a new silk loom to be manufactured here in Saint-Étienne."

"Okay," he continued. "Perhaps you are a purchasing agent, and have engaged in this theft to satisfy an overzealous client. Oui?" he asked, not expecting an answer.

The woman knew what accusation would follow.

"But this."

The Commissioner used the revolver to expose a sheaf of five papers below the plans for the loom.

"These are the production plans for a Lebel Model Repeating Infantry Rifle. These plans were stolen from the Manufacture d'Armes de Saint-Étienne.

"Today, these plans were found within your bodice, wrapped around your abdomen. Nein?"

The woman's sole reaction to the Commissioner's purposeful use of the German negative was to re-pin the strands of her hair that had fallen loose.

"Finally, there is this," he continued. "A map which appears to have been prepared in some haste. Directions from Saint-

Étienne to the Hotel-Dieu de Lyon."

The Commissioner paused to emphasize the importance of his next question.

"Why would a German spy want to travel from Saint-Étienne to the hospital in Lyon?"

The woman reached into her bodice for a handkerchief and dabbed at her nose, perhaps to suggest that the authorities had not respected her as inviolate.

The Commissioner suppressed a sigh.

"You have been our guest for several days. Don't you prefer sunlight to darkness? Conversation to silence? A warm cup of tea to the barrel of a gun? Wouldn't you prefer to remain up here than to return 'down there?'"

The woman ran her hand over the papers before her as if to smooth out a wrinkle. But she did not speak.

"My colleague and I will leave you now. The police officers will stay to assist you in finding your tongue. Adieu."

With that, the Commissioner stood and returned his revolver to the holster around his waist. He glanced at a gendarme who then opened the door for them. The Commissioner motioned for Lepine to exit first, then followed the Prefect out of the room.

The Prefect and the Commissioner walked along a narrow corridor into a common room without speaking, and from there toward a smoke-windowed door with the title *"Commissare"* stenciled upon it.

As the Commissioner opened the door for Lepine to enter, he asked no one in particular for a glass of wine for himself and his guest. Then he shut the office door behind them.

The Commissioner began speaking before Lepine had had a chance to sit. For a moment, Lepine was confused whether he was to sit or remain standing.

"Louis," began the Commissioner. "Saint-Étienne is a sieve.

It seems as if every progressive idea developed here finds its way into the hands of our Prussian counterparts before we have a chance to sit down."

Both men grinned as the Commissioner finally realized his inadvertent breach of etiquette, and he gestured for Lepine to be seated.

"Fabric production. Perfumes. Pharmaceuticals. Weapons. It seems as if our products are in the German market before they leave our production lines," continued the Commissioner.

The Commissioner stood again. Lepine stood, following the lead of his host.

"We were fortunate to arrest this woman as she attempted to secure a carriage to Lyon. Her apprehension was sheer luck.

"These papers literally fell out of her clothing, and one of our officers retrieved them for her as an act of civility. It took a moment for him to realize that the papers she was stuffing back into her décolletage were production plans.

"As you saw, our interrogations have yielded nothing. She has no past. No family. No identification documents. She is an invisible woman. But her method of operation is consistent with a community of invisible women who have materialized throughout France.

"Some might suggest that we French have a reputation of wariness toward strangers. I suggest to you that we require this apprehension to protect France," posited the Commissioner.

The Commissioner did not wait for Lepine to reply, but moved on.

"The map provided directions to her from Saint-Étienne to the Hotel-Dieu de Lyon. It takes little deduction to suggest that she is part of a network of spies that spirit information from town to town using different couriers, and then ultimately out of

119

France. This map excites me because it suggests that Lyon is one of the hubs through which information passes."

Prefect Lepine nodded in agreement.

Two kicks upon the door preceded the arrival of a gendarme with two glasses of wine.

"Merci, Ferdi," the Commissioner said to the officer. "Please close the door as you leave."

Once Officer Ferdi closed the door behind him, the Commissioner continued.

"Louis. Your brother is a physician at the Hotel-Dieu de Lyon? A fine, fine hospital. Yes?" asked the Commissioner.

"Yes," replied Lepine, even though he was uncertain as to which question he was being asked to respond to.

"But I believe that my brother is now a professor at the medical school."

"Even better," replied the Commissioner. "Might I impose on you that you travel to Lyon to see him under the guise of a social visit? Relay to him the peculiar nature of this woman's portfolio, and ask him if there might be a way that the hospital is being used as a conduit for these secrets? Possibly, you could engage in a bit of surveillance while you are there?"

"Of course," replied the Prefect, wondering if the Commissioner knew that he harbored aspirations for police work.

"One more thing," said the Commissioner as he moved toward the door. "I have heard from a colleague in Lyon that a similar 'invisible woman' has been admitted to the hospital. A girl, really. Apparently she was injured when she fell off the equestrian statue of Louis XIV in Lyon. Can you imagine? When she was admitted to the Hotel-Dieu de Lyon, her garb was characterized as foreign and unique.

"Louis. Might you find her and ask her a few questions on

120

our behalf? Probe to see if she might be part of this network? Are our nefarious enemies now using children to steal our secrets? Might she be associated with a foreign regime? Perhaps good fortune has finally played into our hands."

"Aha!" cried Lepine, finally making his contribution. "Even more good fortune than you think, Commissioner! By coincidence, my brother informed me that the hospital is hosting a celebrity sleuth seeking convalescence, and perhaps he might assist in this inquiry!"

"And that 'celebrity sleuth' would be who, exactly?" asked the Commissioner.

"I am sorry, sir. But I have been sworn not to divulge his identity. But it is a happy coincidence, I assure you!" said Lepine excitedly.

"Good luck, then. Please see Ferdi as you leave. He'll provide you with all of the letters of authority that you might need."

The Commissioner clapped Lepine upon his back as the Prefect departed, knowing that there was only one celebrity sleuth in the world worthy of anonymity.

Chapter Fourteen

Charlotte 2.2

Marie Lepine, wife of Prefect Louis Lepine, was repacking her husband's inexpertly packed valise. She knew few of the details surrounding his sudden departure except that he had official business to attend to at the respected hospital Hotel-Dieu de Lyon. In a happy coincidence, she had washed, starched and pressed his shirts several days prior. Lout that he was, and as were all men, he had not observed the pleat lines of her ironing when he packed.

Marie had not yet reworked the contents of his valise before her husband the Prefect returned to their modest apartment.

"Good fortune continues to smile upon us, dear wife. I have made arrangements to share a carriage to Lyon with a prosperous family traveling directly to the hospital."

"Do not celebrate another's misfortune. 'Tis bad luck," she admonished.

"Oh, no dear. I did not mean to suggest that anyone was ill. The father is a physician seeking employment at the hospital," he explained.

"Since you are going to the hospital, are you going to visit your brother?" Marie asked, seeking to decloak his mission.

"Yes," he replied. "I've an official matter to discuss with him, and I may have to stay on with him for several days to conduct some reconnaissance."

"Reconnaissance." She let the word sit on her tongue for several moments.

"Is it dangerous?" she finally asked as she attempted to strap shut the overpacked valise.

"It may be something. It may be nothing," he replied. "It seems that every foreigner in France is a spy."

"Spies!" she repeated, impressed by the exoticism of it all. "Why have they asked you to intervene?"

"Last year, prefects were enrolled to assist the gendarmes in matters of intelligence gathering. So it is my duty." He shrugged. "Keeping order is part of my job, Marie, and I think I do it well."

"Your valise would suggest otherwise," she teased.

He laughed at her wit.

"This preoccupation with spies," pressed Marie. "It is unbecoming of a French gentleman."

"Maybe so," her husband replied. "But this errand will give me an opportunity to visit my brother. And I may get to meet a celebrity of some consequence in my inquiries."

"A celebrity of some consequence," she repeated.

She did not ask him to identify the celebrity of consequence, and he did not volunteer a name.

***

Charlotte was awake but could not raise her eyelids. She knew that she was lying in a bed and had been asleep for some time. She assumed it was nighttime because it was quiet and darkness reigned on the other side of her eyelids. Reflexively, she felt for the band on her left wrist, flipped it, and removed a capsule from a hand-carved cavity. She carefully lifted the capsule to her mouth and placed it under her tongue.

As she began to drift back to sleep, she heard an unusual sound and squinted her eyes open.

Across the darkened room, she could see the outline of a row of beds. She could also make out the figure of a man hovering over a bed in conversation. Although they may have intended for their hushed conversation to be inaudible, it was loud enough to have awakened her.

"They're speaking French just like Dad," she whispered to herself.

"Tu m'as réveillé!"

Charlotte had intended to upbraid the pair in French for having awakened her, but her words were rendered indecipherable by a combination of fatigue and her tongue being distracted with medication.

Charlotte drowsily flipped her wristband back over, dropped her arms back to her mattress, and fell back to sleep.

Chapter Fifteen

Charlotte 2.3

When Charlotte opened her eyes again, it was daylight. Lying on her side, she could see at least ten beds extending down the length of the room and running parallel to her own bed. Lining the opposite wall was an equal number of beds creating an aisle through the center of the room. Each bed's footboard was numbered and had what appeared to be a medical chart hanging from it.

She had a vague memory of a man in conversation across the aisle during the night.

She was in some kind of hospital.

As she slowly rolled onto her back, Charlotte gazed up at the ceiling and waited for her vision to clear. At least twenty feet above her, the aged, cracked ceiling plaster was spotted with brown stains suggestive of water leaks. She focused upon one significant fissure and followed its snake-like pattern across the ceiling from beginning to end.

That could be a map of my life, she thought.

Despite its flaws, Charlotte found the decay more comforting than the latticework of acoustic tiles repeating across the ceilings of every hospital she'd visited.

Turning her head, Charlotte had expected to see a similar row of hospital beds mirrored to her left, but her view was blocked by a sheer curtain gathered into a column. As she centered her eyesight, she saw within the column of gauze a chair with a hollowed out seat. Beneath the seat was a deep bed pan.

That's a toilet!

The thought jarred her. She remembered having been swept into a wormhole of unimaginable colors. She had a vague memory of an arrival and of having sat high above the ground upon the haunches of a stationary horse. She remembered falling. She couldn't recall much after that but for the vague memory of having been awakened by the voice of a man in late night conversation on the opposite side of the room.

Charlotte shifted her attention from the perimeter of the cavernous room to the wooden bed gates on either side of her mattress. Then, she heard around her the voices of women.

"Ses yeux sont ouverts."

"Elle est réveillée."

"Bonjour, ma petite cherie."

Charlotte felt sure that she was hearing the language of France.

A figure, backlit by the windows on the wall opposite her bed, approached from the center aisle and stood at the footboard of her bed. Charlotte's mind flashed back to her introduction to the Aginbyte of Inwit, and her breath caught.

"Bonjour."

The voice was quiet yet warm, with a bit of melody behind it.

Charlotte began to breathe again.

"You've been asleep," continued the visitor in French. "How are you feeling?"

Charlotte heard the room quiet, her roommates focusing on their conversation.

"What day is this?" asked Charlotte in English.

126

The volume of the voices around her momentarily spiked in volume, then returned to silence.

"Je suis désolé mais je ne parle que anglais," the woman responded.

"Quel jour, est-ce?" Charlotte asked, attempting to mimic the woman's dialect.

She was surprised to hear the weariness in her own voice.

"Ahh. Nous sommes le Avril 28," the woman responded.

"Quelle année, s'il vous plait?"

"1887," responded the woman, making a note on the clipboard she carried.

Having satisfied the curiosity of her audience with the mundanity of their conversation, the conversations among the other occupants in the room resumed.

Charlotte continued to converse with the woman exclusively in French, allowing herself to be schooled in local dialect by the woman as they spoke.

"Where am I?" Charlotte asked.

"You are in the women's ward of the Hotel-Dieu de Lyon," responded the woman with some importance.

"Lyon, France?" asked Charlotte.

"Mais oui. Is there another?" the woman asked facetiously and smiled, making another notation on her hospital chart.

"Aren't I supposed to be in London?" Charlotte asked herself aloud, still attempting to shake off the confusion of her extended sleep.

"Repetez?" requested the woman, this time with even greater sympathy.

"Rien," Charlotte answered. Charlotte motioned for the woman to step to the side of her bed so that she could see her.

As the woman slid to her bedside, Charlotte could see that she wore the coif and tunic of a nun. She had a kind, cherubic face, but pale, and smiled frequently.

After giving Charlotte a moment to absorb her appearance, the woman introduced herself.

"Je m'appelle Soeur Collette," she offered through her smile.

"Quel est ton nom?"

"Je suis Charlotte," she replied as she extended her arm through the bed gate.

"Pleased to meet you," replied Sister Collette as she exchanged a handshake. Sister Collette spoke slowly and distinctly, unsure whether Charlotte's odd pronunciations were health-related.

"If you are feeling fit," continued the nun, "Brother Tomas has some simple intake questions to ask you."

"Wait. Please. Sister Collette?" Charlotte tried to delay the nun's departure. She was not yet prepared to be passed off to an unsympathetic male bureaucrat.

"How did I get here?" she asked.

Sister Collette smiled compassionately before she responded.

"I have heard from others that a man and his daughter carried you into the hospital. They said that you'd fallen off the statue of King Louis XIV at the Place Bellecor."

Charlotte did not interrupt her.

"They said that you'd fallen off the statue, fell to the podium and then to the ground, but that you were still conscious after your fall. When you attempted to stand, you went into a seizure and fell unconscious. When you arrived, you were still unconscious."

Charlotte thought about this for a moment before responding.

"Where are my things? My clothes? My backpack?" Charlotte had gotten stuck on the French translation for *backpack*.

Collette understood Charlotte's question from context, and was able to respond.

"We put all of your personal belongings into your valise; your clothes, your book, your jewelry."

Charlotte rubbed her left wrist against her mattress to assure herself that she was still wearing the bracelet laced with her medication.

"Can I have my valise?"

Sister Collette smiled again, equating Charlotte's accelerated speech with an improvement in vigor. She made a note on her chart.

"Your belongings will stay in your locker until you are discharged."

Sister Collette leaned over the bed gate and whispered conspiratorially.

"There are spies and thieves about."

Sister Collette then resumed her posture, chart poised proudly before her.

"That's enough for now, mon petite," Sister Collette concluded. "Nap. I'll ask Brother Tomas to perform your intake once you've awakened."

Brother Tomas arrived in the middle of the afternoon. Charlotte eased through Brother Tomas' intake, having had several hours to anticipate his questions, develop her answers, and even practice her French dialect.

In response to her question about her hospital admittance, he begged Charlotte's pardon for not having been at the main desk at the time of her admittance, and so had few details to share about her arrival.

At the conclusion of his brief intake, Brother Tomas thanked her and wished her good health. As he turned to leave, the women in the ward bade him goodbye with a chorus of bawdy catcalls and whistles, as if the presence of a man in the ward was a unique and unwelcome occurrence.

Upon the departure of Brother Tomas, Charlotte attempted to piece together her arrival in Lyon. She remembered being pursued by the Aginbyte of Inwit down Ivy Hill. She remembered Abbie instructing her on how to escape using the BookMarck she'd stolen from the Aginbyte. She heard herself whisper into the BookMarck her favorite series of books, *The Memoirs of Sherlock Holmes* by Sir Arthur Conan Doyle.

Charlotte had read the entire Holmes oeuvre several times. She admired Holmes for his ability to focus his intellect and purge himself of distractions. She embraced the camaraderie Holmes shared with Dr. Watson and likened it to her relationship with her brother.

But mostly she was enamored of the locales of Holmes' era. So she was disappointed to realize that she had awakened not at 221B Baker Street and the London of Sir Arthur Conan Doyle, but in Lyon, France. She had somehow screwed up her positioning. It was of small consolation to her that Sister Collette had confirmed her arrival in the appropriate time frame, just on the wrong side of the English Channel.

As she inventoried her memory, Charlotte thought of her brother and his foresight in having developed an escape plan for them. As their parents had fallen away from one another, she had come to rely upon her brother's stalwart loyalty. She missed him already.

As daylight started to dim, Charlotte was served a light dinner of broth and bread, which she ate at a gallop. Sister Collette arrived as Charlotte concluded her dinner and noted Charlotte's ravenous appetite on her ever-present chart.

Charlotte watched as the women of her ward retired to their

beds for the evening. Her arrival in France and not England began to prey on her confidence. *How did I mess up my directions to the BookMarck? Has my BookMarck misdirected me? Might it do so again? Where is my backpack? Has my BookMarck even been returned to my backpack? Has it been stolen by 'spies and thieves,' as Sister Collette warned? How will I return home? Will the Aginbyte find me? Will I ever see my family again?*

Relying on the little information provided by Brother Tomas, Charlotte assumed that she had had an episode of MS after she had fallen off of the statue, precipitating two good samaritans, an unknown man and his daughter, to bring her to the nearest hospital.

What happens if I exhaust all of the MS medication that mom had carved into my wristband? Which symptoms of my MS will return? Weakness? Tremors? Imbalance? Speech? How will I pay for my care? Will I be consigned to a pauper's ward? Could I die here? Will I die here?

As the world moved into night, Charlotte's confusion morphed into desperate thoughts. She had denied them for several hours, but then could no longer fight them off. In the anonymity of darkness, Charlotte's body spasmed with tears punctuated by sobs. The sounds of her stifled cries reverberated off of the parquet floors and up into the void of the high vaulted ceiling.

Would she ever see her family again?

As Charlotte grieved, she heard the creak of a nearby bedgate. A small hand pressed her right shoulder with soft assurance. Another equally small hand found Charlotte's right hand and gently squeezed it. A third hand caressed her right hip. In a matter of moments, the women of Charlotte's ward had surrounded her bed, squeezing their arms over and through her bedgates and wrapping her in a blanket of individual hands.

Their caresses were respectful, concerned, loving and, as if

131

these Lyonnais women shared a sensory vocabulary, intended to extend comfort to a frightened girl. Charlotte found herself the focal point of a miraculous ceremony.

Amid the reassuring murmur of female voices, Charlotte's breathing calmed. She opened her eyes to see the blurred nightgowns and chemises of her roommates.

She cleared her throat.

"Merci," she whispered.

As Charlotte repeatedly thanked her wardmates, she could feel herself calm.

Reassured, the chorus of hands began to recede.

Grateful for their intervention, Charlotte allowed herself to savor the touches of these compassionate strangers. That is, the compassion extended by all but one. Down by her right foot, the hand grasping her ankle had no intentionality behind it. Charlotte glanced at the woman but she had already turned away. It was as if the woman had participated so that she could be seen doing so, more interested in being considered as one with the group than extending warmth.

Her panic subdued, Charlotte's focus returned.

Why am I not seeing a connection between Holmes and France?

Charlotte began to rehash each story of Sherlock Holmes in her head, searching for a connection. She welcomed the self-discipline required of this analysis as it distracted her from her uncertainty.

As the women of the ward left Charlotte's bedside and returned to their beds, Charlotte watched the outlier walk across the aisle and made a mental note: Bed Number 3, *third bed from the corner on the opposite wall.*

Chapter Sixteen

Charlotte 2.4

On the morning of her interrogation, Charlotte welcomed what had become the routine of her days. Her life in the Hotel-Dieu de Lyon had fallen into a predictable pattern, giving her the time and space to recover from the trauma of her unusual arrival.

That morning and every morning previous to it, the Sisters of the Hotel-Dieu de Lyon opened the transoms atop the tall windows in Charlotte's ward by pulling down on long drawstrings. The aromas of fresh flowers and baked bread wafted in, displacing the smells of decay and disease that had accumulated during the night. Charlotte could hear the hymns of a Catholic Mass being sung outside of her ward.

Charlotte sat up in bed. She was the first to rise among her wardmates, so she took the opportunity to meditate.

Through the veil of early morning, she focused on the wall opposite her bed, following the outlines of paintings and tapestries long removed but whose shadows had refused to be extinguished with paint and whitewash.

Charlotte concluded her meditation when she heard the closing hymn of the Mass, knowing that the chaplain would now visit her ward followed by the main surgeon.

The chaplain was often called upon to deliver Last Rites to those women in Charlotte's ward who were significantly ill. During one of their many conversations, Sister Collette had confided to Charlotte that the ward, reserved exclusively for women, was referred to as the "feverish" room. Conditions among the women in her ward ranged from tuberculosis to typhoid to appendicitis to smallpox.

As the chaplain attended to several of her roommates, the main surgeon and his medical students entered to conduct medical examinations. Often the main surgeon would return before dinner for a follow-up conversation with select patients, including Charlotte.

Curiously, the surgeon and his students elected to start their rounds that morning with Charlotte rather than visit those beds of her more seriously ill wardmates.

Charlotte's previous conversations with the surgeon and his team had been brief. He would ask whether there had been any significant changes in her condition, and she would disclose that she was well. Charlotte revealed as little information as possible, hoping to discourage the hospital staff from probing too deeply into her identity and her back story.

"Comment vas-tu ce matin, Charlotte?" asked the surgeon.

"Je me sens beaucoup mieux, merci," she responded.

"Bien. Je ne crois pas que nous aurons besoin de vous voir plus longtemps pendant les tournées de l'après-midi."

Upon hearing that she would no longer be seen during his afternoon rounds, Charlotte smiled and clapped her hands.

She did not ask the surgeon what motivated his decision. Had she improved? Was he frustrated by her having stonewalled him? All of that she elected to ignore as she celebrated.

"Do not forget to walk today," reminded the surgeon as he lowered her bedgate.

"Thank you, doctor. When might my belongings be returned to me?" she asked.

Either the surgeon did not hear her question or chose to ignore her because he updated his notes on the surgical chart at the foot of her bed without responding.

One of the students tailing the party elected to respond on his behalf.

"Lorsque le médecin juge que vous êtes guéri et que vous pouvez sortir."

When the doctor deems I've recovered and can be discharged, repeated Charlotte to herself.

Charlotte's task for the day had been set: she'd need to determine what constituted a "recovery" in the eyes of the medical staff of the Hotel-Dieu de Lyon.

First, she'd need to get a look at her medical chart. Charlotte bided her time with breakfast as she waited for the surgeon and his staff to complete their rounds and leave her ward. She discreetly extracted a capsule from the back of her wristband and self-medicated, washing down the pill with warm orange juice and silently thanking her inventive mother.

After the surgeon and his entourage filed out of her ward, Charlotte grabbed her cane, swung out her legs to the floor and slipped the hospital-issued sandals onto her feet.

Charlotte loitered at the foot of her bed, pretending to steady herself. As she fussed with her balance, she casually flipped her medical chart onto her mattress and attempted to read it without drawing the attention of her ward mates.

Charlotte was doubly vexed by the entries made by her surgeon. She would need to translate arcane French medical terminology into English **and** decipher the doctor's poor penmanship in a matter of seconds.

The best she could do was:

The patient is female and appears to be approximately thirteen years of age. Residence: Unknown. Parentage: Unknown. Place of Birth: Unknown.

An eyewitness account by an unidentified male and his daughter puts the patient at the location of the Place Bellecor immediately before her fall from the statue of King Louis XIV. After her fall, witnesses relate that the patient's attempts to move or communicate were frustrated by imbalance, tremors, spasticity, slurred speech and eventual loss of consciousness. She was unconscious when carried into the hospital.

The patient is referred to the women's ward for rest pending a more detailed evaluation.

I suspect that the patient may suffer from paralysis agitante and/or sclerose en plaque. I have requested a consultation with M. Charcot, La Salpetriere Hospital, Paris, France.

I recommend bed rest. No medication prescribed at this time. Once conscious, the patient may ambulate with staff assistance or supportive devices (a cane has been provided at bedside).

Patient's afternoon evaluations are suspended pending her detailed evaluation.

Henri Soulier

Charlotte committed herself to getting herself out of the hospital before "her detailed evaluation."

She formed her plan. Since her arrival, Charlotte had feigned reliance on the cane provided by the hospital to slow herself and create the time she'd need to evaluate her options. If she were to act as if she were gradually weaning herself from her reliance on the cane, her doctors might develop the conclusion that she had indeed "recovered" and was eligible for discharge.

Charlotte discreetly replaced her hospital chart onto the

136

footboard of her bed and faux-limped down the center aisle of the feverish room, pausing to chat with ward mates. Charlotte had not forgotten the kindness of her roommates. Sadly, many of them waved her on as they were consumed by tremors or pain.

The wooden, double doors at the end of the room were large and heavy. The lumber used to fashion the doors was thick and dense, as was the glass of the inlaid windows. On most mornings, the medical staff wedged the doors open to allow themselves unfettered access and egress to the ward as they carried in clean linens and removed waste buckets (or the dead).

But on this day, the day of her interrogation, the doors were closed, and so Charlotte had to lean into them to squeeze through.

Stepping out from the feverish room, Charlotte entered a lobby that Sister Collette had referred to as the Petit Dome. Out of the Petit Dome extended four hallways that the Sisters referred to as *les quatres rangs*. Charlotte felt her spirits rise as she stepped into the space and was greeted by the natural light of the dome above and the fresh air circulating among the four hallways.

She paused at the chapel entrance from which the songs of Mass rose every morning She passed the opened entryway to the pharamacie where she would often be greeted by Sister Collette working behind the counter, but not this morning.

As Charlotte faux-limped past the pharmacie, aSister unknown to Charlotte greeted her and opened one of the many indistinguishable hallway doors into a courtyard of flowers. A path of inlaid stone tiles marked a convalescent walkway, and Charlotte inhaled with satisfaction, having found the flowers whose aroma would find its way into the feverish room every morning.

Charlotte sat down upon a bench and reflected upon the

balance of her day. From midmorning to late afternoon, her ward room would receive patients, families, surgeons, students, new patients, the Sisters, and an occasional visit by the chaplain to give Last Rites. If a Brother were to enter to complete an intake or run an errand, he could expect to be chased out by the sounds of whistles and derisive suggestions.

After taking a moment to acclimate herself to this new sitting area, Charlotte reached into her pocket, pulled out several folded papers and a pencil, and began to write about her liberation from afternoon medical rounds, her medical chart, and her plan to escape.

Cameron Taylor had introduced her daughter to journalling in anticipation of the boredom of hospital evaluations, just as she had anticipated the need to supply Charlotte with a wristband of emergency medication.

Cameron had encouraged Charlotte by gifting her odd and eccentric journals with unique cover designs, different grains of paper or those that could only be accessed with a separate key or numeric passcode.

Charlotte needed little encouragement to write. She had filled journals with strategies from Chess Club, schematics for the successor to the VLCT 1200, stories of hospital interventions, and a multitude of musings. She had filled one corner of her bedroom closet from floor to ceiling with a stack of completed journals.

When Charlotte had asked Brother Tomas shortly after her arrival for some paper and a pencil with which to write, he had refused, citing a scarcity of hospital supplies. So Charlotte had removed several pages crumpled paper from the disposal in the pharmacie, and palmed an orphaned pencil from the same location. With her appropriated tools, Charlotte would spend her afternoons chronicling her life in Lyon, carefully hiding the pages under her mattress when she returned to her room in late afternoon.

Charlotte's dinner would invariably be accompanied by a glass of wine, and she had quickly grown to look forward to it. Who was she to argue if it were considered to be medicinal? She and her roommates would fall into an inevitable drowse after dinner, positioned for a night's sleep with hopes that no one would become ill during the night and suffer aloud.

Charlotte's sleep was interrupted with annoying frequency by the male infidel visiting the patient in Bed Number 3. Although his visit would be considered heretical by her wardmates during the day, there were no catcalls or whistles to chase him in the middle of the night.

Charlotte assumed the woman in Bed Number 3 to be preoccupied with her late night trysts, and so bore her no ill will for having slighted her. Charlotte even considered engaging her in a conversation about her source for paper because the indecipherable words of the lovers' rapture always seemed to be accompanied by the sounds of ruffled materials. Charlotte had not yet figured out how to talk around the intimacies of the relationship to get to the pragmatism of paper, and so had not yet approached her roommate.

Suddenly, Charlotte jumped.

She was still seated on the bench in the garden.

I must have dozed off.

Sister Collette was standing in front of her.

"Good day, ma petite. I'm sorry to have awakened you. How are you feeling? Have you had breakfast? Have you completed your toilet? Did you enjoy your nap?"

Immediately, Charlotte realized that something was amiss. Normally, Sister Collette would address Charlotte with patience, asking one question at a time and waiting patiently for an answer. The rapidity of her questions suggested to Charlotte that Collette was anxious.

"We are going to conduct a more thorough examination of your condition today," continued Collette. "I am to take you to an examination room. It is not far. Why don't you take my arm?"

"Do we have to do this today?" Charlotte asked innocently.

"Unfortunately, this decision was not mine to make," Sister Collette responded cryptically.

Sister Collette helped Charlotte to stand. Although forty years her senior, Collette was about the same height as Charlotte. Collette put the cane in Charlotte's left hand and wrapped Charlotte's free arm around her own. In that fashion, the two walked out of the courtyard and back into the hospital. They passed through the Petit Dome and down a corridor that Charlotte had not yet explored.

Eventually, Sister Collette led Charlotte to another set of double swing doors. The word Amphitheatre was stenciled on each of the doors. Sister Collette opened a door, allowing Charlotte to precede her into the room. At first, their view of the room was blocked by walls that rose high above their heads on either side of them, creating a corridor. The floor elevation gradually declined as they reached the center of the room, the high walls having receded until they fell below their sightlines. Charlotte and Collette could now see at least ten rows of empty seats rising up and around them. At the center of the room was the stage of the amphitheater. On the stage were a table and three chairs.

Two men stood behind two of those chairs. A single, empty chair was positioned on the opposite side of the table, facing them.

Something bad is about to happen to me, thought Charlotte. *This is why Collette is so anxious.*

The first man to speak wore the white laboratory coat of a physician.

"Good morning. My name is Raphael Lepine. I am a

professor of clinical medicine at the Faculté de Médecine et de Pharmacie here in Lyon."

After he concluded speaking, Professor Lepine extended his hand to Charlotte. Once Charlotte took his hand, he bowed from his waist and raised her hand to his lips in the gesture of a kiss. Charlotte scanned the room.

"Allow me to introduce my brother, Monsieur Louis Lepine. He is the Prefect of the Loire."

Charlotte offered her hand to Louis Lepine, and the Prefect repeated his brother's gesture.

Charlotte did not share her name, saving information as currency for the interrogation she knew would follow.

"Madame. If we were to excuse Sister Collette, could you find your way back to your ward?" asked Professor Lepine, addressing Charlotte.

"Yes," answered Charlotte, responding minimally so as to magnify the importance of anything she would later share.

"Thank you, Sister Collette," said Professor Lepine.

"We can manage from here."

Sister Collette stole a quick glance at Charlotte, her eyebrows raised toward her hairline in a sympathetic frown.

As Sister Collette turned to leave, Professor Lepine turned his attention back to Charlotte.

"Young lady. Please have a seat."

Charlotte pulled at the arms of the wooden chair and carefully sat. As the brothers Lepine sat down across from her, Charlotte made note of the formality of their dress. Their white shirts had been pressed. They wore the simplest of contrasting cravats with their jackets, the Professor in his white jacket and the Prefect in a dark dress coat. Behind them rose at least ten tiers of empty seats.

The Professor pulled a pen out of the breast pocket of his lab coat. From the depths of a side pocket, he pulled out a journal of such small size that it momentarily reinforced to Charlotte the value of paper to this society.

As his brother opened his journal to an unmarked page, Prefect Louis Lepine sat back in his chair and folded his arms across his chest.

"Your formal examination should have been done shortly after your arrival, but it was delayed at my request to allow me to participate. I offer that as an explanation and apology for your delayed examination," offered Professor Lepine.

"This doesn't appear to be an examination room," commented Charlotte, attempting to throw the men off of their agenda.

"Young lady. Don't be impertinent," cautioned Prefect Lepine.

Raphael Lepine gave his brother a sidelong glance.

"What is your name?" asked the Professor.

"Charlotte Taylor."

"Would you spell that, please?" Professor Lepine carefully recorded the correct spelling of Charlotte's name at the top of the page as she responded.

The Professor continued.

"Charlotte. Your case has been referred to me," said Professor Lepine as if to imply that the delegation of her file to him was of some importance.

"At the time of your admittance here at Hotel-Dieu de Lyon, you were unconscious. But your case notes indicate that, before falling unconscious, you exhibited symptoms of which I have some familiarity."

The Professor paused.

"Do you know what tremors are?"

"Yes," replied Charlotte.

"In the past, have you occasionally experienced tremors?"

"Yes."

"Do you experience tremors in all parts of your body, or are they isolated to a particular part of your person?"

"All over."

"Do you, on occasion, feel tingling or numbness in your limbs?"

"Yes."

"Does it occur more frequently on a particular side of your body?"

"No."

"Do you experience weakness in your limbs?"

"Yes, but on no particular side," responded Charlotte, anticipating his next question.

"Do you experience loss of vision, or pain associated with your vision?"

"Yes. Again. No particular side. And I sometimes experience double vision."

The Professor paused and looked up from his notes as if intrigued by her response.

"What is double vision?" he asked.

Charlotte did not yet want to attempt to wrest control of the interrogation away from Professor Lepine, but she did want to entice him with a medical concept that would increase her value as a medical asset.

"I sometimes see two images where there is only one."

Charlotte could feel the rhythm of the inquiry change. The Professor's note taking slowed and he had lengthened the pauses between his questions. She felt as if she was scoring points.

"Do you have problems with your memory?"

"Yes," said Charlotte, silently thanking the Professor for giving her an alibi should she not wish to answer a question about her past.

Professor Lepine pushed his pen across the table to her.

"Would you mind picking up my pen?" he requested.

Charlotte picked up the pen.

"Would you hand it to me?"

Charlotte handed the pen to the Professor without hesitation.

"Would you stand up?"

Charlotte pushed her chair back with both feet, held the armrests for support, and stood.

"Would you walk to that guard rail, then turn back toward us?"

"With or without my cane?" asked Charlotte.

"If you are comfortable, without your cane please," responded the Professor.

Charlotte walked without her cane to the partition that separated the first row of seats in the amphitheater from them. She kept her head down to concentrate on her feet. When she turned, she made sure to separate her feet in order to maintain her balance and made it obvious to the Lepines that she had done so. She paused as she turned to face them. The Professor continued to write entries into his journal.

"Would you walk back to us?"

Professor Lepine stood as well but left his journal on the table.

Charlotte walked steadily back toward them but did not sit down. Again, she continued to concentrate on her feet. Prefect Lepine remained seated, his arms folded, his expression impassive.

"Would you touch your nose with your finger? Right hand to nose?"

Charlotte did so, then returned her hand to her side.

"Now with your left hand?"

Charlotte attempted to do so and missed. Purposely. The Professor bent down to the table and scribbled furiously.

"Please sit down again."

Charlotte found an armrest with her right hand before releasing her torso into the seat.

"Do you ever find that your symptoms disappear for a while?" asked Raphael Lepine, waiting for Charlotte to sit before he did so.

"Yes," replied Charlotte.

"Do you currently feel that you are in remission?" asked Professor Lepine.

"Yes," replied Charlotte.

"Might you have any idea why this has occurred?" he asked.

"I think it might be the wine," she joked, and permitted herself a smile.

Prefect Lepine sprang to his feet, surprising both Charlotte and his brother.

"That is a splendid idea," volunteered Prefect Lepine, and he strode out of the amphitheater.

With the departure of his brother, Professor Lepine allowed his torso to fall deeper into his chair, and for his shoulders to fall away from his chin line.

"Mademoiselle Taylor. Allow me to share my curiosity about your symptoms. I was a house officer for Jean-Martin Charcot at the La Salpetriere hospital in Paris. During my association with him, I assisted in his research of the causations of symptoms such as your own. I was in the company of Dr. Charcot in Paris before returning home recently, and I was then commissioned to examine you at my brother's request."

"But that is not really why my examination has been delayed, has it?" Charlotte asked.

Before the Professor could respond, Prefect Louis Lepine

returned with three glasses in his hand, followed by a Brother, frocked in a half-apron, carrying an unopened bottle of wine.

The Prefect set the glasses out on the table before Charlotte, Professor Lepine and himself as the Brother attempted to uncork the unopened bottle of wine.

Prefect Lepine remained standing and turned toward Charlotte.

"You might wonder what role I play here today? Yes?" asked the Prefect.

Charlotte was sensitive to the cadences of speech, and quickly measured Louis Lepine as a bully. Charlotte was prepared for them to play good-cop/bad-cop with her, even if the technique had not yet been identified.

Prefect Lepine's question was followed by the sound of the pop of a cork. The Prefect took the opened bottle of wine from the Brother.

Prefect Louis Lepine then turned back to the table and poured two glasses of red wine, one for his brother and one for himself, leaving the glass in front of Charlotte conspicuously empty.

"Your mysterious arrival in Lyon concerns me," he said.

"I suspect that you are a spy, and that you are engaged in espionage."

Chapter Seventeen

Simone

Aubergois looked up from the crossguard that refused to fit onto his client's sabre. He surveyed the activity around his shop and exhaled in appreciation.

Look at the changes wrought by Abisia Taylor.

Abisai began every morning in the shop by resetting the fires, cutting charcoal, refilling water barrels and repairing the tools which would invariably break at some point each day.

He concluded his work days by extinguishing the fires, cleaning the floors, sweeping the cooled ovens, stowing tools and cutting more charcoal.

Aubergois would later say that he'd never had a more astute or intelligent apprentice. While Aubergois' previous apprentices had only applied themselves while supervised, Abisai worked independently, industriously and required no oversight. Aubergois would always find Abisai sweeping the shop, salvaging a valuable fragment from the fires or stoking the forges with new loads of charcoal.

But what Aubergois found to be most unique about Abisai Taylor was his ability to modify time-worn traditions into greater efficiencies. If Aubergois had a tang in the heat of a forge, Abisai would manage the bellows from an unexpected angle to better focus the applied heat. When the forges needed additional charcoal, Abisai would have already pre-engineered the charcoal so that it scaffolded neatly inside a furnace, creating a focused and uniform burn. When a spark from a forge threatened to expand into a fire, Abisai extinguished the flame with water from previously damaged buckets that he had reclaimed from neighborhood scrap, re-soldered to be watertight and positioned around the shop in strategic locations.

Aubergois returned his attention to the recalcitrant crossguard and the sword. Dusk was drawing near and with it the conclusion of another work day. He carefully wrapped the sword in a cloth and set it aside on an anvil. When he walked into the courtyard to immerse his face and arms in the water barrel, he found not the brackish, stale water that previous apprentices would leave unchanged for days, but the cool, fresh water of the apprenticeship of Abisai Taylor.

Aubergois did not allow his uncertainty about the true identity of his new apprentice to interfere with his desire to protect him. Since Abisai's appearance made him conspicuous, Aubergois had outfitted Abisai in the abandoned work clothes of his previous apprentice. He had one of his journeymen shear the boy's layered hair. He encouraged Abisai's fervor in the shop if only to render him unrecognizable under layers of charcoal and soot.

Aubergois kept Abisai's presence in Paris a secret to all but a precious few individuals outside of his inner circle: his family, the journeymen in his shop, and René and Simone Sansoulier.

Several days after Abisai had begun his apprenticeship, René and Simone had stopped by the shop to inquire of him. Since they'd arrived at midday, Abisai was unable to greet them with anything other than a smile and a bow. Still, he managed to find work in their vicinity in an effort to overhear their conversation with Aubergois.

148

Aubergois shared how he would return to the shop every night with Abisai's supper after which he would tutor his apprenctice in swordsmanship. As Aubergois selectively disclosed the details of Abisai's daily routine to René, he kept Simone in his peripheral vision, affectionately measuring her reactions to the more intimate details of Abisai's life in Paris.

It did not come as a surprise to Aubergois that several days later René returned at his daughter's request and asked if she might be allowed to provide dinner to Abisai on alternate evenings in order to relieve Aubergois of some of the burden imposed by their having delivered to him a new apprentice. Aubergois granted his approval, so long as René served as chaperon by stationing himself outside of the shop during Simone's visits, and that she leave as he returned for Abisai's training.

At first, Simone would arrive with a pretext for her visit, carrying a damaged silver utensil or ornament to ask Abbie if Aubergois might deign to repair it. By her second visit, her affections were obvious to both of them, so she gently abandoned her pretenses and arrived without distressed silver ornaments but with Abisai's dinner. Invariably, Simone would bring a linen upon which to carefully lay out bread and cheese. After their brief minutes together, Simone would take equal care to clean the premises of every crumb that might suggest that she had been there.

Abisai was confused about how to receive Simone. Though he wracked his brain, he could not remember her existence within the narrative of The Three Musketeers. Despite his uncertainty and shyness, Abisai began to look forward to Simone's visits. After Aubergois closed the shop on the nights of Simone's visits, Abisai would rush to complete his chores so that he might have some extra time to wash some of the grime and sweat off of himself.

At first, their conversations were awkward and formal, both of them acutely aware of René's presence just outside the doorway. So, they talked about the weather or his daily tasks.

Until one night, after Abisai had coaxed a laugh from her, he felt courageous enough to ask Simone about her role in his arrival in Paris.

"Was it a coincidence that you and your father were on the Pont Neuf when I arrived?" Abisai asked.

Simone gave him a long look before she responded, as if she were weighing a risk.

Her hand wandered up to his shorn hair and she smiled.

"You were so different when you first arrived. When I first saw you, you looked so much a boy. Now, you look like a man.

"My father and I. We serve as ambassadors of safe harbor when individuals arrive out of the BookStream and into a narration. We attempt to remain neutral in the war between the WordSmythes and the Repositors."

Abisai looked at her, stunned. The fragments of a thousand questions flashed through his mind,

"So you welcome visitors into *this* BookStream of *The Three Musketeers*?" asked Abisai.

"Oui. Into this and other BookStreams," responded Simone as if to urge him to ask his next question.

"Simone. At the time that I arrived here, might you and your father have also welcomed a girl who is about three years younger than me into the BookStream of *The Memoirs of Sherlock Holmes*?"

"I really shouldn't. There are rules…" Simone resisted, half-heartedly.

"Might this have been someone that you love?" she asked.

"My sister. I have been so concerned about her safety. Please?"

Abbie was asking and pleading simultaneously.

"Yes. My father and I did welcome Charlotte Taylor safely into the BookStream of Sir Arthur Conan Doyle."

Abbie leapt from his seat and caught her in his arms. She laughed as he held her.

"Are you for real?" he asked.

"Are you real?" she smiled as she teased him back.

"No. C'mon. I don't remember your name being in *The Three Musketeers*."

"I am as real as you want me to be," she responded.

Simone separated herself from his embrace and cleared their dinner before Aubergois' returned , removing every suggestion that a small meal and a meaningful conversation had occurred.

As she moved toward the doorway, she stopped and turned back toward him.

"Abisai Taylor. Sometimes, when my father and I find an arrival to be objectionable, we absent ourselves from the narration of a BookStream rather than serve as an ambassador to a malefactor."

Abbie paused to absorb what sounded like a warning.

"Au revoir, mon amour," she said.

And with that, Simone ducked out of the shop and into the darkness.

After his evening's training and Aubergois' departure, Abbie laid awake upon his bed of straw for hours. He could not calm himself from the excitement of knowing that his sister had been confirmed safe. Simone had relieved him of one of the most significant uncertainties that had vexed him.

Abisai was anxious to greet Simone on the occasion of her

next visit. He had developed so many questions about her role in the BookStream that he'd had to create categories of inquiries in his mind in order to try to maintain some sort of order.

But Simone did not return for their next supper. As he replayed their last conversation in his head, Abisai realized what Simone had been trying to tell him.

When my father and I find an arrival to be objectionable, we absent ourselves from the narration of a BookStream.

Aubergois returned that evening and dispatched Abisai to his training with an urgency that suggested to his pupil that their reverie was over.

Chapter Eighteen

The Kill Zone

"Only engage an adversary after you've developed a plan of attack," coached Aubergois.

"Your plan of attack must be calculated to force your adversary to reveal a weakness."

Abisais was a quick study, having fenced in middle school and high school. Even so, Aubergois trained Abisai starting with the basics of fencing. The swordsmith divided each of their torsos into four imaginary quadrants. Then, he introduced attacks, defenses, and advancements based on consequent blade positions.

After each foray, Aubergois questioned Abisai about his intention. How much preliminary information was necessary to form a successful attack? Should Abisai precede a bona fide attack with an advance or a retreat? Should Abisai thrust forward and pressure his adversary to reveal his defenses? Should he beat the blade of his opponent to break his guard? Should he press his opponent's blade point with his own and break his guard? Should he then advance his press into a glide along his opponent's blade, keeping it at bay, in hopes of developing his own advantageous blade position? Or should he advance his press into a traverse and slide his blade down to the hilt of his opponent? Should he plan for a single engagement, or a double engagement, and at what speeds?

Aubergois would listen patiently to Abisai's explanations, then offer corrections and advice as to how he might improve or vary his approach based upon his intention.

The blue-white sparks of swordplay and the sounds of clashing blades would rise into the night, attracting visitors. After finishing their work, a small audience of the shop's journeymen would gather, share their dinner, and watch as Aubergois walked Abisai through an accelerated primer in swordsmanship. When Aubergois overheard a journeyman attempt to place a wager on Abisai's next error, Aubergois banished the offender from the shop, after which the crowd observed the house rules of a respectful quiet.

On occasion, Aubergois and Abisai would inflict bruises and superficial cuts upon one another, even though their swords were buttoned. To simulate battle conditions, Aubergois insisted that the wounded swordsman fight through the pain and dress a wound only upon the conclusion of the evening's lessons.

One journeyman attended every evening's training session. He did not work in the shop during the day, but would join the other journeymen at the day's conclusion to watch Abisai's training. Although he wore a tunic in the style of the other journeymen, he was the only one who remained hooded throughout the night. Aubergois would occasionally consult with the unknown journeyman during Abisai's training, as if he had some special knowledge of sword fighting.

Then, one night, Aubergois retired from their training earlier than usual and suggested to Abisai that he seek an evaluation from the hooded journeyman.

Thus began Abisai's training in fighting a taller opponent.

The hooded journeyman invited Abisai to put down his sword and sit upon a shop bench. Although Abisai was unfamiliar with his new tutor, he trusted Aubergois' judgment. So Abisai seated himself. The journeyman asked him to inhale deeply through his nose and exhale slowly out his mouth, to drive all other thoughts out of his head, and to listen to the strategy that he was about to share.

Once he saw that Abisai was still and listening, the journeyman said to him.

"Close your eyes, Abisai. Concentrate on what I am about to say:

Observer

Conserver

Controler

Presser

"Have you heard me?" asked the journeyman.

Abisai nodded in nonverbal assent but kept his eyes closed.

Then, the hooded journeyman repeated the list, and again Abisai nodded his head.

"Repetez," ordered the journeyman.

Abisai was able to repeat the entire list.

"Very good, Abisai. You may open your eyes. That concludes tonight's training. If you can repeat that mantra tomorrow night, we continue your training. If you fail, I will bid you *adieu.*"

The hooded journeyman stood, bowed to Aubergois, and left.

Abisai spent the following morning in a walking daze, repeating the mantra while cutting charcoal and cleaning forges. The journeymen in the shop grinned and teased him, unaccustomed to seeing him stumble about. Occasionally, one of them would interrupt with a rhyme or a ribaldry but Abisai would good-naturedly shake him off and continue with his incantation.

That night, the hooded journeyman asked Abisai to repeat the list.

The room quieted. The journeymen, having spent the day teasing him, now leaned forward to silently root for the apprentice's success.

Observer

Conserver

Controler

Presser

The journeymen, breaking shop protocol, cheered Abisai's success. Several small flasks appeared to pass through the crowd. Aubergois dropped his head to hide his smile.

The hooded journeyman retreated to the sword wall and withdrew two sabres, handing one to Aubergois.

Abisai then watched as the hooded journeyman converted each word of the list into action, using Aubergois as his taller adversary.

"Analyze your taller opponent's preferred distance, his parries and his basic fencing style. When he thrusts, how much distance does he cover? When he thrusts AND lunges, NOW how much distance does he cover? Is he guileless and fighting without artifice, or is he cunning and purposefully keeping his stride shortened to lure you into his kill zone?"

"When he recovers from a lunge, is it effortful or effortless? Is he slow afoot or agile? Long limbs often require more energy to move. It is often difficult to negotiate big feet. This is how you evaluate areas of attack."

Throughout his instruction, the hooded journeyman demonstrated how Abisai could feint or goad Aubergois into an attack in order to diagnose his tendencies.

"Who will lead this gavotte? If your opponent dictates the fighting style, he will exhaust you. He will capitalize on your smaller frame by forcing you to keep up with him, spending your energy to cover the same distance that he does. Don't fall into this trap. Be clever. Conserve your energy. You want to exhaust your opponent while conserving your vitality. Use your smaller size and speed to induce him to use his energy. A smaller target is harder to hit, so be so."

"While you are evaluating him, keep your blade parallel to the ground or at your side to make it difficult for him to beat or bind your blade. If you must hold him off from a distance, tilt your sword slightly up to threaten his sword hand. If you must address him with your sword, keep your blade moving so that it cannot be easily taken."

Once the hooded journeyman was satisfied that Abisai understood, he moved into the third tier of the mantra.

"Control the distance between you and your opponent, and you will control the duel. Most importantly, avoid being at the distance where he can hit you but you can't hit him."

With that, the journeyman grabbed the blade of Aubergois' sword and put it to his chest, then swung his blade helplessly at Aubergois' distant torso without being able to touch him.

"Stay out of the reach of his blade until you have completed your analysis. Have a plan. Once you have identified a weakness in his repertoire, make full use of your speed and agility for a decisive engagement."

Abisai nodded in his understanding. The journeymen in the shop murmured their approval. Then, the hooded swordsman moved to the final stage.

"Fourth. Control his blade. At what angle does he attack

you? How does he reposition his blade and strike after your parry? A larger adversary will often rely on size to intimidate, and he will compound that intimidation by beating on your blade with his, or using his strength to transfer his blade positioning."

The journeyman exchanged a signal with Aubergois, and Aubergois struck down on the journeyman's blade, which fell out of the journeyman's hand and to the ground. As the journeyman bent to retrieve it, he felt the buttoned point of Aubergois' sword at his neck.

The point having been made, Aubergois withdrew his sword, and the men smiled at one another.

"What to do then, other than defend yourself?"

The hooded journeyman paused, and Abisai anticipated this next to be critical instruction.

"To attack, get your body inside the danger zone of his sword. To do so, you must step inside his sword. His sword point must end up behind your body."

"How do you get inside the circumference of his swordpoint? If you can parry his advance, you may be able to bind his sword and advance past it."

The journeyman turned his head away from Abisai and engaged Aubergois' sword at the high line. He moved in slow motion as he purposefully bound Aubergois' sword and carried it down to his low line, then stepped toward his feigned adversary and past his sword point.

Having successfully penetrated Aubergois' kill zone, the journeyman backed out.

"If you can successfully displace his blade, you might employ your own beat attack and step in. If he counterattacks, you may control his blade and step in."

The hooded journeyman gestured to Aubergois to attack

again. Their swords clashed. Aubergois did not buckle under the attack of the hooded journeyman. Then, the journeyman counterattacked and bound Aubergois' blade, pushed it outside the profile of his own smaller body and stepped inside Aubergois' kill zone.

At the conclusion of this foray, the hooded journeyman raised his sword to touch the sword of Aubergois, and the men bowed deeply to one another. Then, they calmly sheathed their swords.

The hooded journeyman turned to Abisai who had remained seated on the bench throughout.

"Once you are inside its defenses…"

The hooded journeyman paused, then took one step toward Abisai and crouched so that they were eye to eye.

"Once you are inside its defenses, kill it."

The hooded journeyman trained Abisai every night for ten consecutive nights.

On the eleventh night, the journeyman did not return to the shop.

Abisai continued to train every evening with Aubergois, who was a skilled swordsman and insistent taskmaster in his own right. But Abisai missed the hooded journeyman. They had formed a relationship, bound through the sweat, grime, blood and exhaustion of their grueling nights. The name of the hooded journeyman was never disclosed to him and Abisai knew better than to ask lest he risk a breach in etiquette.

Several nights after the departure of the journeyman, Aubergois dismissed Abisai at the conclusion of the night's training. All of the curious observers departed. Aubergois toweled the mixture of charcoal and sweat from his chest and

159

arms, then pulled out two benches and invited Abisai to sit across from him.

Aubergois set two goblets onto the bench, reminiscent of their first evening together. The swordsmith raised a half-cask from the floor and filled each of them with wine.

They drank together, Aubergois drinking first. Then, he spoke in a timbre with which Abisai was unfamiliar.

"Abisai. As of tonight, your apprenticeship concludes. I thank you for your service. You are the finest apprentice this shop has ever enjoyed."

Aubergois refilled his goblet and pointed it toward Abisai as if to toast him before drinking deeply once again.

"As you might suspect, I often transact business with members of the King's Musketeers. Several years ago, I was asked to repair a sword that harkened back to the time of King Francis I. The hilt of the sword was encrusted with precious stones, several of which had dislodged over the course of time. The owner of the sword entrusted me with its repair. Since that time, that Musketeer and I have developed a trust for one another.

"If you and your sister are indeed being pursued by an adversary much larger than yourselves -and I believe that you are-," he added parenthetically, "you will require greater protection than I can offer you here. Therefore, tomorrow I have arranged for you to have an audience with the Musketeer of whom I speak."

Aubergois stood and quaffed the balance of the wine in his goblet. He nodded his head toward Abisai's bed. Abisai was at first confused, but then wandered over to his bed as Aubergois prepared to leave. On it lay a short sword and a scabbard.

Abisai stood above the weapon, dumbfounded. After a minute had passed, Abisai unsheathed the sword. Even in the dim light, Abisai could see that the blade had been honed to rapier thinness and polished to reflect the light as might a mirror.

As Abisai turned to thank him, Aubergois interrupted him.

"I will return your valise to you when we arrive at the Musketeer's lodgings tomorrow. He will be witness to the official conclusion of your commission. He has an apartment on Rue Férou, within steps of the Luxembourg. We are expected tomorrow at eight a.m.

"His name is Athos."

Chapter Nineteen

Charlotte 2.5: An Interrogation

Prefect Louis Lepine sat down next to his brother, Professor Raphael Lepine, and across from Charlotte. He removed a small journal from an interior breast pocket of his dress coat, then brought a small pencil to his tongue before asking his first question.

Charlotte resisted the impulse to remind Prefect Lepine of the toxicity of lead. Instead, Charlotte instructed her inner-author to keep track of his questions so that she could accurately record them in her journal.

"Charlotte Taylor. Where are you from?" opened the Prefect.

"North Orange, New Jersey," she responded.

Prefect Lepine paused before writing.

"Ah! Of course! England!" he said, associating her answer with a group of islands in the English Channel near France.

"When were you born?" he continued.

"July 12," she responded.

"And the year?" continued the Prefect.

"2013."

Prefect Lepine paused but did not raise his eyes from his notepad, maintaining his stoic demeanor. In his peripheral vision, Prefect Lepine caught his brother's look-away to hide a brief smile.

The Prefect had always disdained his brother for his lack of professionalism. Prefect Lepine satisfied his condescension by delivering a swift kick to his brother's ankle under the table, sobering him.

"How did you come to know René Sansoulier?" asked Prefect Lepine.

"I don't recognize that name," Charlotte replied.

"No, eh? Perhaps this? How did you come to know Simone Sansoulier?"

"I don't recognize that name either," responded Charlotte, this time genuinely confused.

Adhering to the guidelines of classical interrogation, Prefect Lepine did not disclose to Charlotte that he'd identified the father and daughter who'd brought her to the hospital.

"Do you read your medical chart every morning?" asked the Prefect.

Charlotte did not respond. She recognized that Louis Lepine was probing her for behaviors that he might consider to be suspicious or seditious. Were she to admit to reading her chart, how would she be able to explain her ability to do so, given the limitations of child literacy in that era?

The Prefect watched her. Charlotte did not meet his eyes, focusing upon the table. Several moments passed before Prefect Lepine conceded the exchange to her silence, and moved on.

"Do you often walk in the hospital corridors alone?"

"Sometimes," responded Charlotte.

"Why? Do you have clandestine meetings with your confederates?"

There it was. Prefect Lepine had wasted no time in exposing his strategy. He had obviously interviewed people in the hospital who had observed her at one time or another, and had pieced their testimonies together to accumulate circumstantial evidence of espionage.

Prefect Lepine did not wait for Charlotte to answer.

163

"Why were you seated on the statue of King Louis XIV at the Place Bellecor?" he asked.

Charlotte shook her head before she answered.

"I don't know how I got up there."

Professor Raphael Lepine interrupted his brother's inquisition, his instincts having been aroused by Charlotte's confusion.

"What do you mean that you don't know how you got up there? Were you in a trance?" asked Professor Lepine.

Several moments had elapsed since Prefect Lepine had accused Charlotte of being a spy. During that time, she had shaken off her surprise and was evaluating her options. Were she to continue to stonewall the Lepines with minimal information, the Prefect would surely incriminate her.

Her mind raced forward as she deflected their questions.

Did the authorities of this era in French history try children for espionage? If I were convicted, would my punishment stop me from getting home?

Charlotte decided that stonewalling the Lepines would not work, and shifted her strategy.

"I live in North Orange, New Jersey in the United States of America, in the twenty-first century. I was exercising one morning by rolling my VLCT 1200 up Ivy Hill when I was threatened by the Aginbyte of Inwit. To escape from the Aginbyte, I tried to spirit myself to England by using an incantation but unintentionally arrived on the statue of King Louis XIV at the Place Bellecor instead. I think that I passed out after dismounting. The next thing I remember, I woke up and was in the Hotel-Dieu de Lyon."

If they diagnose me as delusional or psychotic, thought Charlotte, *I'd have a better chance at gaining freedom from a hospital than some pauper's detention center.*

Charlotte was careful not to mention the existence of her

BookMarck, just in case the thieves referred to by Sister Collette elected to search through her backpack to corroborate her story.

Charlotte sat back in her chair and exhaled. Charlotte had spoken softly but with enough conviction to suggest that she believed herself to be telling the truth. She was satisfied with her performance.

"May I have a sip of wine?" she asked.

"No," responded the Prefect curtly.

Defying his brother, Professor Lepine slid his untouched glass across the table to her. As she took two deep quaffs, she could not help but notice the Professor grimace in pain and reach down to his ankle.

"Tell me, Charlotte. What is the relationship between France and Germany in the twenty-first century?" asked the Prefect as he closed his journal and pocketed his pencil.

"Germany and France are member nations in a cooperative called the *European Union*. Among other things, they share a common currency called the Euro," she replied.

Up to this point in her interview, Prefect Louis Lepine had maintained his composure except to deliver several kicks to the ankles of his brother. But apparently he could no longer hold his temper at Charlotte's suggestion of a European alliance.

"European Union, you say?" he blustered, apoplectic with rage.

"Such talk is treason!"

The balance of the Prefect's remarks were lost to Charlotte in a cascade of half enunciated words and spittle.

"I'm not done with you yet, you impudent child," he choked out as he rose from his chair.

"I'll not allow you or anyone like you to frustrate my career in police work. You will see me again once I have interviewed René and Simone Sansoulier.

"You are dismissed!" he yelled, disrupting the air around him with a backhanded wave.

Professor Lepine rose and extended his hand to Charlotte.

"Allow me to squire you back to your ward?" volunteered the doctor.

Charlotte had not internalized the impact that the interrogation had had upon her until she attempted to stand. She held onto the table to steady herself.

Although the interrogation had drained her, something about the Professor's last remark gnawed at her despite her fatigue.

"Professor Lepine. Would you please repeat what you just asked?"

"I asked if I might squire you back to your ward?"

"That's it, Professor!" she cried, her excitement engulfing her,. "That's the story I'm in! *The Adventure of the Reigate Squire*. I remember the story!"

She paused before she shared her deduction, the enormity of which both surprised her and restored her faith in her BookMarck.

"Sherlock Holmes is here! In France!"

The Lepine brothers pulled their gazes away from Charlotte to stare at one another in disbelief, their facade of calm atomized by their shock and confusion.

"Young lady, how could you possibly know that?" asked Professor Lepine.

Charlotte sagged forward toward the table, but Professor Lepine caught her before she fell.

"You're exhausted. We will continue this at another time," pronounced Professor Lepine, his decision directed more to his brother than to Charlotte.

As Prefect Louis Lepine scrambled to re-open his notebook and find his pencil, Raphael Lepine moved Charlotte forward toward the queue leading to the exit of the amphitheater.

Professor Lepine looked back at his brother one last time before he and Charlotte disappeared behind the heightening walls. He had rarely seen his brother Louis so shaken by the uncertainties of the world.

As the ascending walls of the corridor began to swallow the pair, Charlotte glimpsed a lone figure sitting high above her in the shadows of the back rows of the amphitheater. He had evidently positioned himself directly behind her after she was seated so that he could eavesdrop upon her interrogation. She could see that his long interlaced fingers were clasped around one knee of his pinstriped charcoal trousers, his torso bent forward in rapt attention.

Chapter Twenty

Another Interrogation

Abisai and Aubergois arrived at Athos' apartment at least ten minutes before their scheduled appointment. It was an easy matter for them to negotiate the streets of Paris before eight o'clock in the morning, crossing the Seine and walking southeast on the Rue Danton, passing the Église Saint-Sulpice along the Rue Palantine until ultimately arriving at the Rue Férou.

Earlier, Aubergois had hoisted Abisai's knapsack over his shoulder as they had left the shop.

"May I carry my valise?"

As Abisia's confidence in Aubergois' character had grown, his concern about the location of his knapsack had waned. But now that Aubergois had reintroduced it to his field of vision, Abisai needed to possess his BookMarck.

"As I said, I will deliver it to you when your apprenticeship concludes," Aubergois responded.

Once outside of Athos' apartment, Aubergois and Abisai were greeted by Athos' manservant, Grimaud. Grimaud did not utter a word in greeting them. He exchanged a deep bow with them then gestured for Aubergois to enter and ascend the stairs to the apartment. All of this was communicated by hand gestures and body language.

Aubergois called back to Abisai as he climbed the staircase.

"Wait here. I will call for you once Athos is prepared to meet with you. I won't be long,"

As Aubergois left them, Grimaud leaned his back against the building to wait, and Abbie did the same.

At first, Abisai was grateful not to have to engage Grimaud in conversation. This was Abisai's first opportunity to be away from the heat and grime of the swordsmith shop since his arrival in Paris, so he felt as if he were on holiday. As he waited, he watched as the rays of the rising sun worked their way down the facade of Athos' apartment. He was charmed by the sounds of horse hoofs on the cobblestones of a nearby street. His sense of smell was stimulated by the unmistakable aroma of breakfast bacon.

After he had satisfied his senses with this new and interesting venue, Abisai attempted to communicate with Grimaud.

"Pardon me, Monsieur Grimaud," he began. "I do not wish to offend you. Are you unwilling to speak to me? Might I have somehow offended you or your master? If so, I apologize."

With this unsolicited apology, Grimaud's initial skepticism of Abisai relaxed. He responded to Abisai in a whisper.

"Indeed, Monsieur Abisai. I am pleased to speak with you. But I am reluctant to do so in the vicinity of my master, or I will surely err and be subjected to his righteous wrath."

Abisai was well aware of Grimaud's fear of Athos, having previously read of it in *The Three Musketeers*. But now finding himself in the physical presence of the deferential manservant, Abisai sympathized with him.

"Would you show me, then, how you communicate with him?" requested Abisai.

Grimaud mimed several situations that might incur Athos' wrath. Abisai found it easy to decipher Grimaud's signing and nodded his understanding. Grimaud, finding a sympathetic and receptive audience in Abisai, smiled and nodded back.

Abisai liked Grimaud, but their moment of camaraderie was

169

short-lived. They heard the sounds of laughter from an approaching party, obviously indifferent to the sweet silence of the morning.

"The Cardinal's Guard," whispered Grimaud to Abisai. "They walk past this way every day at this hour, although they pretend it to be happenstance. It is more like surveillance."

Grimaud gently pushed Abisai to the wall on the opposite side of the narrow street and mimed for him to adopt an appropriate demeanor, hands behind his back, head down and eyes averted.

As three Guards appeared around the gentle curve of the Rue Férou, they raised their heads to appraise Grimaud. One of the Guardsmen unsheathed his sword and spanked Grimaud on his buttocks as he passed. Grimaud maintained his submissive posture, attempting to be invisible.

The Guard, satisfied with Grimaud's acquiescence to being subservient, turned his eyes back to the street to develop some new mischief. Not one of them looked at Abisai.

Grimaud dared a quick glance across the street at Abisai. Abisai's hand had gone to the pommel of his sheathed sword. Grimaud shook his head vigorously to dissuade Abisai from interceding on his behalf. Seeing Grimaud's prompt, Abisai's hands returned to his back, and the two of them resumed their submissive postures until the sounds of the Guardsmen's boots vaporized into the sounds of the Parisian morning.

"Not everything is so offensive that it rises to the level of swordplay," advised Grimaud with a grin. "Particularly when it involves a servant."

"This too will change in time," whispered Abisai through clenched teeth, prompting an appreciative look from the manservant.

A moment later, Aubergois opened the door and stepped into the street. As he did so, Grimaud squeezed past him in a rush and hurried up the staircase.

"Impudence," muttered Aubergois after Grimaud with a look of annoyance.

"Abisai. They are ready to see you," said Aubergois, recovering himself.

"They?" repeated Abisai.

Aubergois did not respond.

Abisai followed Aubergois up the narrow staircase. As they climbed, Abisai felt a sense of unworthiness about himself. How quickly he'd purged the luxury of North Orange, New Jersey, for the humility associated with serving a swordsmith's shop.

As they reached the top of the stairs, Grimaud squeezed past Aubergois once again, but this time to descend the staircase, eliciting one of the few oaths that Abisai had ever heard Aubergois utter. Abisai thought for certain that Aubergois would have turned and kicked at Grimaud in annoyance had his apprentice not been behind him.

Athos' apartment consisted of two clean, furnished rooms. Upon the walls hung swords and framed portraits of the past.

Abisai's brief inventory of the walls was interrupted by the sound of Aubergois' voice.

"Monsieur Porthos. Monsieur Athos. Monsieur Aramis. Allow me to introduce you to my apprentice, Abisai Taylor."

As Aubergois offered this introduction, he bent low from his waist and extended his right hand before him, palm up, as if offering an aperitif. Following Aubergois' lead, Abisai bowed even lower from his hips. Since he could not see if their bow had been acknowledged by the three Musketeers, Abisai waited for the swordsmith to release before rising.

"Abisai," pronounced Aubergois with formaility. "In the presence of these witnesses, I hereby release you from your apprenticeship."

The Musketeers offered polite applause through their gloved hands as Aubergois shuffled backwards and deeper into the apartment as if to disappear.

Abisai's focus quickly fell upon the Musketeer introduced as Athos, whom he recognized as the hooded journeyman from his evening training in Aubergois' shop. Athos purposefully pulled back his hood.

Despite their recognition of one another, neither Athos nor Abisai acknowledged their familiarity other than to share a momentary gaze.

Porthos was the first to speak.

"Aramis. Look upon our comrade Athos, and then look at Monsieur Abisai Taylor," he requested. "Do you see the similarity?"

"Mon Dieu, Porthos. You are right! The similarity is astounding," replied Aramis.

Then Porthos directed his remarks to Athos.

"If I didn't know better, friend Athos, I would swear that Abisai Taylor could be your younger brother," observed Aramis.

To Abisai's eye, the resemblance did not seem quite as pronounced. But then, he did not spend a lot of time looking at himself.

Porthos, who stood to Abisai's left, was a mountainous man whose clothing was calculated to accentuate his size. He wore a cerulean blue doublet, over which he wore a gold baldric, over which was a crimson cape. Yet, the most conspicuous aspect about him was the massive rapier that hung from his waist.

The Musketeer to Abisai's right had been introduced as Aramis. Of the three, it was Aramis who appeared the most self-absorbed, what with the calculated perfection of his mustache, his clear complexion and the alignment of his white teeth in which he took obvious pleasure displaying.

"Gentlemen. I am humbled to meet you," said Abisai, and he bowed again.

Abisai was cross-fired with internalized questions. *Am I now part of the mythology of The Three Musketeers? Would every edition of the book now include some reference to me?* But his questions were dwarfed by his acknowledgement of the moment.

I am in the presence of three of the greatest fictional heroes in all of literature.

"Monsieur Aubergois reports that you have done an admirable job as his apprentice over a short period of time," Porthos said. "Well done, boy."

"Over the years, we have all benefited from the swordsmithing skills of Monsieur Aubergois. We respect him and we trust his judgment," added Aramis.

Witnessing them in conversation, Abisai now vaguely recalled reading that Porthos and Aramis shared a symbiotic relationship, one often playing off of the other.

"Your appearance, your dialect and your demeanor suggest that you are not a native of France. Pardon me if I offend, but you speak as if you hail from another land. Where are you from?" asked Porthos.

"You are correct, Monsieur Porthos. I am from America," replied Abisai.

As he began to explain his presence in Paris, he sought Aubergois' support. But Aubergois had removed himself and stood at a distance, his eyes down and arms crossed in a position of impartiality. His message was clear. Abisai was on his own in his interview before the Three Musketeers.

"Monsieur Aubergois has explained to us that you seek our help and protection," Porthos said. "We have been discussing this matter for at least a week, and we have some inquiries."

"I believe that this belongs to you," Athos suggested in as non-accusatory a manner as he could manage. Athos turned to a table behind him, picked up a book and tossed it to Abbie's feet.

Abbie immediately recognized it as his copy of *The Three Musketeers*.

"Athos reports that he found this in your valise. What is this?" asked Porthos.

"It is a book of your adventures," replied Abisai.

"How can it be so thick?" asked Aramis. "We are young and we have just started adventuring. How can an account of our foibles be so voluminous?"

"It is a fable. It is an imagining," answered Abisai in an attempt to explain.

"Please understand. We cannot read English," Porthos explained.

"Or little else," muttered Athos under his breath, his eyes on Abisai.

Porthos ignored the jibe of his comrade and pressed his inquiry.

"We have spent the better part of our week attempting to decode this missive. We have recognized our names and the names of some of our colleagues among these pages, but little else.

"And then there is the matter of your arrival in Paris," Porthos said, switching topics to make his point. "You were first seen upon the statue of our beloved King Henry IV. This is disrespectful, no?

"Allow me to suggest a scenario. You are a disrespectful lout who seeks to infiltrate our ranks with a request for aid. You are a spy. For whom? The Cardinal? More likely the English!" accused Porthos, working himself into a froth.

"Are you not a spy for the English?" cried Aramis, attempting to match his comrade's level of outrage.

"By God, boy! Explain! Who are you?"

The question resonated in Abisai's ears, having been asked by Augergois weeks before. But, in anticipation of a moment similar to this, Abisai had rehearsed his answer.

"I am not from this place, but from America. And in America, I am not of this time, but of a different time," Abbie said.

Aramis raised his eyebrows to his hairline and Porthos leaned forward as if he were not hearing accurately.

Aubergois remained silent, his gaze fixed upon the book at the feet of Abisai. Athos betrayed no emotion.

"I am here because my younger sister and I are being pursued. I came here to lure my pursuer away from my younger sister, who is hiding in a different place and in a different time."

Porthos began to shuffle about in impatience, his annoyance fueled by his inability to grasp what Abisai was suggesting. Aramis played off of Porthos' agitation by crossing his arms and tapping his feet. He looked to Athos for unanimity, but Athos remained nonplussed.

"My pursuer is known as the Aginbyte of Inwit. The Aginbyte is large, even larger than Monsieur Porthos. The skull of the Aginbyte is exposed and pulses with light as if to evidence its intentions, and so it is hidden beneath a hood. Large hands. They look more like slabs of meat than fingers and palms."

Porthos and Aramis stilled, and they gazed back at Abisai with recognition.

"But the most telling characteristic is that the Aginbyte does not walk. It appears to glide over the surface of the earth."

"I know this Aginbyte," Porthos said with incredulity. "Whatever be its name, it is a member of the Cardinal's Guard."

"I, too, know this… this… thing. It is a formidable foe," agreed Aramis, staring at Abisai and nodding with familiarity.

175

"You exhibit an extraordinary amount of courage, baiting this adversary to pursue you so as to protect your sister," continued Aramis.

"In inciting its anger, you must have done so in pursuit of a righteous cause, for no one is more corrupt than the Cardinal and the Cardinal's Guards."

Porthos took a step toward Abisai, extending his hand.

"It matters not to me where you come or from whence you came, Abisai Taylor. We share a common enemy. I am prepared to protect you."

Abisai bowed and accepted Porthos' hand.

Aramis followed Porthos, clapping both Porthos and Abisai upon their shoulder blades.

"This union should lead us to the blade of our adversaries. For that, we thank you for the opportunity, Abisai Taylor."

As Porthos and Aramis embraced Abisai, Athos turned and looked back at Aubergois with satisfaction. The look they exchanged suggested that they had managed to steer Porthos and Aramis to their own conclusion without a strenuous argument.

"Indeed, Abisai Taylor. From this day forward, you may count yourself as a friend of the three Musketeers," proclaimed Porthos.

"God help you," teased Athos.

"Grimaud," called Athos. "Five glasses and a bottle of fine wine. We will toast our new union."

"The protection that you seek, Abisai Taylor. Of what nature is it?" asked Aramis.

"I do not want my sister or family threatened. If it arrives here, I want to stop it here," replied Abisai.

"Indeed," cried Porthos.

"Well said," seconded Aramis.

As Grimaud poured, the Musketeers strategized ways to best

protect Abisai and vanquish their enemy. Their animated conversation veered sharply between tactics and braggadocio. Minutes turned into hours, attenuating Athos' hospitality and forcing Grimaud to exhaust all of the wine and foods in the apartment.

Finally, after it became obvious that they could not reach agreement as to what would be the best plan to follow, they fell into an awkward silence.

"I've an idea," said Porthos, driven to discomfort by the unique occasion of silence among Musketeers. "The evening is still young. Why don't we seek the counsel of our Captain, Monsieur de Treville?"

"Yes! Why not? Our Captain will empathize with the plight of young Abisai and may organize a sequence of Musketeers to protect him," responded Aramis with enthusiasm.

"Nonsense," postured Porthos. "We three can protect him!"

As Aramis and Porthos argued over who would be better suited to protect Abisai, Athos approached the swordsmith.

"Monsieur Aubergois," said Athos, turning toward the swordsmith. "On behalf of my compatriots and me, I thank you for this introduction. Might I impose on you one more time?"

"I am at your service, Monsieur," responded Aubergois.

"Would you locate the additional Musketeers that we spoke of earlier in the week and insist that they now join us outside my apartment, tout de suite? If we are to face this formidable foe, I believe that we will need to increase our numbers."

"But of course," responded Aubergois, and he bowed as he prepared to leave their company.

As he moved to the door, he hesitated.

"Monsieur Athos. How am I to impress upon them that this request is made in an official capacity?"

They all pondered the question until Aramis pulled from his sleeve a finely embroidered handkerchief.

"Should they question your commission, then proffer this.

177

They will undoubtedly recognize it as mine," volunteered Aramis, handing the handkerchief to Aubergois.

Aubergois bowed to all once again and turned to leave. As he passed Abisai to descend the stairs, he quickly squeezed his forearm in affection.

As Aubergois left to summon the additional Musketeers, Athos pulled Abisai to a side to speak in confidence.

"I have a story to share with you.

"I, too, shared the skepticism and cynicism of Aubergois and my comrades. I was not sure that your cause merited placing our lives at risk for you. Then, before you were formally introduced to us by Monsieur Aubergois, Grimaud rushed up the stairs and insisted upon speaking to me alone. Poltroon that he is, I was about to box his ears for his impudence. But I gave him an audience.

"Now, this is extraordinarily courageous behavior for Grimaud. He is deathly afraid to speak to me, and he endorses no one, other than myself. So, anything he does dare say to me must be taken as likely credible.

"Grimaud told me of your willingness to come to his defense out on the street this morning. He said that you have a generous spirit, and that this era needs you.

"So, his endorsement of your character and his obvious affection for you have erased my uncertainties."

As Athos concluded his comments to Abisai, he noticed that Porthos and Aramis were strapping into their scabbards in the manner so as to appear before their Captain, M. de Treville.

"So. Is it to Rue du Vieux-Colombier we go?" asked Athos.

"We go!" said Porthos.

As Porthos and Aramis moved toward the door, Athos picked up Abisai's knapsack. He removed three bricks from its interior, and replaced it with three books: *Frankenstein*, *The Memoirs of Sherlock Holmes* and *The Three Musketeers*.

"Allow me the honor of carrying this for you," said Athos, and he slung the khaki strap onto his shoulder.

Chapter Twenty-One

Charlotte 2.6

Professor Lepine opened every door for Charlotte between the amphitheater and the feverish ward. Charlotte thanked him each time he did so, and each time he appeared to want to say something more, but could not find his words.

As they passed the chapel and approached the pharamacie, he realized that he'd only one opportunity left before they arrived at the double doors separating them from Charlotte's ward.

"I don't believe that you are a spy," he finally said.

Charlotte looked at him but did not respond, hoping that he would continue to fill the silence.

"Speaking to you in any capacity, especially expressing my opinion of your innocence, prejudices my brother's investigation. So, I am conflicted. Do you understand my reluctance to defend you?"

"Yes," responded Charlotte. "I understand."

"And your alibi," continued Professor Lepine. "It is absurd."

His words reverberated through the empty hallways.

"To be honest, I don't recall if delusionment or psychosis is symptomatic of paralysis agitante or sclerose en plaque. It has been a long time since I have studied with Monsieur Charcot. Yet, if you are in fact delusional, it would explain the fantasticalness of your story, and absolve you of any guilt for perjury."

Professor Lepine stopped walking. Charlotte stopped as

well. He looked at her squarely in her eyes when he spoke as if probing for a malady.

"To my mind, there are two explanations as to how you might know that Sherlock Holmes is in France. One is that you are part of a spy network that has developed this intelligence."

"Not true," she replied.

"Agreed," he said.

"And the other?"

The Professor did not respond to her question directly.

"Tell me again how you know that Sherlock Holmes is in France."

Charlotte paused to piece together her explanation.

"Dr. Watson, Mr. Holmes' colleague, records and publishes many of their adventures. I have read these stories in their entirety several times. And I remember that in at least one of them, titled *The Case of the Reigate Squire*, Mr. Holmes is in France."

"In fact," continued Charlotte excitedly, "in his memoirs, Dr. Watson purposefully misdirects the reader, suggesting that Mr. Holmes is treated at the Hotel Dulong in Lyons. But no such hospital of that name exists. But there obviously IS a Hotel-Dieu in Lyon, isn't there? Dr. Watson purposefully misleads his readers with a game of phonetics."

"Incredible," said Dr. Lepine, shaking his head.

Charlotte did not confide to Professor Lepine that, since Professor Lepine was sharing the fictional BookStream of Sherlock Holmes and Dr. Watson, that he too was a work of fiction and had no real existence other than in a reader's imagination.

As they walked toward the swinging doors to her ward, Professor Lepine continued.

"Still, it is eminently convenient to identify you as an agent in a network of foreign interests that use this hospital as a drop box to export French commercial secrets."

181

Charlotte put her hand on the door, then paused. She withdrew her hand and took a step backwards.

Lepine noticed her hesitation.

"What?" he asked.

"Professor Lepine. There is something that I need to tell you. I don't know if it means something, or if it means nothing. But I think it is important that you know."

"Every evening, a nightly meeting occurs between a Brother of the hospital and the occupant of Bed Number 3 across the floor from me. They share whispered conversations, and I could swear that they are exchanging papers. Although I thought it might be a romance, the ward is hostile to men and he takes a great risk in entering the ward every evening."

Lepine listened intently, then asked Charlotte to repeat her observations as he withdrew his small notebook and pencil from the interior pocket of his cloak .

When she had finished, Professor Lepine stared at the door in front of him, momentarily lost in thought.

"Is this part of your delusion?" he asked himself aloud.

"Or is this real?"

He pushed at the swinging door with his hand to locate Charlotte's empty bed, then scanned across the room to Bed Number 3.

He pointed.

"Is that it? Is that her?" he asked.

Charlotte focused her head behind his index finger.

"Yes," responded Charlotte. "That's Bed Number 3."

"I think that this will conclude our promenade," he said. "I have no desire to arouse the catcalls of your roommates."

Charlotte stepped through the double doorway.

"Thank you for this information, Charlotte Taylor of the twenty-first century."

Chapter Twenty-Two

The Rue Férou

If the Musketeers had intended a discreet exit from the apartment of Athos, it was poorly executed. Knowing full well that the homeowner of Athos' apartment was a handsome hostess, Porthos and Aramis allowed their boots to reverberate down the stairway in hopes of rousing her attention.

As they exited the doorway into the Rue Férou, they were greeted by three additional Musketeers. Since only Athos was familiar with the three additional Musketeers, several minutes were spent with introductions.

"Dear Porthos and Aramis. Allow me to introduce Musketeers deMatteis, Soulliat and Marceau," said Athos by way of introduction.

All bowed low to one another, some sweeping their arms across their torsos to accentuate their salutations.

"What has become of Monsieur Aubergois?" asked Athos.

"Ah! Having found us and directed us here, Monsieur Aubergois elected to return to his shop and begs your pardon in doing so," replied the Musketeer known as deMatteis.

"A gallant fellow is Aubergois! And a skilled artisan to whom I owe the integrity of my sword," added Musketeer Soulliat.

"Before leaving, he did give us a sense of what you sought from us. But is his former apprentice about?" asked Musketeer Marceau.

"Ah! Forgive me!" cried Athos.

With one hand pulling the shoulder strap of the knapsack tightly to his shoulder, Athos walked to the back of their group and gently guided Abisai by elbow to the front of the assembly.

"Gentlemen. Allow me to introduce young Abisai Taylor. It is his safety with which I entrust you," said Athos.

Again, all bowed to one another.

With the introductions having been completed, the Musketeers shared their common interests and relationships, the noise and enthusiasm of their conversations reverberating against the walls and cobblestones of the Rue Férou. Any party in Paris seeking six Musketeers and Abisai at that moment would have found it an easy task.

Finally, Porthos shouted above the din.

"Let us away to our Captain, Monsieur de Treville. His counsel will assist us in protecting our young charge."

Musketeer deMatteis had neither the charisma of Porthos nor the vanity of Aramis, but he did fashion himself as a bon vivant. Although he dressed modestly, he had taken pains to clean and press out his doublet. He was clean-shaven except for a thin mustache so waxed as to appear frozen upon his face.

"I think we all agree that seeking out the counsel of our Captain is a wise decision. However, before your man Aubergois called us to action, we were enjoying a warm and gracious reception in a cabaret that is conveniently located on this very street. Perhaps we might rejoin our company and share a toast to our good fortune before our audience with Monsieur de Treville?" asked deMatteis of the group.

The convolutions of the debate that followed far outweighed the slightness of the proposal. Nevertheless, after seriously weighing the amount of time needed to gain the hotel of M. de

Treville in the Rue du Vieuz-Colombier, the group decided that a brief quaff was in order and moved en masse to the cabaret.

Under any circumstance, it would have been difficult for six Musketeers to enter any cabaret and remain inconspicuous, but they tried their best. They minimized unwanted eyes on Abisai by encircling him, using their size and their garments to camouflage him from all but the most discerning of spectators.

Upon their entry into the cabaret, the host instantly recognized them as Musketeers and treated them with the deference accorded them in the hierarchy of Paris, clearing out local customers from a corner and making a great show of preparing a table for his auspicious guests.

Not a moment expired after they were seated before a member of the Cardinal's Guard appeared before them.

"Ho, Musketeers," said the Guard.

"Ah, Captain Jussac," replied Aramis, recognizing the visitor. Jussac was known locally as an experienced fighter and a fine blade.

"Gentlemen, I wish you a 'good evening.' How fare thee?" asked Jussac.

Abisai struggled to hear the conversation over the noise of the cabaret. But it did not take long for the Captain to fix Abisai in his gaze while continuing to speak to Aramis.

"I must ask that one of your party accompany me."

Immediately, Abisai felt the collective musculature of his chaperons tighten about him. Marceau's hand fell to the pommel of his sword.

"Monsieur. We are here for a brief toast before we go off to an appointment with our Captain. You surely know our Captain, Monsieur de Treville. And surely as you know him, you realize the importance of punctuality to him. Why, should you delay us, it could inflate to a *cause celebre*! We cannot be delayed! Why not visit us with your request tomorrow?" replied Aramis, feigning joviality as he prepared to defend Abisai.

"My orders are to remove from your company one that the Cardinal has identified as a spy. Should you not acquiesce, then all of you will be charged with espionage. Please follow me."

Jussac turned on his heels and exited the cabaret.

"What should we do?" asked Marceau of the company.

"How could he possibly already know that Abisai is with us?" asked Porthos of Athos.

"We've not left your apartment but for ten minutes."

Abisai recollected the thirty minutes of carousal outside of Athos' apartment that preceded their arrival at the cabaret, but did not correct Porthos' impression.

He did, however, suggest a theory.

"I think I know," volunteered Abisai. "When I was waiting for my audience outside of Monsieur Athos' apartment, three of the Cardinal's Guards passed us. They teased Grimaud as they passed and pretended to pay me no mind. I thought it innocent enough, although their behavior toward Grimaud annoyed me. But now, I suspect that they pretended to focus on Grimaud while evaluating me."

"Quite right, young master," said Athos, endorsing Abbie's theory. "There are six Musketeers in our company, and there is but one of Captain Jussac. I think we can convince the good Captain that his maths will not redound to his benefit today. Let us step outside and persuade him."

"It is possible that a company of the Cardinal's Guards awaits for us outside as well," volunteered the Musketeer Soulliat.

"What awaits us outside, awaits us outside. Let us discover what our future holds, shall we?"

With that, Athos moved toward the exit, and the Musketeers and Abisai followed.

186

***

As the Musketeers filed out into the street, Soulliat's comment proved to be prescient. In the darkness of the Rue Férou, Abisai thought he saw at least six men in the uniforms of the Cardinal's Guards waiting for them. They stood in the formation of a triangle, with Captain Jussac at the apex facing them.

It was difficult for Abisai to define any one Guard other than their Captain. A Guard in the rear of the formation clearly sought anonymity, crouching below the shoulder line of the other Guards. A Guard stationed off of the right shoulder of Captain Jussac wore a black mask that covered his face from chin to nose. Abisai thought he saw something familiar about him.

"Come forward and surrender, young man, unless you wish to see these Musketeers upon our blades," said the Captain.

Abisai had difficulty translating Jussac's words. Abisai had grown accustomed to the courtesies extended to him. Those in his company would quickly apprehend his delay in translating their French, and so had spoken slowly and clearly to aid his understanding. Captain Jussac was neither aware of the challenges of French to Abbie's comprehension, nor would he have likely cared had he been aware.

Then, Abisai felt a pull upon his sleeve. Marceau was gently moving him toward the southern intersection of the Rue Férou and the Rue de Vaugirardas. Porthos meandered in the same direction, his size, personality and presence influencing both the Cardinal's Guards and the Musketeers to follow him.

"Perhaps the Captain would enjoy the continuance of this conversation behind the Luxembourg?" offered Athos in an effort to distract the Guards from focusing on Abisai.

187

"Your invitation to duel is in violation of our edicts. I will add it to the list of offenses with which you will be charged," accused Jussac, taking the bait.

Jussac and Athos continued to exchange vague threats, allowing the company to gradually shift over to the spaciousness of the corner of Rue de Vaugirard. The masked Guard must have realized the strategic advantage that Porthos had gained on behalf of his comrades, because he swore at Jussac in annoyance. Then, the masked Guard twisted his torso into the center of the formation and barked an order to the Guardsmen.

Upon his command, two of the Cardinal's Guards unsheathed their swords.

One killed deMatteis as he stood, and another severely wounded Soulliat.

Outraged by the breach of etiquette and unfair advantage taken by the Guards, the Musketeers shouted their objections in unison. The courageous Soulliat cried out in pain but stood his ground.

The five standing Musketeers unsheathed their swords and surrounded Abisai to protect him.

Recognizing that the Musketeers would never surrender after having been ambushed, the Guard in the rear of the formation abandoned his anonymity and unfolded its torso to its full height, standing at least one head above every other swordsman in the Rue de Vaugirard.

"Aginbyte!" whispered Abisai and Athos in unplanned unison. Abisai looked at Athos in wonderment.

The Aginbyte of Inwit was cloaked in the garb of the Cardinal's Guardsmen except that it wore a black skullcap and hood pulled tightly around its head to hide the globe that was its skull.

"Pardon the unfortunate breach in etiquette," rumbled the Aginbyte to the Musketeers in unassailable French.

"I only wish returned to me what is mine. You are harboring a thief."

Athos hugged Abisai's knapsack closer to his body, unintentionally drawing the focus of the Aginbyte.

"My BookMarck," growled the Aginbyte, eyeing the knapsack.

Aramis proclaimed the boy's innocence and began to list the infractions suffered by Musketeers at the hands of the Aginbyte.

While Aramis attempted to distract the Aginbyte, Athos leaned back to Abisai.

"They are six," Athos whispered to Abisai with urgency. "We are five, and with the mortal blow to Soulliat, we will be four in a moment's time.

"Secret yourself under that arbor," Athos said as he nodded toward a small group of trees on the far side of the Rue de Vaugirard.

For a brief moment, Athos turned away from the growing threat to give Abisai his attention.

"I won't leave you," whispered Abisai in return.

"You'll do as I say," commanded Athos. "Tonight, your time will come to engage in battle. Await your fate under that arbor and prepare to defend yourself. Remember what I've taught you."

Abisai heard in Athos' voice the intonation of the hooded journeyman, and dropped his objection. Obscured by the darkness and the circle of Musketeers in front of him, Abisai slipped out of the circle and backed his way across the street, kneeling beside one of the trees in the arbor. Although the Aginbyte attempted to follow him with his eyes, Athos continually shifted his position to remain between the Aginbyte's gaze and the boy.

As the Guardsmen circled the Musketeers, the Aginbyte moved forward to engage Athos. The difference in size between them was obvious to all.

Porthos called out to his comrade.

"Athos. Allow me to engage the blade of this Aginbyte?" requested Porthos.

"I think not, but I thank you, friend Porthos. The Aginbyte covets the contents of this valise," replied Athos, pressing the strap to his chest.

"I will relinquish it only upon my death and perhaps not then."

"Then take this," responded Porthos, who gracefully flipped his great sword to Athos, its hilt falling neatly into Athos' palm.

"It has the heft to slay dragons."

"Merci, mon ami," Athos said and, with a wry smile, gently tossed his sword to Porthos in exchange.

Aramis paused to address the wounded Soulliat.

"This is not your fight, friend Soulliat. You may retire without disgracing your uniform," said Aramis.

"But it is my fight," responded Soulliat. "The blade of a Guard carries my blood, even if it be but a flesh wound."

A knowing smile passed between Aramis and Soulliat. Aramis, who had seen the sword of a Guardsman pass through the body of the gallant Soulliat, knew that Soulliat had sustained a mortal blow. The only question that remained was how long the wounded Soulliat could stand and fight.

Captain Jussac sensed that the pall of dishonor had fallen over his company. He knew that the death of deMatteis and wounding of Soulliat were acts of cowardice, reinforced by the sight of the valiant Soulliat remaining on his feet and preparing to defend Abisai.

"You are accused of harboring a spy and a thief," cried Jussac to the Musketeers, attempting to rally the Guardsmen out of their malaise. "If you relinquish the spy to us, we will arrest you but allow you to sheath your swords."

"You have already spilled our blood, Monsieur," replied Aramis. "In doing so, it is *you* who have decided the matter."

"Have at you, then!" cried Jussac.

The Musketeers rushed upon their adversaries with ferocity, intent on avenging the death of deMatteis. Porthos sprang toward two of the Guardsmen to dispel any notion that they might have an advantage over him. The Musketeer known as Marceau received Captain Jussac. Aramis charged at his Guardsman with the intention of concluding his match quickly. And the wounded Soulliat paired off against the masked Guardsman.

All but Athos rushed into battle. Athos carried the sword of Porthos but held it back. He watched as the Aginbyte of Inwit unsheathed its massive sabre and extended it toward Athos, rotating the tip in a slow circle to outline Athos' torso. Athos kept his blade in motion to prevent it from being taken by his taller adversary, yet maintaining it parallel to the ground so that it would be difficult to beat or bind.

The Aginbyte attacked first, thrusting its sword at Athos but keeping its feet in place. Athos measured the significant distance covered by the Aginbyte with the mere extension of its sword arm; he made a mental note of how much effort it then took the Aginbyte to recover its massive frame.

The Aginbyte accompanied its second thrust with a lunge, but Athos deciphered the move as more feint than an attempt to harm him. Athos parried the thrust, sweeping the blade of the

Aginbyte to his right and away from the line of his body. Again, Athos stayed within himself, using a minimum of movement to mask his fighting style, all the while measuring the Aginbyte's speed and ability to cover distance.

From the arbor, Abisai measured the Aginbyte's movements as Athos had taught him. It was curious to Abisai that the Aginbyte had elected to pivot and lunge as would an earthbound swordsman, and not to slide along the surface of the street. *Was the Aginbyte suppressing its ability to glide to be inconspicuous among the Cardinal's Guards? Had the Aginbyte lost the ability to surf when it lost its BookMarck to Charlotte? Or was it baiting Athos into a false rhythm, preparing to use its glide at its most advantageous moment?*

I'm in a book! This is crazy, crazy, crazy! What happens to me if I am killed in a work of fiction?

Before this thought could percolate into panic, Abisai's attention was jolted back to the battle before him.

Athos defended himself from the Aginbyte's attacks and feints. As he did so, Athos would glance over in the direction of Abisai as if to say: "Do you see? Are you measuring? Are you memorizing his tendencies? His rhythms?"

Finally, the Aginbyte must have completed its own analysis of Athos' defenses, because it attacked Athos with unexpected speed, bringing his blade to Athos' chest. Athos, feigning a retreat, spun into the circumference of the Aginbyte's sword.

Inside the kill zone of the Aginbyte's sword, Athos beat the Aginbyte's blade in hopes of displacing it. But the Aginbyte's sword did not move, and Athos felt the shock of his own blow reverberate through his own sword and up into his forearm. In need of time and space, Athos controlled the Aginbyte's sword long enough to retreat out of harm's way.

Abisai recognized that Athos had been moving with a purposeful slowness to mask his agility, and was varying his footwork to disguise his natural lines of attack, all in the hopes of gaining a moment when he might marshal his advantages and strike the Aginbyte with one mortal blow. But after having tested the superior strength of the Aginbyte, Athos realized that he would need to attack relentlessly or he would lose the slim advantage of his superior experience and stamina.

The Aginbyte raised its shoulder and dropped its forearm so that its long blade pointed at Athos from an intimidating height. Athos gave Abisai one more sidelong glance, and attacked.

Athos lunged forward and unexpectedly raised his blade to extend over that of the Aginbyte. With surprise as his ally, Athos' sword circled over the top of the Aginbyte's blade and, with astounding leverage, moved the Aginbyte's blade up and outside the line of Athos' body.

Athos continued to control his opponent's sword by gliding his own blade up that of his opponent, keeping it in opposition until Athos' hilt was to the middle of the Aginbyte's sword.

The Aginbyte, sensing the fragility of its position, attempted to retreat. Athos, now relentless, redoubled and followed him in. Having successfully collapsed the distance between himself and the Aginbyte, Athos released the Aginbyte's sword and, sensing the moment to be his, lunged under the Aginbyte's hand, thrusting his blade at the massive torso.

Realizing that it had relinquished far too much space to Athos, the Aginbyte threw back its left shoulder as Athos' blade slid past its chest. Athos' sword blade plucked the threads of the Aginbyte's baldric but did not pierce. But before Athos could withdraw, the Aginbyte slapped its own blade to its mighty sternum, freezing Athos' blade to its own chest.

With Athos momentarily pinned, the Aginbyte leaned its massive frame down to face Athos.

"You have vexed me for eons," it swore.

Athos did not reply, but collapsed his thighs into his calves while simultaneously tugging his sword down with both hands, freeing it from the Aginbyte's trap. As Athos retreated, he heard the Aginbyte's blade cut the air above him.

Athos sprang out of his crouch and attacked again, staying low and lunging forward. Again Athos' blade was met by the resistance of the Aginbyte. Athos used the resistance of the Aginbyte's sword to scrape down and drive its threatening blade outside the line of his body.

Suddenly, the Aginbyte's sword went slack, withdrawing its resistance and pitching the imbalanced Athos forward.

Athos' battle instincts screamed.

He knew he had been duped.

Despite this realization, Athos was too late to prevent the dagger in the Aginbyte's free hand from plunging into his back.

Chapter Twenty-Three

Athos

Athos heard the dull thud of penetration, then felt his torso punched forward from the force of the Aginbyte's blow.

From his hiding place, Abisai had seen the Aginbyte raise the dagger high above the head of Athos and had jumped forward as he followed the arc of the descending blade. Too late to warn Athos, Abisai froze in place. To Abisai's surprise, Athos did not react in pain.

Athos, even more surprised than Abisai, felt no pain. He twisted his torso in the direction of the embedded dagger and watched as three books fell to the ground: *Frankenstein; or, The Modern Prometheus*, *The Memoirs of Sherlock Holmes* and *The Three Musketeers*.

The Aginbyte's intention was now obvious. The Aginbyte had managed to shred the underside of Abisai's knapsack and empty its contents to the ground.

Athos watched in bewilderment as the Aginbyte ignored their duel and bent its mammoth frame to inspect the books. But before Athos could attack, he heard an unfamiliar voice behind him.

"Aginbyte. Must I finish all that you start?"

Before he could react, Athos felt the piercing pain of a sword blade travel through his right shoulder and into his chest. Ambushed, he did not cry out so much as audibly gasp for breath.

Athos' vision blurred and he fell to his knees. He felt the blade twist inside him as his assailant inartfully tried to withdraw it. From his knees, Athos recognized the motionless body of Soulliat lying next to him, and realized that his comrade had succumbed to his wound. Athos did not need to raise his head to deduce that his assailant was the masked Guardsman.

Athos remained on his knees, motionless, more apparition than Musketeer. It was the unnaturalness of Athos' immobility that pulled the eyesight of the Aginbyte away from the scattered books.

The Aginbyte pivoted from its crouch to face the masked Guardsman.

"Have you no sense of honor?" accused the Aginbyte. "Have you no sense of propriety? You stink of the twenty-first century. Having a sword in your hand does not entitle you to a street brawl! It is a sacred instrument!"

The masked Guardsman pulled his bandana down from his mouth so that the Aginbyte would not mistake his words.

"You have been seduced by a code of honor that never existed. Do I have to remind you that we're occupying a work of fiction?" hissed the unmasked Guardsman as he pulled his mask back up to his nose.

"You would do well to remember that we answer to a higher order!"

The Aginbyte of Inwit, synapses firing beneath its skull cap, withdrew the sword of the masked Guardsman from Athos' shoulder as carefully as could be managed before handing it back to the Guardsman, seeking to minimize Athos' pain. Athos cried out in agony and completed his fall to the ground. Absolutely vulnerable, he could feel the boots of Aramis pass over him to defend him from the masked Guardsman as well as to continue to engage his own adversary.

I must remember to thank Aramis, thought the fallen Athos.

The Aginbyte returned its attention to the books that had spilled to the ground. A sliver of phosphorescence peaked out from between pages 121 and 122 of *The Three Musketeers*. The Aginbyte bent its great bulk to the ground, intent on recovering a BookMarck.

The BookMarck refused to acknowledge the Aginbyte with a celebration of light.

Interesting, thought the Aginbyte.

Still bent, the Aginbyte reached to remove the BookMarck from its sanctuary between page 121 and page 122. But before it could pull the BookMarck from between the pages, a sword point pierced the aged cellophane of the book cover.

"Je te de en garde!"

As the Aginbyte released the book to the ground, the sliver of exposed BookMarck rejoiced with a kaleidoscope of colors. The Aginbyte swiveled toward the voice of a new adversary.

"Abisai."

Chapter Twenty-Four

Luck

Abisai stood over the Aginbyte, sword in hand, face reddened with rage.

"I say thee, en garde," he yelled again, pressing the flat of his blade to the shoulder of the kneeling Aginbyte.

The Aginbyte turned and raised itself to its full, intimidating height.

"Abisai," responded the Aginbyte calmly. "You needn't die today. I seek only that which belongs to me."

Athos, hearing Abisai's engagement of the Aginbyte, raised his chest off of the cobblestones and, with a sweep of his arm, gathered beneath him the three books and the knapsack, collapsing upon them.

For a third time, Abisai called out the Aginbyte.

"En garde!" he yelled, tears flooding his eyes.

As the Aginbyte slowly unsheathed its massive sword, Abisai used the back of his sleeve to clear his vision, and prepared for the fight of his life.

***

Porthos, Aramis and Marceau could not break off their own duels to assist Abisai. Porthos and Aramis occupied two blades each, while it took all of the skill that Marceau could manage to fend off Jussac's talented blade.

"All eyes, Abisai!" cried out Porthos. "Watch for his swordplay!"

"Defend, Abisai!" yelled Aramis. "Draw in only on your own terms."

Abisai positioned himself between the Aginbyte and the prone body of Athos.

"Do you really think that your children's sword will defeat me where Athos' has failed?" asked the Aginbyte.

The words had no sooner left his lips when the Aginbyte lunged toward Abisai, gripping the hilt of his sword with both hands. He windmilled his great blade above his head, marshaling speed for a devastating downstroke that would shatter Abisai's blade.

As the Aginbyte's blade descended, Abisai sidestepped, holding his blade parallel to the ground.

As the Aginbyte's sabre struck Abisai's short blade, Abisai released his sword and allowed himself to be disarmed. The Aginbyte, not expecting the foray to be unopposed, became a prisoner of its own momentum and pitched forward, the massive blade sweeping downward and cleaving the cobblestones of the street.

Porthos had positioned his duels so as to keep his eye on Abisai. He stole a glance at Aramis and Aramis returned his glance with a wry smile. The Musketeers appreciated the irony of Abisai's feinting the Aginbyte as the Aginbyte had duped Athos.

"Bravo to you!" yelled Porthos.

"You are a quick study, my boy!" added Aramis.

As the Aginbyte attempted to pull its embedded sword out from the street, Abisai gripped its right glove and drove his knee into the exposed arm of the Aginbyte, forcing its elbow joint into an unnaturally obtuse angle and eliciting a bellow of pain.

Abisai silenced the Aginbyte by driving his left palm into its jaw.

The Aginbyte, swordless, backed away to locate Abisai through stars of pain.

As its vision cleared, Abisai brandished the Aginbyte's massive sword.

"'Children's sword' be damned!" yelled Abisai. "Perhaps your own steel will do you?"

"HALLOOO!" shouted Porthos in appreciation. Aramis was so distracted by the sound of Porthos' voice that he allowed one of the Guardsmen to beat down on his own blade and splinter it. Offended, Aramis buried his gloved fist into the nose of his adversary. As the Guardsman dropped his own sword to reflexively bring his hands to his face, Aramis grabbed the falling sword before it grounded and ran the Guardsman through with his own blade.

Aramis turned quickly to finish off the masked Guardsman.

"Coward!" yelled Aramis.

"Drop your swords and yield!" cried the masked Guardsman.

Aramis pinwheeled to see the masked Guardsman press his sword point into the flesh of Abisai's neck, indenting his skin but not yet drawing blood.

Abisai, feeling the swordpoint, turned his head as much as he dared toward his assailant.

For the second time that night, Abisai felt a familiarity about the masked Guardsman.

"I say thee, YIELD OR I KILL THE BOY!" he yelled to the remaining Musketeers.

"Spare him!" responded Porthos. He carefully stepped back and conceded his duels by raising his sword before his face.

Aramis and Marceau followed Porthos' example. The clamor of swordplay in the square was replaced with silence, broken only by the pants of the exhausted swordsmen.

"You are the luckless mother of treachery," groused Aramis,

annoyed at himself for having allowed the masked Guardsman to slip away and ambush Abisai.

Prompted by that epithet, a wave of recognition swept over Abisai.

"Mister Luck?" Abisai asked in English, keeping his head immobile.

"Yes, Abisai Taylor."

Luck pulled the mask from his face. The bridge of his nose and his cheekbones were lined with grime and perspiration, but his identity was unmistakable.

"Your luck has obviously run out," he added with a self-satisfied grin.

"I've waited years to say that!"

Luck, keeping his arm extended and his swordpoint at Abbie's neck, moved to face him.

"The only thing that prevents me from killing you is the integrity of Dumas' book," whispered Luck as he leaned toward Abisai.

"In *The Three Musketeers*, only two Musketeers lose their lives at the battle of the Rue du Vieux-Colombier. You survive only because, if I were to violate the narrative of the book, I might be consigned to this hell hole forever."

Luck paused and gave Abisai a long look, then continued.

"Perhaps you knew that? Perhaps that explains where you found the courage to confront the Aginbyte. Oui?

"No, Abisai Taylor. You will not die here today. Your punishment will be to remain in this BookStream forever."

But Abisai had stopped hearing Luck's voice to focus his memory of *The Three Musketeers*, specifically upon the battle of the Rue du Vieux-Colombier.

Only two Musketeers lose their lives at the battle of the Rue du Vieux-Colombier.

201

Abbie did the math.

DeMatteis. Soulliat.

Athos is still alive.

Of course he's still alive. He has an entire book to live through.

"Vive la France," Luck added derisively as he withdrew his swordpoint from Abisai's neck and walked away.

The Aginbyte of Inwit ruefully rubbed its jaw and returned to where it had last seen the BookMarck. Scanning the motionless body of Athos, it was obvious from his odd positioning that the Musketeer had swept the contents of Abisai's knapsack under his torso before losing consciousness. The Aginbyte lumbered toward the prone Musketeer.

Athos' torso was bathed in a red aura, nearly imperceptible to all but those who were familiar with it.

Healing element, thought the Aginbyte. *Athos has Abisai's BookMarck.*

The Aginbyte bent low and extricated a crumpled BookMarck from Athos' right hand.

As he watched the Aginbyte remove the BookMarck from Athos' grip, Abisai noticed that the BookMarck remained muted as if refusing to celebrate being possessed by the Aginbyte.

Instead, Abisai's attention was drawn to the continued coloration of Athos' body in the faint, red aura of the healing factor.

If the Aginbyte has my BookMarck, what is healing Athos?

Abisai's confusion was quickly interrupted by the voice of Ronald Luck.

"Arrest them!" he ordered.

Having allowed Porthos, Aramis and Marceau to sheath their swords, the exhausted Guardsmen prodded the Musketeers into a loose formation of prisoners and moved them forward at swordpoint.

As Abisai moved to join the prisoners, the Aginbyte bent toward him.

"I have *your* BookMarck.

"Now, I want *my* BookMarck. If you tell me where your sister is, I'll let her live. Is it to be Mary Shelley or Sir Arthur Conan Doyle?" asked the Aginbyte.

Abisai took a moment to assess the risks. The Aginbyte obviously knew that Charlotte had escaped to one of the three books that had fallen out of his knapsack.

"*The Memoirs of Sherlock Holmes.* Sir Arthur Conan Doyle," answered Abisai.

The Aginbyte rubbed its jaw and gave Abisai a long look, evaluating his sincerity.

As Abisai joined his party, Captain Jussac and the remaining Guardsman marched their prisoners back up the Rue Férou. As they walked, Aramis influenced them toward the whitefaced, brick wall defining the right side of the streetline.

"At the ready," he whispered to them.

From the rear of the procession, the Aginbyte conferred with Luck.

"He says that Charlotte Taylor's location is not in the BookStream of *Frankenstein* but in the BookStream of Sir Arthur Conan Doyle."

"The boy would never intentionally disclose her true location," Luck suggested to the Aginbyte. "She is undoubtedly in the BookStream of Mary Shelley's *Frankenstein*. Travel to the *Frankenstein* BookStream and recover your BookMarck. Should you capture or kill Charlotte Taylor, better still."

"What of you, Censorium Luck?" asked the Aginbyte.

"I will enter the BookStream of H.G. Wells' *Time Machine*," Luck responded. "If Charlotte Taylor eludes you, she will need to enter the realm of the *Time Machine* to return home, and I will capture her there. If you are successful in subduing her and recovering your BookMarck, then I will be conveniently positioned to return home using the Time Machine."

"As you wish, Censorium," responded the Aginbyte.

"And this time," chided Censorium Luck, "hang onto your BookMarck? Your hitchhiking on my BookMarck drains the energy out of the entire system. Try to manage your own itinerary."

The Aginbyte raised the BookMarck of Abisai Taylor.

"Mary Shelley. *Frankenstein*," said the Aginbyte, ignoring Luck's final insult.

"H. G. Wells. *The Time Machine*," said Luck as he raised his BookMarck.

Hearing the voices of the Aginbyte and Luck behind him, Captain Jussac turned back to them for his instructions.

"Pardon, Monsieur Luck, but is our destination the Bastille or Fort L'Eveque?"

"Mon Dieu," cried Jussac.

Hearing the incredulity in the voice of their Captain, all of the Guards turned around to see the cause of his outcry.

The two BookMarcks responded to the commands of the Aginbyte and Censorium Luck by transforming their corporeal forms into kaleidoscopes of elemental color. Once decomposed to lightform, their corporealities collapsed into two lightstreams and exploded into opposite directions, leaving behind auras of phosphorescent color.

The Guardsmen stood in awe, transfixed by the light show.

Aramis leaped upon their opportunity to escape.

"Now!" he whispered with urgency. He took two steps to the white wall, found a toehold upon a damaged brick and vaulted himself to the top of the wall. Once perched atop the wall, he extended his hands down to assist his comrades' escape. With the Guardsmen engrossed, Abisai scaled the wall with ease.

Porthos did not enjoy the good fortune of his comrades. He

struggled to pull himself up, requiring Aramis and Abisai to pull him up by his arms while Marceau pushed him up by the seat of his pants.

Once safely on the other side of the wall, Aramis addressed them hurriedly.

"Porthos and I are going back to the square to retrieve Athos. Marceau, you take Abisai back to Aubergois and hide him there until this furor abates. And there is sure to be a furor."

As they rose to leave one another, Aramis grabbed Abisai's right elbow, and pulled him in for a quick embrace.

"You disposed of yourself courageously today, Abisai Taylor," said Aramis. "I say to thee 'Well Done.'"

With that, Marceau hurried Abisai back toward the Quai de Feraille. Aramis and Porthos, using the garden wall as concealment, doubled back to the square.

After the last of the phosphorescence had diffused into the air, the Cardinal's Guards shook off their amazement and turned back to find that their prisoners had disappeared as well. Dispirited, exhausted and confused, they shared an oath to never repeat to anyone the events that had occurred that evening and that their secret would die with them.

Chapter Twenty-Five

Le Comte de la Fere

Following his battle at the Rue Férou, Abisai returned to the smithing shop of Roland Aubergois to hide. Since he believed his BookMarck to have been taken by the Aginbyte of Inwit, the BookStream of *The Three Musketeers* had become his exile and Aubergois' shop had become his prison. No matter how he gameplayed his situation, he could not formulate an escape plan.

Despite his resignation, Abisai carried out his duties with aplomb. Aubergois would arrive every day to the shop having been swept and the furnaces afire; such was the character of Abisai Taylor.

On the Friday morning after his return, Aubergois arrived with Abisai's breakfast as was their routine. Upon seeing Aubergois walk into the shop, Abisai bade the swordsmith good morning before turning toward the courtyard to wash.

"Bonjour, Abisai. Last night, I received a visitor. Do you remember Grimaud? You know him as the valet of Athos?"

Abisai turned and faced the swordsmith, wiping his blackened hands on his smock.

"This Grimaud," continued Aubergois. "He is an eccentric character. Does he actually speak to you? He tried to communicate with me with gestures, and I was within an inch of spanking him with my blade before he discovered his tongue and deigned to share a few words with me."

Abisai stopped wiping his hands and stood motionless, listening.

"He shared the news that Athos is alive and in passable health. I had heard rumors of this myself. Apparently, Athos and several other Musketeers were involved in an altercation two days ago at the convent of the Carmes-Deschaux. Whatever. He wishes to see you at his apartment tomorrow morning at eight."

Abisai felt his heart gallop and his blood course through his ears. *I am to have an audience with Athos.*

"Monsieur. Would you allow me to accept this invitation?" Abisai asked the swordsmith, accompanying his request with a bow.

"Of course," responded Aubergois. "You may leave early tomorrow morning. Do not set the furnaces. Instead, use your time to gain his apartment with caution. Do not allow yourself to be seen."

Abisai was reminded that the Cardinal's Guards still suspected him to be a spy and wanted him apprehended.

"Before you go, be sure to arm yourself. I suggest that you select one of these."

Aubergois moved toward the sword wall and pointed toward the five short swords mounted on the wall.

Abisai dropped his head before he responded.

"Merci, Monsieur Aubergois. I have already cost you one sword when I allowed myself to be disarmed. I don't have the right to another."

"Nonsense. I do not present this to you as a gift. You have earned it. Now, let's speak no more of it. There's work to be done."

Abisai saw a rare smile fly across Aubergois' face, then disappear.

207

Abisai set upon his day's work with renewed vigor, relieved that he would be in the company of Athos the following morning.

***

Abisai traveled across Paris to Athos' apartment before dawn the following morning, keeping to the shadows and doing his best to avoid being seen. Once he arrived, he presented himself to Grimaud and they enjoyed a brief reunion before Grimaud led Abisai up the stairs and into Athos' apartment. Grimaud kept Abisai in the outer room while he informed his master of his arrival. It took several minutes for Grimaud to reappear.

When Grimaud finally led Abisai into the inner apartment room, Abisai stole a quick glance around, then bent low before the Musketeer. He waited to be acknowledged.

"Good day to you, Abisai Taylor. Please rise."

"Good day to you, Monsieur Athos. You appear to have recovered remarkably well."

Athos looked very much himself to Abisai except he remained seated on his bed to receive him.

"Yes, a remarkable recovery indeed," responded Athos with enthusiasm. "Although the Guardsmen of his Eminence left me for dead, I was hardly so. Luckily, although the sword of that masked Guardsman pierced my arm and chest, it did not touch my heart.

"And I have been about some business since last I saw you. I have happened upon a new acquaintance: a Gascon who calls himself D'Artagnan. Are you familiar with him?" asked Athos.

Abisai thought he heard a hint of suggestive mischief in Athos's voice. But Abisai remained respectful and responded that he had never met D'Artagnan.

"No?" continued Athos. "Ah. Well. He reminds me of you in some respects. In time, this D'Artagnan may gain my regard. That is, if I am not forced to kill him first.

"In any event, this D'Artagnan shared with me the recipe for a balsam that has sped my recovery. He said that it is his mother's recipe; that he'd tried it himself and it well cured him. He has shared it with me and, indeed, it has assisted my recovery."

Again, Abisai felt that Athos was probing him.

"I was impressed with the courage of this D'Artagnan. In this, he reminds me of you as well."

As he completed his greeting, Athos rose from his bed and leveled his eyes upon Abisai. If Athos' voice had been previously mirthful, he now spoke in earnestness.

"Aramis told me of your courage in disarming the Aginbyte," Athos confided. "He said that you stood over me after I was bladed, and that you may have saved my life. For this, I thank you."

Athos bowed slightly, and Abisai returned his bow.

"Perhaps now, I can return the favor."

As Athos turned to reach behind him, Abisai saw Athos briefly blanche with pain.

"Monsieur. I am appreciative of your attention, but I am not wounded," said Abisai, expecting Athos to offer him the balsam.

But when he turned back toward Abisai, Athos had in his hands a BookMarck, its chaincloth of colors pulsing in the morning light.

Abisai's stoicism disappeared. He took a step backwards to stabilize himself as the room began to spin about.

Athos extended the BookMarck to Abisai.

"I believe that this belongs to you, Abisai Taylor," Athos said, for the second time in a week.

"What? How?"

Athos allowed himself a slight chortle at Abisai's expense. Then, he winced as he extended the BookMarck to Abisai with his right arm.

"Would you please take this?" insisted Athos. "This position is causing me some pain."

"Sir. I cannot take your BookMarck," replied Abisai.

"It is not my BookMarck, Abisai Taylor. It is *your* BookMarck."

Athos tilted the BookMarck into the morning light, hoping to illuminate its serial number.

After a momentary adjustment, the embossed serial number appeared on its surface.

Sure enough. The inscription read: *BookMarck 501.23.*

"This is my BookMarck," repeated Abisai, incredulously.

As he accepted his BookMarck from Athos' hand, the BookMarck pulsed with the celestial colors of joy.

"But how? I saw the Aginbyte take my BookMarck out of your hand."

"No. You saw the Aginbyte take *my* BookMarck," responded Athos.

Athos paused, allowing his words to hang in the air.

"Any questions?" Athos asked as he smiled.

"You own a BookMarck? Then you must be a WordSmythe?" Abisai finally asked.

Athos ignored the question.

"I have learned to love France, especially the Paris of this era. It has become my home. I no longer see the need to leave."

Athos paused to look about the apartment. He did not hide his affection for his surroundings.

"Besides," he added, "books have been written about me. Oui? How dare I leave this BookStream?"

As Abisai attempted to absorb the conversation, Athos called out an order.

"Grimaud. Two glasses of wine."

Grimaud's head and shoulders appeared in the doorway as he bowed in acquiescence, exposing his proximity to the doorway and his penchant for eavesdropping.

"When you first arrived at his shop, Aubergois had misgivings about you. You must admit that the circumstances surrounding your arrival were a bit suspicious, as if you'd rode into Paris with King Henry IV.

"On the day of your arrival, Aubergois wasted no time in examining your valise and was astonished by its contents, particularly by a book about Musketeers. Aubergois does not understand English but was conversant enough to see names that he recognized. Further, the three books in your valise were produced with a methodology he'd never seen before, piquing his curiosity as a master craftsman.

"Not knowing what to make of you, Aubergois absconded with your valise on the night of your arrival and delivered it to me.

"I must pause now and offer my apologies for our indiscretion. I hope that you can forgive us?" asked Athos.

"Forgiven," replied Abisai, too curious to interrupt Athos' narrative.

Grimaud entered the room with two goblets but hesitated, uncertain as to where to serve them.

"Of course. How silly of me. Abisai. Please sit in that armchair to relieve Grimaud of his confusion. Grimaud. I will sit upon my bed. The nightstand will do."

"And pack Abisai's BookMarck away for him. It sits between page 121 and page 122, I believe."

Grimaud deposited the goblets, carefully took Abisai's BookMarck from his hand and backed out of the room, wordlessly.

Athos continued.

"As you may know, Roland Aubergois and I have shared a relationship of trust that extends back for years, so for him to seek my counsel in the middle of the night was not taken lightly by me. Luckily, I was in this apartment that evening and was able to receive him.

"Along with your valise, Aubergois shared with me your fantastical story about leaving America to bait a pursuer away from your sister. It was then that I became truly concerned. Who were you? Were you a spy for the Cardinal? For the King? For the Prussians?

"Or worse yet, were you a Repositor sent to hunt *me* down? Aubergois does not know of Repositors, but he does know that I have enemies, and it would not be the first time that they'd sought to approach me through my comradeship with Aubergois.

"Finally, when Aubergois revealed your name to me, all the pieces fell into place for me. And I said to myself, *'Abisai Taylor? Could it truly be that the brother of Charlotte Taylor has arrived into this BookStream?'*"

"'The brother of Charlotte Taylor?'" Abisai repeated in annoyance.

"I found the contents of your valise to be consistent with your explanation of being a member of the Taylor family. Of course, I am familiar with Dumas' classic novel, *The Three Musketeers*. I live it."

"Then, your performance as an apprentice to Aubergois convinced me of your sincerity and your integrity. Once I was convinced, I enrolled Aubergois as well, and we pledged to protect you. With Aubergois' help, we secreted you in his shop, which may be the safest location in Paris. As you began to assimilate into our culture, I made it my business to monitor your training. When I had finally developed some time to absent myself from my King and my Captain, I assisted Aubergois in his instruction of you and your swordsmanship."

The light of realization began to grow in Abisai's mind.

"I did not oversee your occupation of Paris to apprentice you in the shop of a swordsmith. I oversaw your occupation of Paris as an ally to defeat a longtime nemesis of both the WordSmythes and the Musketeers, the Aginbyte of Inwit."

Athos paused for a drink, and invited Abisai to do the same.

"What was revelatory to me when Aubergois asked for me to rifle through your valise was finding your BookMarck among the pages of *The Three Musketeers*. How careless of you!" scolded Athos.

"Once I'd had a chance to evaluate it away from Aubergois, I found your BookMarck to be unique in several respects. It hails from the five hundred series of BookMarcks which has developed a reputation for reliability over the years. But far more unique is that your BookMarck has a healing property among its attitudes. Did you know this?" asked Athos.

Abisai nodded his agreement, thinking back to how his BookMarck had repaired the seriously injured ankle of the librarian as if dispensing "red light therapy on steroids."

"Since my own BookMarck does not have a healing property, and realizing that we were both likely to have a difficult and painful road ahead, I kept your BookMarck on my person at all times.

But also I carried my own BookMarck, waiting for the appropriate moment to play bait and switch with the Aginbyte. The Aginbyte almost got your BookMarck when he gutted your valise, but once you distracted him, I was able to sweep your BookMarck, your books and your valise under my body, and induce the Aginbyte into taking *my* BookMarck from my hand.

"So, I must beg your forgiveness for yet another indiscretion," begged Athos. "You thought your BookMarck lost to the Aginbyte, but it has remained with me for over a week. The Aginbyte has my BookMarck."

As he spoke, Athos massaged his right shoulder as if to alleviate pain or loosen stiffness.

And with that gesture, the reason for Athos' miraculous recovery became obvious to Abisai. It had nothing to do with the balsam of D'Artagnan.

"I must thank you," said Athos. "Though your graciousness was unknown to you, my recovery would have been far more arduous without your BookMarck and its healing element."

Athos stopped talking again to allow Abisai the chance to absorb the nuances of his apprenticeship.

"By now, the Aginbyte has realized that it has been hoodwinked with an inferior BookMarck. I can assure you that the Aginbyte will not be happy about it.

"Compounding the Aginbyte's annoyance will be the recognition that my BookMarck is a conduit in the BookMarck system. Should the Aginbyte use it frivolously or in defiance of BookMarck protocol, my BookMarck will lose its energy and the entire BookStream transit system will seize up.

"In fact, the Aginbyte's trip into the BookStream of Mary Shelley may near exhaust my BookMarck, leaving the Aginbyte stranded.

"However, if it exhausts, it will also leave you and your sister stranded in your respective BookStreams as well, so there is some immediacy about finding your sister and returning home."

Athos allowed those words to remain in the air, and Abisai began to feel the weight of his future.

"I have a strategy to share with you," said Athos. "I think I might have a plan to reunite you with your sister.

"You believe her to be in London, yes?"

Abisai nodded in agreement.

"She is not. She is here in France, but in a different BookStream than ours, and in a different era. I have an idea how we might attempt to get a message to her. What say you?"

Abisai's jaw dropped, dumbfounded. Not twelve hours before, he was convinced that he was stranded forever and would never be able to assist Charlotte. Now he had his BookMarck and the possibility of contacting his sister. Abisai shifted his weight forward in his chair to attend to every detail of Athos' plan.

"Ironically, I think we can use this balsam as a pretext to do so," continued Athos.

With the suggestion that his sister might need the balsam, Abisai snapped back into the conversation.

"What?" said Abisai, more alarmed than curious. "Are you saying that my sister has been hurt? Is that why she needs this?"

"No," responded Athos. "But I do think it will be of assistance to her. And it gives us the chance to deliver to her a message from you as to how she might meet you and return home together."

Athos spent several minutes laying out his thoughts and what a message intended to span centuries might need to include. Then, Athos had Abisai sit at the secretary in his apartment.

"Grimaud! Pen, ink and paper!"

Grimaud was already standing next to his master with a quill pen, a small pewter dish of black ink and a roll of parchment paper.

Abisai followed Athos' instructions and finished writing the note to his sister. As he allowed the ink to set, Abbie shook his head in bewilderment.

"There is so much about this that I don't understand," he confided to Athos. "What is all this that I have fallen into?"

Athos pondered the best way to respond. As he strolled around his apartment in thought, he walked under a painting of a

215

nobleman. The similarity between the portrait and Athos was unmistakable.

"It is not my place to explain all this to you. But let me tell you two things about the BookStream," offered Athos.

"One: The BookStream has its own internal logic. It makes intelligent decisions. One might suggest that the BookStream is a sentient intelligence. And since BookMarcks are the ambassadors of the BookStream, it appears that BookMarcks have an innate sense of intuition as well. So, if you are good of heart, you may find that your BookMarck will assist your purposes and discourage your enemies.

"Two: The BookStream has a sense of humor. It was not in error that you were deposited in Paris aboard the horse of King Henry IV. You were having a bit of a joke played upon you."

Athos looked at Abisai with genuine affection.

"Are you certain that you want to leave?" Athos asked Abisai. "You might consider remaining in this realm. You are clever. You are good with a sword. Perhaps someday, someone might write of your adventures?"

Abisai rose from his chair and stood before him, speechless, his palms extended in a gesture of stupefaction.

Athos laughed, grimaced and massaged his shoulder.

"Then, return you to Aubergois, but do so with care. Try to keep yourself from being recognized. Grimaud will give you a cloak so that you blend into the populace of Paris. He has sewn your valise together as best he could. Once you've arrived at Aubergois' shop, you should prepare to depart for the BookStream of *The Time Machine* as quickly as possible."

"As for me," concluded Athos, "I will deliver your note as we have discussed."

Athos exchanged a handshake with Abisai.

"We may not see each other again. I bid you *adieu.* I wish you good luck in reuniting with your family."

With that, Grimaud entered the room to escort Abisai out. He wordlessly showed Abisai that he had secured his BookMarck between page 121 and page 122 of *The Three Musketeers* and had returned it to his knapsack along with the other two novels.

As they moved through the outer room, Abisai took a moment to loiter under the painting of the nobleman. He stole a quick glance at the small plaque attached to the bottom frame of the portrait.

It read: Le Comte de la Fere.

***

Before leaving Abisai for the evening, Aubergois paused in the doorway of his shop.

"What is your intention?" he asked.

"I leave tonight. I have an appointment with H.G. Wells," teased Abisai.

"H.G. Wells? I don't know that name. Who is that?" asked Aubergois.

"An author. I think he fancied the wife of Ernest Hemingway," Abisai said with a grin.

Chapter Twenty-Six

Charlotte 2.7

After recording the unpleasantness of her interrogation into her faux journal, Charlotte did not see the Lepine brothers again. Instead, her life fell back into the routine of the Hotel-Dieu de Lyon. When she wandered the hallways on her afternoon walks, she always found the doors to the amphitheater to be locked so securely that one might think they'd been so for centuries. She even managed to push her interrogation into a distant part of her memory.

That is, she did not dwell upon it until a morning when she was awakened by the unfamiliar sound of furniture being moved about. The rays of the rising sun had not yet reached the high windows of the feverish ward, and the world appeared gray through the filter of her eyelashes. Her focus fell upon a pair of angular legs in a chair that had no business being next to her bed, the familiar ash gray pinstripe fabric of a trouser leg crossed over the other.

Charlotte pushed herself up into a sitting position, pulling her threadbare flat sheet to her chin and exposing her feet and ankles in doing so.

The posture of her visitor suggested a man who was used to waiting. As Charlotte raised her eyes to his face, she was startled by the intensity of his gaze as if he was unaware of or unconcerned with the proprieties of staring down a youthful woman in her bed clothes. She immediately looked away.

"Good morning, Miss Taylor. You speak English, do you not?" asked the visitor.

Charlotte nodded in assent.

"Grand. Allow me to introduce myself. My name is Sherlock Holmes."

Holmes rose from his seat, reached over the bed gate, and gently shook her hand. Charlotte, upon hearing Holmes introduce himself, became a maelstrom of activity, her hands attempting to simultaneously rub her eyes, fix her hair, wipe residual drool from the side of her mouth and pull herself into a complete sit while keeping her sheet at her collar line.

Charitably, Holmes finally averted his eyes while Charlotte fumbled about herself. He distracted himself by lowering the bedgate that separated them. With her bedgate down, the two shared unobstructed views of one another.

"Pardon me, Miss Taylor. I should have asked if I might lower your bedgate. Is that all right?" he asked, too late to be courteous.

"Yes, Mr. Holmes," Charlotte said, as much to hear what her voice would sound like that morning as to respond.

Holmes reached down to a side table next to her bed that had never existed before and raised to her a drinking glass.

"I have taken the liberty of rearranging some furniture and ordering you a glass of orange juice. Perhaps you will consider it a peace offering for my having interrupted your sleep," he said as he carefully handed the glass to Charlotte.

Charlotte had never expected much of hospital galleys, partially because she was just grateful to be fed and partially because she'd never had great expectations about hospital food. But when she accepted the glass and coquettishly tipped the

219

liquid to her lips, the icy cold tang of freshly squeezed orange juice rushed into her mouth with an unexpected intensity and reminded her of a previous life that had existed outside of this fictional hospital in this fictional France.

"Thank you," Charlotte said after she'd completed half of the contents. "I don't think I've ever had a better glass of orange juice."

"Indeed," Holmes responded, reaching forward to relieve Charlotte of the glass, tilting it with curiosity as if seeing a glass of orange juice for the first time.

After setting the glass on the miraculous side table, Holmes' attention returned to Charlotte.

"Miss Taylor. I greet you this morning as a colleague. We have never met, yet I owe you a debt of thanks. You have fulfilled a commission for me."

Charlotte had been expecting Holmes to continue her interrogation. Holmes' gratitude was unexpected, and she remained wary in the event this was some clever trap devised by the Lepine brothers.

"I don't understand," she responded as she loosened her death grip on her topsheet.

Holmes' eyes did not wander from her face, reading her.

"Several months ago, I was hired by the French government to ferret out a cabal of spies who were moving manufacturing secrets out of France. I undertook a series of investigations that led me to suspect that this hospital, the Hotel-Dieu de Lyon, was being used as a hub to move information out of France."

Although she did not interrupt him, Holmes' use of English precipitated in her a moment of homesickness.

"So it was discreetly arranged that I would be admitted to the Hotel-Dieu. If I were recognized, my alibi was to be that I was recovering from the rigors of several recently concluded investigations. In order to support my cover story, hospital officials sent a telegram describing my illness to my associate in London, Dr. Watson."

"I *know* this story," Charlotte said, unable to control her enthusiasm.

"The Reigate Squire!" she said with recognition.

"Pardon me?" asked Holmes.

"Oh no. No. I apologize. Please continue," urged Charlotte, catching herself.

"I arranged for Prefect Lepine to question you while your medical condition was monitored by Doctor Lepine. I attended your interrogation. Once you'd arrived in the amphitheater, I slipped into the top row behind your seat where it would be impossible for you to see me.

"You see, for a time, you were my principal suspect in this matter.

"But then, while you were exiting the amphitheater, I overheard your enthusiastic deduction that I was in the hospital, a truth that had only been disclosed to several hospital officials, the Lepines and Dr. Watson on the other side of the English Channel.

"If you were in fact a spy, it would have been counter-intuitive for you to share your knowledge of my presence with your interrogators. Your enthusiastic, voluntary admission against your own self-interest exonerated you in my mind.

"I fear that the time has come to admit to you that you were not so much a patient of the hospital as a detainee of the French authorities, holding you on a probationary basis until I could arrive and observe you.

"Would you like another drink?"

Charlotte shook her head to decline, her confidence growing that good news awaited her at the conclusion of Holmes' tale.

"As further evidence of your innocence, Doctor Lepine told me of your having observed a series of late night clandestine exchanges between a Brother of the hospital staff and a patient in Bed Number 3.

"Relying upon your information, I arranged with the Commissioner of the Saint-Étienne Police Department to allow a recently apprehended woman to escape from the Saint-Étienne prison along with the documents she'd allegedly stolen. It was an easy matter of having Gendarme Ferdi leave a few doors unlocked and a few papers scattered about her interrogation room.

"I had hoped that, as a fugitive, she would lead us to her contact point here in Lyon. Sure enough, those papers were discovered in your ward last night. You see, based upon the observations you'd disclosed to Dr. Lepine, I had your ward under surveillance. Last night, I arrested the Brother you'd identified as he was transferring to the 'patient' in Bed Number 3 production plans for a Lebel Model Repeating Infantry Rifle, stolen from the Manufacture d'Armes de Saint-Étienne. After placing him in the hands of the authorities, I had the hospital discharge the patient in Bed Number 3 in the early hours of the morning. She will be followed to her next contact point."

Charlotte stole a look across the ward and found that Bed Number 3 was indeed vacant, its bed linens having been stripped and the mattress rolled into a spiral.

"We have, of course, judiciously changed the production plans so that the rifle will literally and figuratively blow up in their faces," added Holmes parenthetically.

"French authorities will follow her and will arrest any

additional agents in the pipeline," concluded Holmes.

"So, on behalf of the government of France, I am here to officially thank you.

"Miss Taylor. You have been released by the City of Lyon and discharged by the hospital. You are free to go," said Holmes.

"Allow me to suggest that you finish your juice before you leave. It is very good."

Holmes uncrossed his legs as if to rise but paused to address Charlotte again.

"By the way, Sister Collette asked if I might deliver this to you from the pharmacie. It appears to be an ancient pouch with which I have some familiarity. Typically, this type of cloth was used in medieval France to wrap salves or balsams. As you can see, any balsam that was within this cloth decomposed long ago. Curiously, however, there appears to be a handwritten note in the package that has survived the centuries."

Holmes carefully handed the pouch to Charlotte. The sack appeared to have held an object that might have been the size of a small apple, but its contents had long since disintegrated into dust. The pouch was tied with a piece of twine that held in place a piece of yellow parchment.

"Given the decomposition of the balsam and the appearance of the fragment, I would hypothesize the note to be some two hundred years old," opined Holmes.

"The curious part of this business," continued Holmes, "is that no one in the pharmacie can remember ever having seen these items until yesterday. They were found in the pharmacie box reserved for your bed. Thinking that this might be a recent medication prescribed by a doctor, Sister Collette inquired of all of the hospital physicians to identify who had prescribed it, and none of them admit to having done so.

"It leads one to suspect that it miraculously appeared out of the void. Which would be preposterous, wouldn't it?" asked Holmes, with no expectation of an answer.

Charlotte carefully unfurled the parchment to the extent that she could without cracking it.

The parchment had curled with age, and the ink had faded. But Charlotte was able to read several phrases from the browned and stiffened missive:

Charlotte Taylor –
Meet me H Wells' The Time Mac ine in Chapter.
Bro A

Charlotte read the note several times, trying to appreciate all of its implications. Her brother was alive. He had found a way to communicate with her. He had developed an escape plan.

Several entries in the note had blurred or disappeared over time, including the middle initial of author H.G. Wells. But the most egregious loss was the disintegration of a chapter number.

Charlotte felt her excitement transition to panic. She knew the novella titled *The Time Machine* by H.G. Wells. She remembered having seen a copy of it in her brother's bedroom. He may even have stuffed a copy of it into her backpack before she escaped into the BookStream. But she knew nothing of the story itself and certainly could not identify the most appropriate chapter to which she might meet up with her brother.

Holmes cleared his throat to interrupt her interior conversation.

"Once Sister Collette brought the existence of this package to my attention, I was bound by my retainer to analyze the package and read the note," confided Holmes.

"I remembered having seen a copy of *The Time Machine* in your saddle bag. Its contents now being relevant, I took the opportunity to read the novella."

Holmes leaned forward to be sure that only Charlotte could hear his voice.

"Assuming, for the moment, that the narrative that you provided to Prefect Lepine were true," he whispered, "and that you are from North America of the twenty-first century, and further assuming that you can, in fact, travel from book to book, then were I you I would consider directing myself to Chapter Ten *'When Night Came.'* If I wished to reunite with my brother, this would seem to me to be the most logical time and place to do so."

"Oh my God," Charlotte exclaimed. "You believe me?"

Charlotte's face flushed red as she turned it away from Holmes and faced the far wall of the hospital ward. In providing her backstory to the Lepines, had she exposed to Holmes that he was no more than a work of fiction?

If Holmes had made this connection, he did not immediately expose his realization to Charlotte.

"Prefect Lepine believes not a word of your testimony, but he is parochial and short sighted. Doctor Lepine does not believe your narrative either, but he is convinced that **you** sincerely believe in the truth of your narrative. His is the conclusion of a clinician and is non-deductive."

"And you? What do you believe?" asked Charlotte as she focused on the far wall of the ward.

Holmes sighed. He spoke slowly as if selecting his words with care.

"Someone who loves you, most likely your mother, has fashioned a bracelet that you wear. The material of your bracelet, the tool that must have been used to craft the individual cavities in which you store your capsules and the production values of the medication in your bracelet – please forgive my having given it a slight turn while you were sleeping – are all unique and rare if they exist at all in this time and place.

"Despite the fact that you are in a hospital, you self-medicate. Whereas your wardmates consider their hospital charts to be inviolate and would never dare to touch them let alone have the educable skills to read them, you not only read them but you then comment upon them in a journal composed of pharmaceutical papers you've stolen. All of this suggests a level of education and sophistication that does not exist among children of this era.

"But what do you believe?" repeated Charlotte.

"Miss Taylor. I offer two questions for your future consideration. Question Number One: Upon what facts do you rely in order to conclude that you are more real than I?"

"Because I started this journey from my home, my reality," responded Charlotte.

"And Question Number Two: Upon what facts do you rely that your "home" is the one true home and not also a work of fiction, the authorship of which you are simply unaware?"

Charlotte swung her face forward, her brow furrowed, her lips pursed in thought.

"If you insist that your pathway home lies through *The Time Machine*, then by all means pursue it. I only ask that you follow your assumptions to their logical conclusions before acting upon them."

Holmes stood and gently deposited Charlotte's backpack upon her mattress next to her exposed feet.

"Don't forget to take your medication."

Holmes bowed to leave, and had taken three steps toward the

double doors when he pirouetted on his heels and returned to Charlotte's bedside. He raised her bedgate.

"I must ask you, Miss Taylor, how an act as innocuous as an early morning visit between a man and a woman in a hospital ward might have aroused your suspicions? It could have been a medical examination. It could have been a romance. How did you deduce it to have been an act of espionage?" he asked.

She remembered the catcalls of her ward mates, creating an air of hostility toward all men and how it would disincentivize any Brother from entering the ward.

She remembered the sounds of papers being exchanged in the middle of the night.

But mostly, she remembered the disinterested caress of the patient in Bed Number 3.

Charlotte could not believe that her life had led her to this moment, when she could share a moment of literary intimacy with her hero. Maybe Holmes was a fictional character. Or maybe he was more real than she. But Charlotte adored him as she might her own father.

So she sobbed, releasing the pent-up tears of her incarceration and interrogation.

Holmes stood above her, patiently awaiting her answer.

Then, through her tear-filled eyes, she met Holmes' gaze fully for the first time that morning.

"It was elementary."

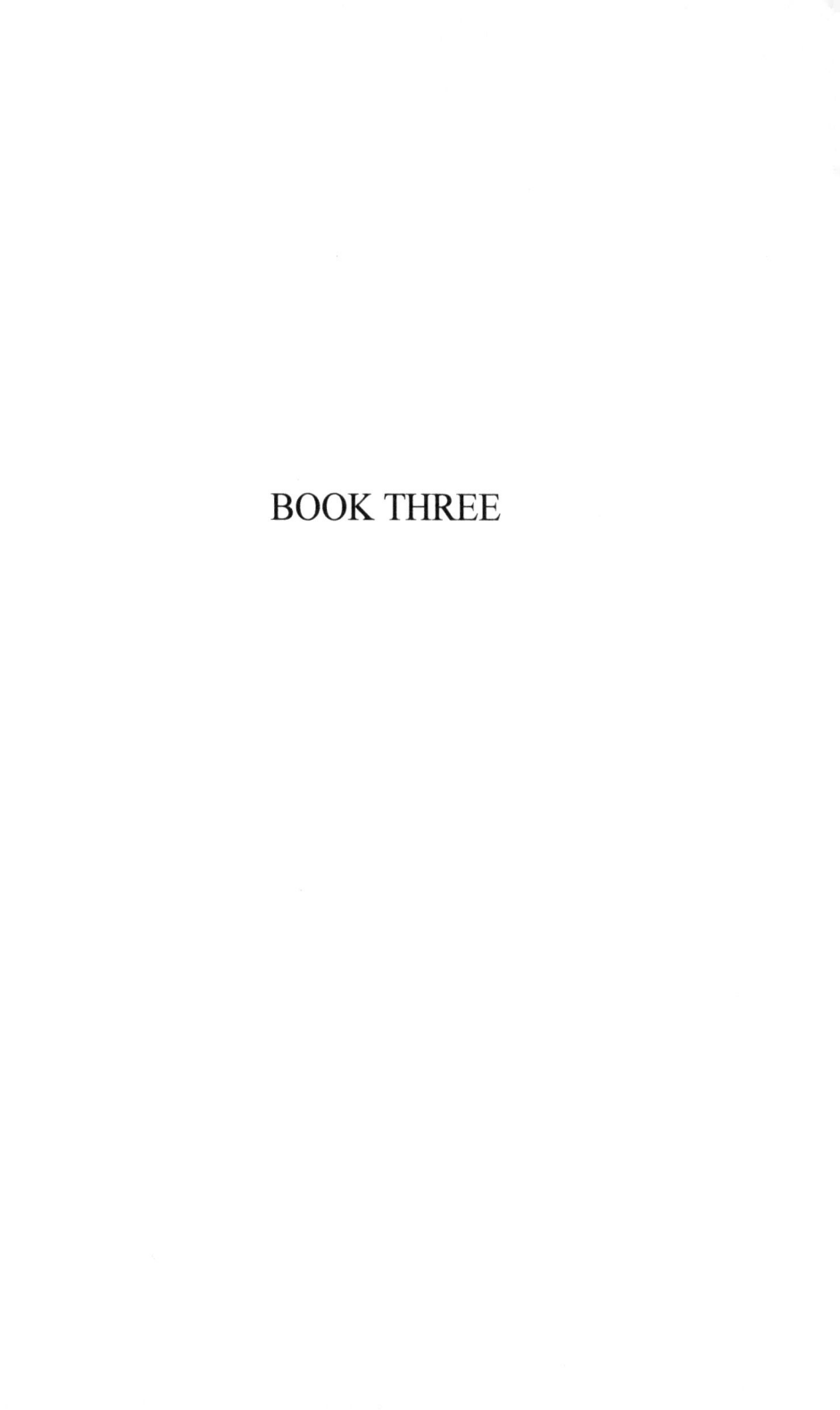

BOOK THREE

Chapter Twenty-Seven

Morlocks

Charlotte opened her eyes to a starlit night. She could make out a distant treeline illuminated against a dark blue sky.

A moment later, she sensed that her body was on an incline and that she was suspended significantly above the ground below her.

She could feel the onset of panic and her body threatening to spasm. She tried to orient herself in space, but was inhibited by her unwillingness to raise her head.

Uncertain about whether her slightest movement might cause her to slide over a precipice from this unknown height down to an unknown surface, Charlotte lay there, immobile, taking shallow breaths, listening to the sounds of the night, trying to figure out where she was.

She inventoried her body. She was lying face down on a slick surface. She lay headfirst, her feet elevated behind her. She became aware of the pressure of blood in her temples as it accumulated in her head.

Charlotte strategized that by tightening her shoulder blades to the center of her back and raising her head, she might be able to reconnoiter without disturbing her torso or precipitating a fall.

As she knitted her shoulder blades and used the muscles in the back of her neck to raise her head, she felt the annoying familiarity of her body sliding uncontrollably down an inclined ace.

Charlotte spread out her arms and legs and inflated her
nach in hopes of maximizing her surface area and slowing her
. She pressed the tips of each of her ten fingers into the surface
the incline, hoping for a purchase. But the slick, impervious
face would not respond with any resistance.

As she slid, she heard the voices of Doctor Wojszek and Miss
right.

"A loose limbed fall is less likely to result in broken bones,"
unseled Doctor Wojszek.

"Where's your fucking helmet?" asked Miss Wright.

Then she was airborne. She hoped that the thick air of that
moisture-laden night might offer some resistance and slow her
all.

Since Charlotte's head, shoulders and arms cleared the
precipice first, her legs and feet followed and torqued her into a
slow-motion midair somersault.

As she tumbled in the air, she saw not the green grass of the
mildewed lawn but a blanket of blue light accelerating toward
her.

Her tailbone hit the surface first, briefly bouncing her back
up into the air, landing her face first into a bed of wet grass.

Something had absorbed her impact.

"That was too easy," she whispered aloud after spitting out
several blades of grass.

Charlotte could feel her heart beating in her chest.
Adrenaline continued to course through her body. She'd not yet
steadied herself long enough to consider what had occurred when
a pair of hands were upon her, a right arm across her back with
its hand grabbing her right shoulder, and the left hand trying to
cup her mouth to silence her.

Reflexively, she pushed the hands away and attempted to wriggle free, her left hand still clenching her BookMarck. Charlotte tried to remember the defensive options that she'd been taught in school when she heard a man's voice in her ear speaking softly and pressing her to action.

"Charlotte Taylor. Please be quiet. Abisai sent me." He then released her, as if to prove his sincerity.

She peered into the dark, trying to distinguish a face.

"Who are you? Where is Abbie?" she gasped as he removed his hand from her mouth.

"Shhhh! Morlocks," he pleaded with her.

"What's a Morlock?" she asked.

"Cannibals!" he whispered.

"Cannibals? That, I know," she responded.

With the assistance of the stranger, Charlotte was able to stand. The man did not hesitate, but took her hand and started to run. Charlotte allowed herself one look back. She had slid off of a pedestal that reflected a blue-green tint of oxidation in the moonlight. Upon the pedestal sat the statue of an apparition, wings afly.

Charlotte allowed the stranger to assist her. They climbed up onto a hillside so thickly wooded that she would have missed their destination had not the man pulled her through a clearing.

Charlotte ducked her head and followed the man through an entranceway created by the bent boughs of trees, thick and thin. The perimeter of the clearing was lit with torches uniformly spaced about six feet apart. The stranger released Charlotte's hand and gestured toward a wooden pallet.

"Please sit," the man requested as he handed her his canteen.

"You've had a long trip."

Charlotte gratefully drank as she watched the man walk to

the edge of the encampment, pull up a torch, and use it to light a pre-arranged stack of kindling and firewood next to the pallet. The fire caught quickly.

The warmth of the fire brought Charlotte's attention to her clothing, her T-shirt and jeans having been saturated from having wicked the residues of rain off of the pedestal as she had slid.

"You've been expecting me," Charlotte said gratefully as the man made a slight adjustment to the log burn.

"I think I remember what a Morlock is." Charlotte had tried to read her copy of *The Time Machine* before she'd transported herself out of the Hotel-Dieu de Lyon.

"That's an ambitious read for someone of your youth, isn't it?" the stranger finally said, more observation than question.

"I read a lot of what my brother reads for class," Charlotte replied.

"But I don't remember this location from the book. What is this place?"

Charlotte remembered that, after Holmes' departure, she'd torn through her backpack in a frenzy until finding that her BookMarck was safely secured between pages 120 and 121 of *The Time Machine*. Relieved, she allowed herself a breakfast, and then extended carefully worded good-byes with her ward mates.

Charlotte had exited the feverish ward through the heavy double doors for what she'd hoped was the last time. The chapel was empty as she had hoped. She emptied the contents of her bag into a pew and changed into her T-shirt and jeans. She folded her hospital gown, placed it on the bench, held her BookMarck aloft, and spirited herself into Chapter Ten of *The Time Machine*. That was her last memory of corporeality until she found herself on the slick wet surface of the statue.

"You might want to put that somewhere safe," suggested the

stranger, nodding his chin toward the BookMarck in her hand.

Sure enough, she was still holding her BookMarck.

"Who are you?" she asked as she opened her backpack.

"Please call me Conrad. I am a WordSmythe. And I am an author. Perhaps you've read me?"

Charlotte wasn't sure whether *Conrad* was a first or last name, so she chose to detour the question.

"I'm Charlotte Taylor," she responded by way of an introduction, momentarily forgetting that Conrad had already addressed her by name.

"Where are we?" she asked.

"This is a fictional world created by author H.G. Wells," responded the stranger. "This is Richmond, England in the year 802,701 and we are occupying the narrative space between the sentences and paragraphs of *The Time Machine*.

"Abbie and I staked out this area before you arrived. This encampment should not interfere with the events of the novella."

Charlotte appreciated Conrad's obvious attempt to feed her information in manageable bytes of clarity and kindness.

"This location had the additional benefit of putting us very close to the actual Time Machine."

So much for clarity, thought Charlotte.

"The Time Machine?" she repeated.

"The Time Machine has been hidden by the Morlocks inside the pedestal of the statue upon which you arrived, but we know it to be there. Abbie arrived here several days ago. After I greeted him, he told me that he had attempted to leave you a message so that you might follow him into the BookStream of Chapter Ten of *The Time Machine*. And here you are. I am really quite impressed that he was able to contact you."

"Where is Abbie?" she finally asked.

"The Morlocks took him last night," he responded.

"What?"

"If you look out over this hillside, you can see the lights of at least five other encampments. This is a queue of Repositors and WordSmythes waiting to use the Time Machine to return to their homes. It is the easiest way that we have found over the years to leave the interior narrative of books and return to our respective realities. So, we sit here together in an uneasy truce fashioned over decades, respecting this Time Machine as our shared method to return to our homes.

"In appreciation of this precious exitway, this area has become a demilitarized zone where Repositors and WordSmythes have agreed to wait in peace for their respective turns at the Time Machine. Similarly, the geographic area on the 'other side' of this BookStream in Richmond, England, has also become an area of neutrality where we can arrive without fear of being ambushed.

"This truce had never been breached until last night.

"Your brother took the early watch and I was sleeping. Someone must have extinguished our torches. It was not bad luck or fate. It had to be an intentional act of sabotage. And it constitutes a grave violation of our truce with the Repositors. Someone was willing to risk the peace that keeps this zone demilitarized in order to prevent you and your brother from returning home.

"After the torches had been extinguished, the Morlocks must have broken into our camp. I was awakened by his exhortation for me to run. I was likely saved by the light of this campfire."

"Is he alive?" she asked.

"As they dragged him off, he was indeed alive," Conrad responded.

"Did you follow him?" she asked.

"I did. And I am fairly certain of the Morlocks' destination. But Abbie saw me in pursuit, and insisted that I return to camp and wait for you."

"We need to find him," said Charlotte. She winced in pain as she stood upon the wooden palette.

"If we pursue him, we will lose our spot in the queue to use the Time Machine. Your next chance to leave would then be governed by the book's narrative. Worse yet, if this act of sabotage concludes the truce between the WordSmythes and the Repositors, this fragile arrangement could devolve into conflict and strand you in this BookStream."

"Thank you, Conrad," she said. "Now let's go."

"Are you sure you are physically up for this? Now that you have arrived, I can pursue the Morlocks alone. You will be safe here as long as you keep the torches lit at night. The Morlocks are averse to light."

"If I stay here, I will need to sleep at some point and the saboteur might extinguish the fires again," responded Charlotte.

She paused to consider Conrad's motivation in asking her to stay.

"Are you thinking that I inhibit your pursuit? Will I slow you down?" she asked.

"No. Abisai was taken toward an area that had been previously known as East Sheen. The topography is flat and far less arduous than that which the Time Traveler must contend with, and we will not cross his path. These are but small advantages."

Charlotte stood patiently, knowing that Conrad had something else to share.

"One large advantage that you have is that you possess the

237

BookMarck of the Aginbyte of Inwit. You may not have noticed it, but the Aginbyte's BookMarck has an element that allows one to glide the terrain, including suppressing the effects of falling. The BookMarck cushioned your fall when you slid off the pedestal. This is a large advantage for us. For you."

Charlotte's mind flashed back to the blue light she thought she'd seen as she had fallen.

Charlotte reached back into her backpack for the BookMarck.

"We have to go now," she said. "We have to save him."

Conrad grabbed two torches from the perimeter of their encampment and handed one to Charlotte.

"One more thing before we go," Conrad added. "Abisai went to considerable trouble to leave me a final message before he insisted I return for you. But I don't understand it."

"What is it?" she asked.

"As the Morlocks dragged him away and I turned back to camp, he hollered after me: 'Tell Charlotte to avoid *bad luck*'!"

Charlotte paused before she stepped off the palette, one finger tapping the side of her cheek.

Then she realized who had extinguished the torches.

***

Conrad's evaluation of the terrain proved to be accurate. The topography was relatively flat, occasionally interrupted by high grasses or tangles of bushes suggesting years of neglect. Occasionally, the light of their torches would reflect off of a large building, each one of a varied style and material, some of which had been left to ruin.

The herd of Morlocks who had taken Abisai had sufficiently

trampled the wet grasses to create an easily identifiable route for Charlotte and Conrad to follow.

"Do you know who is in the queue for the Time Machine?" Charlotte asked during one of their infrequent pauses.

"I did recognize some faces. Yes."

"Was the Aginbyte of Inwit among them?"

Word of Charlotte's confrontation with the Aginbyte of Inwit had spread quickly in the community of WordSmythes. Conrad paused to appreciate her.

"The Aginbyte is not in the queue. And I do not believe the Aginbyte to be in this BookStream," answered Conrad. "In fact, I have heard that the Aginbyte has been purposely marooned in the BookStream of Mary Shelley's *Frankenstein*. Some sort of punishment for his having lost his BookMarck to a mere child."

They exchanged smiles.

***

Conrad insisted upon taking the lead, so Charlotte followed some ten feet behind him, keeping him in her view. They hurried along the vestiges of deserted roads that were now only memories. Charlotte saw pathways that may have at one time been streets now covered with soil and overgrown with foliage. There was no evidence that the offroad farmland had been tilled. There were no factories. No one sold goods. It was as if the Thames River had reclaimed its dominance of its valley, encouraging the growth of evergreens, tree ferns and grassland.

Occasionally they would see a structure that resembled a cupola, under which sat a circular passageway whose entrance was rimmed with bronze. Conrad would stop at each one, examining the ground for unnatural depressions or evidence of recent activity. Each underground silo was coupled with a nearby tower. Charlotte assumed they shared some functionality, although she could not guess what it was.

After what felt to Charlotte like several hours of following Abisai's trail, Conrad stopped abruptly and raised his hand. Although the night was otherwise dry and still, Charlotte heard the sounds of wind rustling through the trees accompanied by the sporadic pattering of raindrops.

Conrad motioned to Charlotte to approach him. He watched as she skimmed silently toward him, having mastered the glider element of the Aginbyte's BookMarck during their night's trek.

"Do you hear that?" he asked.

She nodded in assent.

"That is the sound of the Morlocks. They are stalking us."

Involuntarily, Charlotte scanned their perimeter.

"Do you remember Wells' description of a Morlock's appearance?" asked Conrad.

Charlotte shook her head that she did not remember.

"They are subterraneans. In the dark," described Conrad, "they will appear to be small white spirits. Were you to see them briefly in the light, they would appear to have large eyes. Hair flows from their scalps to their backs. And they are fast. Very, very fast."

Conrad knew that this description had unsettled her, so he accompanied his warning with a reassurance.

"They have an extreme sensitivity to light. If you carry your torch, they will not approach you."

***

Conrad and Charlotte pressed on through the night but were

unable to catch up to Abisai and the herd of Morlocks. Charlotte's mind raced forward to daybreak. If Conrad was right, the Morlocks would gone to ground and taken Abbie underground with them.

Conrad must have had the same thought because he turned back toward Charlotte and pantomimed that he was going to extinguish his torch in a pool of water standing nearby. He motioned for her to stay well behind him.

Charlotte vigorously shook her head in disagreement.

Charlotte watched smoke rise as Conrad extinguished his torch. She could still see the faint outline of his torso in the moonlight. She could not recognize any of the constellations in the night sky except for the moon and the stars of the Milky Way. An unfamiliar red star showed on the horizon to the south.

At first they waited in silence, the Morlocks having abandoned their mask of faux wind and rain. Then, they were upon Conrad. He did not resist as the Morlocks pulled him down to the ground. It took only a moment for the Morlocks to fall back into a sort of formation and continue their progress, Conrad now submerged among them.

Charlotte understood Conrad's plan: the most efficient way to slow the Morlocks and track them to their lair would be for Conrad to give himself up for abduction.

Charlotte followed from a distance, torch alit.

***

Charlotte recalled having been chased plenty of times during her childhood in North Orange. But she had never been so hoodwinked as the Morlocks had done to her that night. The Morlocks had not stalked them from their rear or flanks, as

241

convention would suggest, but had stalked them by fronting them, drawing them deeper into the countryside until the brink of daylight. Now, having apprehended Conrad, it appeared that they had abandoned their purposeful pace, and pushed forward to find an underground accessway before dawn broke.

Charlotte pressed to keep Conrad and the Morlocks in her field of vision. Even with her ability to skirt the terrain, the all night pursuit was wearing upon her. Her right shoulder ached, and she could feel her left foot begin to balk.

Night had begun to transition into dawn. Up ahead, the emerging daylight illuminated the now familiar sight of a cupola and bronze silo that it protected. This had to be the destination of the Morlocks.

"No!" she yelled. "No! No! No! No! No!"

She leaned her body forward to speed toward Conrad and the Morlocks, touching off sparks as the flame from her raised torch swept the canopy of low slung branches over her.

Charlotte had hoped to startle or frighten the Morlocks with her bravado. Indeed, the head of every Morlock in the herd turned toward the sound of her voice. But she failed to startle them. Instead, they seemed to focus on her, the pupils of their large eyes dilating as if to memorize her appearance. Several of them started back toward her, but reconsidered and drew back as morning sunlight began to reflect off of mildewed leaves.

The Morlocks funneled into the silo, comically climbing over one another in their impatience, leaving the impression of a sink full of bodies siphoning down a drain.

With the withdrawal of the last of the Morlocks, the clearing around the cupola revealed the body of Conrad lying in front of the well mouth, motionless but breathing. Charlotte rushed forward to examine him in the light of her torch and pallor of dawn. She found no evidence of wounding or blood.

"Charlotte?"

She turned immediately toward the sound of her brother's voice.

In the half light she saw the outline of a figure propped up against a large tree. Its legs were hidden in the tall underbrush, but the cut of his shoulders and the way he carried his head were unmistakable.

"Charlotte?" he called again.

"ABBIE!" she cried. She ran to him, slid to his side, and they wrapped their arms around one another.

"Ouch," she yelled as she recoiled from him. Something sharp and inflexible had pinched her hip.

"You have a sword!" she giggled.

"I have a sword!" he repeated proudly, then buried his head into her shoulder to cry as daylight broke over the horizon.

Chapter Twenty-Eight

A Plan of a Higher Order

"I don't understand," Charlotte said to her brother. "I thought for sure you were Morlock breakfast."

"Me too." Abisai grinned. "Just before dawn yesterday, they forced me down into an underground silo and spent a lot of time sniffing me and touching me and licking me. It was disgusting."

Charlotte shivered. She remembered the gaze of the Morlocks upon her.

Abisai turned to look at both Charlotte and Conrad as he spoke.

"But I think they abandoned me. I don't think twenty-first century humans suit the advanced tastes of the Morlocks. That might be why they abandoned you, as well," Abisai said, directing his comment toward Conrad.

"Maybe that's why the Time Traveler survives the Morlocks in the novella. Human beings of their past are unpalatable," agreed Charlotte.

"Interesting theory, although I've experienced evidence to the contrary during my visits here," responded Conrad as he attempted to wipe the accumulation of grime and Morlock saliva from his face.

"Once they abandoned you, why didn't you come back to the encampment?" Conrad asked Abisai.

"I guess I passed out," Abisai responded. "Climbing down

244

into that silo was exhausting. Then, after a couple of minutes, they abandoned me and pretty much disappeared. So I crawled back through the passageways and back out of the silo. But I was wiped when I got to the surface."

"Wiped," Conrad repeated aloud, bemused. Charlotte could see Conrad turning the phrase in his head.

"Conrad. Thank you for staying with Charlotte," Abisai said, and he raised his hand.

"My pleasure, old boy," responded Conrad, returning Abbie's handshake with vigor.

***

Although Abisai, Charlotte and Conrad were beset by different levels of fatigue, the threat level posed by the Morlocks provided them the incentive to return to their camp before nightfall. Abisai and Conrad relieved Charlotte of her pack to reduce the pressure on her sore back. With the withdrawal of the Morlocks to their underground lairs, there was no longer a need to be stealthy, and Conrad and Charlotte found their return trip to be much shorter than their expedition out to rescue Abisai.

The threesome reached camp by midafternoon. Once they arrived, Conrad organized them. He resuscitated their fire from the still-warm embers, lit the torches around the perimeter of the campsite, and began to prepare a meal from the stores he kept within one of three tents in the encampment. Abisai and Charlotte helped where they could, but they were reluctant to interfere with Conrad's routine.

When he was finally satisfied with the condition of the campsite, Conrad addressed them both.

"Eat something. Take a nap. Then, you both are leaving,"

Conrad said.

"But the queue?" asked Abisai. "Haven't we lost our place in the queue?"

"If you recall from your reading of *The Time Machine*, the Time Traveler takes an extended trip away from the Time Machine to visit the Palace of Green Porcelain. He is on that trip as we speak."

"During the Time Traveler's absence, everyone in the queue uses the Time Machine to return to their respective eras. Today is no exception. All the fires on the hillside seem to have been extinguished. To my knowledge, everyone who has sought to use the Time Machine has done so but for you."

Abbie and Charlotte scanned the hillsides and saw no sign of smoke or fire.

"We cannot lose this chance," continued Conrad. "Now that we have the opportunity to get you home, let's take it."

Conrad organized them into a watch. While one would sleep, two of them would remain awake. Conrad heaped so much wood upon the fire that one might think it would burn for days.

Abisai and Conrad took the first watch. Charlotte fell asleep almost immediately. As Conrad expected, Abbie dropped into an involuntary sleep, fending off his exhaustion as long as he could.

Conrad remained on duty all afternoon, allowing Charlotte and Abisai to sleep through their watches.

***

Once the sun started to descend, Conrad roused Abisai and Charlotte from their sleep. He had prepared a meal composed entirely of local fruits, including a floury fruit with a unique three-sided husk. At various times during the meal, both

Charlotte and Abisai asked Conrad if he could identify the ancestors of the plants they ate, but Conrad conceded that his guess would be no better than theirs.

As they broke camp, Conrad packed a crowbar and two lighted torches, one for himself and one for Charlotte and Abisai.

"What's the crowbar for?" asked Charlotte.

"To pry open the panels at the bottom of the pedestal," responded Conrad.

"Is that the same pedestal that I fell from when I arrived?" she asked.

"Yes, it is," said Conrad.

As they traveled to the pedestal, they saw not a single creature. To Conrad's surprise, the bronze valves securing the panels of the pedestal had been opened and slid down into their grooves.

"This is not good for us," said Conrad. "This configuration of the bronze valves suggests that the Time Traveler will be returning to this site shortly. We need to move quickly."

As the three entered the chamber inside the pedestal, Conrad placed his torch in the only wall sconce to keep the room lit.

Then, he turned to Abisai and Charlotte.

"Over the years, the WordSmythes and the Repositors have developed the tools to operate the Time Machine. We'd customarily have to wait for the Time Traveler to fall asleep, then crib from his pockets small levers needed to operate the Time Machine. More recently, we've copied the levers and produced them ourselves."

Conrad fished through his pockets and produced two small metal cylinders. He placed one in Charlotte's hand, and one in Abbie's hand.

"These two levers fit into two studs on the sides of the Time

247

Machine. Familiarize yourselves with how they fit before you attempt to operate the machine."

Then, Conrad pulled out of the inside breast pocket of his blazer a piece of cardboard in the shape of a half moon and held it before them.

"The Time Machine does not have the calibrations to deliver you to an exact point in time. So we have created these time maps. If you were to click this particular map into the support next to the lever, you can calibrate your return date to within twenty-four hours of your departure."

With that, he handed the time map to Charlotte.

"Since the Time Machine originates out of Richmond, England, you'll be returning to this very spot in Richmond, England when you return to your own era. Don't worry. The physical site to which you'll be returning is a neutral location, and you'll be greeted by a non-adversarial host who will assist you in disembarking. Then your host will arrange for the Time Machine to be returned to this moment so it remains in the continuity of the story.

"I'll stay outside. If I knock, that means that the Time Traveler is approaching. If so, you'll need to hide and postpone your trip. You cannot deprive the Time Traveler of his use of the Time Machine within the chronology of the story, or you will reduce this BookStream to chaos.

"Questions?" asked Conrad.

"Only a thousand," responded Charlotte.

"Good luck."

Conrad embraced them both. Then warned them.

"Keep your wits about you. Remember that secreting the Time Machine inside this pedestal was a trap that the Morlocks had set for the Time Traveler. Don't be caught unawares!"

248

Conrad stepped out of the room to secure the door and watch for the Time Traveler. While the room was dimly lit by the torch and the waning daylight from the opened panel, Abbie took Charlotte's backpack and carefully deposited it into a corner of the room with his knapsack. Returning to his sister, they quickly installed the two levers and familiarized themselves with the Time Machine.

Then, without warning, the bronze entryway panels clanged shut. The crowbar that Conrad had wedged into the door jam to keep the panels ajar snapped in two and fell harmlessly to the ground, its purpose defeated.

Then, as if a line of dominos were falling in sequence, Abisai and Charlotte watched in dismay as the vibrations of the closed panels jarred the walls of the room, dislodging their torch from the wall, and dropping it into a mound of loosely packed sand, extinguishing their last source of light. Abisai cursed his carelessness for not having checked the room for sabotage while he had the light to do so.

"Who put that sand there?' asked Charlotte as she lifted the torch and blew upon the last of its orange embers, hoping to resuscitate it.

Abisai swore an oath as he helped Charlotte into the saddle of the Time Machine. He recognized the sound of onrushing Morlocks.

Abisai positioned his body to create a barrier between his sister and the frenzied Morlocks, but they ignored him and reached around him to pull Charlotte out of the saddle. He grabbed for her, and their fingers briefly touched, but she was quickly submerged in a sea of Morlocks. Abisai tensed his body to defend himself, but found it was unnecessary. He was being ignored.

Disoriented by the darkness, Abisai stood still and thought he could see Charlotte's silhouette as she was pulled down into a silo in a corner of the pedestal chamber.

As the Morlocks pulled her down, she made only one sound.

"Go!" she yelled to her brother.

Chapter Twenty-Nine

The Time Traveler

As Abisai climbed down into the silo in pursuit of his sister, he realized that he had underestimated the Morlocks. They were not just instinctual beings. They had the ability to strategize and to deceive. That the Morlocks had abducted him and seized Conrad only to release them both because they were inedible made no sense.

He and Conrad had been used as bait.

"Could it truly be that the brother of Charlotte Taylor has arrived into this BookStream?"

It was Charlotte they wanted to capture all along.

The Morlocks had drawn Charlotte out of the campsite, knowing that she would pursue her brother. Then they had attempted to isolate her by taking Conrad. But they had not anticipated her enhanced mobility, thanks to the glide element of the Aginbyte's BookMarck.

Rather than exposing their purpose, the Morlocks bided their time, recognizing that Abbie and Charlotte would need to use the Time Machine to escape the BookStream. So, they strategically retreated inside the pedestal room and waited to capture Charlotte within the confinement.

As he descended into the silo, Abisai struggled with one element of the conspiracy. Fear of light made the Morlocks unlikely suspects to have extinguished the torches in the campsite two nights previous. Since they could only get into the pedestal room when the panels were open (allowing light into the room), it was not likely that the Morlocks had loosened the wall sconce and deposited loose sand beneath it. If the Morlocks had not done so, and if the Aginbyte were indeed marooned in another BookStream, who did?

Of course.

Bad luck, Abisai repeated to himself.

The silence of Abisai's descent was suddenly interrupted by the unmistakable voice of his sister.

"Charlotte!" Abisai yelled after her.

Abisai abandoned his careful rung by rung descent and pushed away from the ladder with his feet, skipping ten rungs at a clip, then recapturing a rung and repeating his accelerated descent.

From a tunnel running perpendicular to the silo, Abbie heard a torrent of profanity that could only be his sister. He folded his body to approximate the height of a Morlock and vaulted across the chasm below him, rolling into the low-ceilinged tunnel. Once in, he scrambled through the darkness toward her voice.

Abisai had run-crawled no more than twenty yards when the horizontal torso of a Morlock rolled past him.

"Charlotte," he called as the Morlock rolled by. "Yell so I can find you!"

"Abbie!" she screamed. "The little shits are biting me! Hurry!"

Abisai drew his sword, the sound of steel resounding through the passageway.

"Keep yelling!" he responded as much in instruction to his sister as an attempt to scare the Morlocks.

"Abbie! Look out! They're headed your way!"

Suddenly, as if the Morlocks had shared some inaudible signal with one another, the herd abandoned Charlotte and rushed toward Abisai. Abbie pressed his back into a sidewall in an attempt to elude the onrushing Morlocks, but the herd ignored him and ran back up the silo. Once the last of the Morlocks had passed him, he was able to follow his sister's recitative of profanity to find her.

"That's quite a vocabulary, sister. Have you been bitten?"

"Ugh. These soft, little pukes. Their fingers were all over me. And I've been bitten on the arm. I really didn't want to scream. But once I was bitten, I lost it."

Abisai tried to see if her skin had been broken, but was frustrated by the darkness. He did not want to touch the wound lest he infect it.

"C'mon, Charlotte. We've got to get you out of here. Can you climb?"

"Definitely. Let's go!"

"Do you have the Aginbyte's BookMarck?"

"No," she replied. "It's in my backpack."

"Too bad. We could use that floating element right now."

Charlotte entered the silo to climb to the surface, and Abbie followed. At first, Charlotte climbed with ease, the fitness of her upper body hoisting her torso. But her legs fatigued quickly and her energy level soon lagged.

"How far down are we?" she finally asked.

As Abbie began to reply, Charlotte yelled in excitement and scrambled over the lip of the silo into the pedestal room. Abbie crawled in behind her and was greeted with the room awash in moonlight from the opened panel.

In the moonlight, the room seemed to have an unfamiliar vacuity. It took them a moment to realize that the Time Machine was gone.

253

"Oh no," groaned Charlotte as she looked about, appreciating her own absurdity in scanning the room as if the Time Machine could be secreted in a corner of the pedestal room.

Abbie ignored his sister's dispiritedness and grabbed her by the hand, extending her arm into the dim light to examine her. Although he could see bite marks on her forearm, her skin had not been broken.

"If I'm understanding the rules of these BookStreams correctly," she said as she pulled her arm away in impatience, "we interlopers get to do whatever we want 'in between the paragraphs' so long as we don't upset the continuity of the narrative. If that's true, and the Time Traveler has gone, then the Morlocks are free to come after us."

"We'd better get back to camp," Abbie said in agreement.

As they moved to leave, the room was illuminated with a flash of intense white light, then darkened immediately.

"Maybe it was some sort of chronal aftershock?" Charlotte suggested.

"Chronal aftershock?" repeated Abisai with a grin. "I'm impressed!"

The chamber flashed white again, originating from the spot vacated by the Time Machine, then darkened.

Before either of them could guess what was happening, the flashes of light accelerated to approximate the effect of a strobe light.

"Do you see that? There's an image in there!" Abisai said, pointing to the center of the light source while gently moving his body between the image and his sister. He unsheathed his sword.

"Yes. I see it," responded Charlotte as she deftly moved in

front of him again.

The duration of the flicker increased until it became a sustained throbbing light source. They strained to define the image inside the strobe light, covering their eyes with their hands and peaking through the gaps in their fingers.

As the flickering light accelerated into a sustained image and then reality, Charlotte and Abisai recognized Conrad at the controls of the Time Machine.

Then, as if to confirm his corporeality, Conrad fell out of the cockpit to the ground, groaning and retching.

Abisai knelt next to Conrad who was convulsing in a series of spasms.

"Charlotte. Have you got something in your bag? An epi-pen? Maybe something like a spatula so we can keep him from swallowing his tongue?"

"I think he's coming out of it, Abbie," she said as she knelt beside her brother.

As his body slowly relaxed, Conrad rolled out of his fetal position and onto his back. He opened his eyes.

"You made it!" whispered Conrad.

"YOU made it!" responded Charlotte.

"You need to rest, Conrad," Abbie said.

"Nonsense," Conrad responded as he propped himself up on his elbows.

"What happened? Where did you go?" asked Charlotte.

Conrad shook his head violently, then paused as if to recollect what had happened.

"I was outside the pedestal room when the panels shut on my crowbar and snapped it. Then, when I heard Charlotte yell at you to 'Go!' I'd assumed Charlotte had been taken by the Morlocks," Conrad said.

"You and I were used as bait," Abisai volunteered. "The Morlocks wanted Charlotte all along. And they got her."

Conrad did not immediately reply, but took a look at Charlotte with a renewed appreciation.

"I followed Charlotte and the Morlocks down the silo," said Abisai. "When I drew my sword, I think that might have scared them off."

Conrad smiled kindly at the boy.

"While you were in the silo," continued Conrad, "the Time Traveler returned to the Time Machine. The Morlocks left Charlotte because the novella calls for them to attack the Time Traveler as he leaves. So, the Time Traveler may have unintentionally saved your lives by drawing the Morlocks away from you."

Conrad grinned and clapped Abbie on the shoulder.

"You are a gallant soul, Abisai Taylor," said Conrad with kindness, having burst Abbie's theory around the impact of his having unsheathed his sword.

Abbie looked glumly at the Time Machine.

"I don't understand," Charlotte said. "If the Time Traveler left after having evaded the Morlocks, why is the Time Machine back?"

"At the conclusion of the novella, the Time Traveler and his Machine travel farther into the future, and then return to Richmond, England in the late nineteenth century. I knew that you needed the Time Machine, so I left my hiding place and, unbeknownst to the Time Traveler, boarded his Machine as a stowaway. I even assisted him in beating off the Morlocks from the rear of the Machine as he attempted to depart, though he had no idea I'd done so.

"Once we returned to the Time Traveler's home, the Time

Traveler left his machine to narrate his story to his colleagues. He is likely doing so at this very moment. But while he is engaged in that extended conversation, I have commandeered his Time Machine and returned it to you, all without disturbing the storyline."

"So we can't use our BookMarcks to return home?" asked Charlotte.

"Not yet," responded Conrad.

"You need to get home quickly. When you arrive, you'll likely be greeted by a host or chaperon. Remind them to return the Time Machine to me so that we do not disturb the continuity of the book."

Abisai and Charlotte helped Conrad to his feet.

"I have fitted the levers into the studs, and I will calibrate the Machine for your return. Get yourselves in."

Abisai climbed into the Time Machine. Charlotte climbed onto his lap. Conrad showed them how the levers were calibrated and how far to pull back on the lever to de-accelerate through time.

"What about you?" asked Charlotte. "You have already been a stowaway. Come back with us."

"Thank you, Charlotte, but I will get into the next queue to return, and await my next assignment from the WordSmythes."

The WordSmythes. Abisai had forgotten about them in the frenzy of events.

"Thank you, Conrad," said Abbie and Charlotte, and they both reached for him. Conrad embraced them, then backed away from the Time Machine.

"Bon voyage," he said.

Charlotte wrapped her arms around her brother as he pushed forward on the lever with both hands.

Chapter Thirty

Home*

In the days following their arrival home, Charlotte would tease Abisai about their return, about his dizziness and nausea, about his falling to the floor to stabilize himself as had Conrad, and about how Abbie unintentionally jettisoned her to the ground.

But instead of arriving in France upon the statue of a horse, or onto the blue-green metallic surface supporting a winged apparition, they found themselves sprawled out on a clean, mauve colored carpet whose tight weave felt warm, welcoming and very twenty-first century.

Charlotte sat up. She observed with appreciation the blue haze around her. The Aginbyte's BookMarck had again buffered her fall, this time from the Time Machine. But Charlotte made a mental note that something was amiss. Her floor strike this time was more severe than that which she'd experienced when she'd arrived in Richmond of 802,701 as if the power of the Aginbyte's BookMarck was waning.

When Abbie finally pushed himself into a sit, he realized that they'd fallen off of a circular, raised platform that sat in the center of a series of concentric raised circular stages, all suspended above the main floor.

They looked up and focused on the Time Machine, well lit for the first time in their experience. Steam rose from its metallic surfaces, as if it had just concluded traveling at an incredible speed. It sat upon the topmost platform of the concentric stages like a grand piano positioned for a concert in the round. A three-tiered staircase sat on one side of the cockpit of the Time Machine, suggesting that its point of arrival had become so predictable that a permanent staircase could be secured to the floor.

As Charlotte and Abbie looked about, they saw that they had arrived into a large auditorium.

"I think that there are people sitting in these seats," Charlotte said as she nodded toward the darkened hall.

"We've got to get this Time Machine sent back to Conrad," reminded Abbie.

As if on cue, a figure in the uniform of a hazmat engineer climbed up the stairs to them.

The figure extended a hand to Charlotte and Abbie, greeted them and helped them to their feet.

"Welcome back," said a female voice from inside the hazmat headgear. "If you'll allow me, I just need to take your vital signs and attend to Charlotte's abrasion."

The hazmat woman scanned their foreheads, then reached into her side bag and withdrew antiseptic and gauze. After she had completed wrapping Charlotte's forearm, she flashed a thumbs up sign to someone below their platform. She bowed to them and stepped down off the stage, passing a man dressed in a white button down shirt and black trousers. The man bounded up the five steps from the auditorium floor and offered his hand to them in greeting.

"Charlotte. Abbie. Welcome home. I'm Baldwin and you are in Richmond, England. The year is 2022."

He smiled as if genuinely happy to see them both, then laughed as he watched them absorb this information.

"This is a safe house built on and around the fictional departure spot of the original Time Machine of H.G. Wells," he continued. "By safe house, I mean that this location is a no-conflict zone. Years ago, the Repositors and we WordSmythes agreed that BookStream travelers could arrive here without fear of being ambushed."

Abbie briefly considered asking Baldwin if he'd heard that the truce had been violated in the BookStream of *The Time Machine*, but elected to allow the moment to pass.

"The families of Repositors are sitting to your right," continued Baldwin, "they are waiting to greet returning family members."

Abisai and Charlotte both turned their heads to the right, straining to see into the darkened auditorium. Row after row of stadium seating rose to the rear of the auditorium, obscured by the glare of the spotlights focused upon them. Suspended above the main floor of the auditorium was a balcony with more seating. The darkness was punctuated by the outlines of scattered, seated individuals, their anonymity preserved by the brightness of the stage and the darkness of the auditorium.

"Is the Aginbyte of Inwit out there?" Charlotte asked.

"No," replied Baldwin. "He has been marooned in the TimeStream of Mary Shelley's *Frankenstein*."

"And Ron Luck?" asked Abbie.

Baldwin turned to Abbie, his eyebrows arched at the prescience of the question.

"Funny you should mention it, Mr. Taylor," responded Baldwin. "Censorium Luck arrived earlier today. He left immediately."

Abbie quietly fumed at Luck's having remained a step ahead of them. His inner conversation was interrupted by Baldwin's next announcement.

"…And in the olive seats to your left are the families of WordSmythes."

Baldwin watched Charlotte and Abbie turn their heads to the left side of the auditorium. The layout of the left side of the auditorium appeared to them to be identical to the right side.

When he was satisfied that they had acclimated to their surroundings, Baldwin spoke again.

"I am going to take my leave of you," he said, "and return the Time Machine to Conrad so that it is ready for the Time Traveler."

Charlotte reached out to Baldwin's arm as if to ask him not to leave them in another unfamiliar place.

Baldwin looked at Charlotte and acknowledged her gesture.

"Ms. Taylor. Do you see those two people to your left in Olive Row Two? I believe that's your mother and father."

***

As the Taylor's family left the auditorium, Gus and Cameron Taylor took the lead, hand in hand, sharing obvious affection. Occasionally, they would lean into each other to exchange a comment accompanied by a smile or a laugh. They would frequently turn back toward Charlotte and Abisai as if to ensure that they were still following.

Earlier, after Baldwin's departure, Gus and Cameron had rushed onto the stage and embraced their children. After their tear-filled reunion, Cameron and Gus laid out their plan to walk through the Kew Gardens of Richmond, then arrive back at their hotel for a meal, showers, and several days of sleep.

Charlotte walked next to Abbie for several moments in

silence as they followed their parents.

"I have a question," she finally said.

"Okay," Abbie replied.

"Our BookMarcks can only transport us book to book. Conrad said that we would return to the physical departure point of the Time Machine in Richmond, England, and so we have."

"Yes. So what?" asked Abbie.

"Well, doesn't that mean that we are still in the BookStream of The Time Machine only in the year 2022 instead of the year 802,701?" Charlotte asked, keeping her eyes on her parents' clasped hands.

"What do you mean?" replied Abbie.

"Think back. You used your BookMarck to leave our reality and enter the BookStream of *The Three Musketeers*. Then you used your BookMarck to go from the BookStream of *The Three Musketeers* to the BookStream of *The Time Machine*.

"I follow you so far," responded Abbie.

"My BookMarck transported me from our reality into the BookStream of *The Adventure of the Reigate Squire*. Then, following your clue in the balsam, I used my BookMarck to follow you into the BookStream of *The Time Machine*."

"Yes," Abbie agreed.

"But we have not used our BookMarcks to transport OUT of the BookStream of *The Time Machine*. We used the Time Machine to travel here from the year 802,701 to the year 2022."

"And your point is…?" asked Abbie.

"My point," responded Charlotte with some anxiety, "is that the Time Machine cannot transport us out of the BookStream. It can only transport us to a particular year within the BookStream of *The Time Machine*. So, we are still in the BookStream of *The Time Machine,* only now we are in the year 2022, not year

802,701."

"Okay," said Abbie, growing more concerned.

"What if our BookMarcks cannot get us out of the BookStream and back into the reality of our real mother and father and our real home? What if our BookMarcks only allow us to travel in a facsimile reality of the BookStream?"

Charlotte paused as Abisai attempted to process her thought.

"And wouldn't that explain some of the weird shit going on here?" asked Charlotte, and she nodded her chin toward the clasped hands of their seemingly reconciled parents.

"Those are not our *real* parents. Those are our parents in the BookStream of *The Time Machine*."

It took a moment for Abbie to understand what his sister was suggesting. But once he understood, he shifted his gaze from his parents' interlocked hands to his sister's face, hoping that she would answer her own question.

"There has to be another way home," he finally offered.

But she did not respond to his suggestion.

That would be too easy.

Printed in the USA
CPSIA information can be obtained
at www.ICGtesting.com
LVHW050924131223
766380LV00008B/163